Tripping the Ballerina

Tripping the Ballerina

Paul Ware

Copyright © 2001 by Paul Ware.

Library of Congress Number: 2001116576
ISBN #:   Softcover   0-7388-6754-3

All rights reserved. No part of this book may be reproduced or transmitted in any form or by any means, electronic or mechanical, including photocopying, recording, or by any information storage and retrieval system, without permission in writing from the copyright owner.

This is a work of fiction. Names, characters, places and incidents either are the product of the author's imagination or are used fictitiously, and any resemblance to any actual persons, living or dead, events, or locales is entirely coincidental.

This book was printed in the United States of America.

To order additional copies of this book, contact:
Xlibris Corporation
1-888-7-XLIBRIS
www.Xlibris.com
Orders@Xlibris.com

Contents

Chapter 1 9
Chapter 2 22
Chapter 3 35
Chapter 4 50
Chapter 5 64
Chapter 6 78
Chapter 7 94
Chapter 8 108
Chapter 9 120
Chapter 10 136
Chapter 11 150
Chapter 12 166
Chapter 13 179
Chapter 14 194
Chapter 15 207
Chapter 16 220
Chapter 17 234
Chapter 18 247
Epilogue 263

To Luc,
the other good thing
that came out of Saint Petersburg.

Chapter 1

He came to on the carpet of his boss's office. There was a sour taste in his mouth and he found it hard to swallow without hurting his bruised neck. A sharp pain in his stomach reminded him where the big man had first hit him.

Just an hour previously, life had seemed a lot simpler to Mels L'vovitch Katz. And the long midsummer day was far from over.

A light breeze from the Gulf of Finland ruffled the surface of the river, making the afternoon sunlight dance in reflection on the buildings that lined the Neva embankment. Mels ambled back to his office at the Geophysical Institute in a contented mood. *Why hurry back?* he thought. The only meaningful task he had been assigned in the last year had been training the visiting Vietnamese delegation and he knew most of them were still back at their hostel, clearing up after the meal they had just prepared for him. If he had known them a little longer he might have been tempted to ask just where they had obtained all that food. It was hard enough to get plain Russian fare in Leningrad these days, what with the American grain embargo and most of the produce being diverted to Moscow for the Olympics. He got on well with the Vietnamese but there were still questions that, well, one just did not ask in front of a whole group, especially people one had only known for a few months. Unlike most Russians, Mels normally never drank alcohol—he hated the loss of control. But this time he hadn't been able to resist: Georgian *Tsinandali* was something special and it had been years since he had even seen it in the shops. *Maybe the Vietnamese are getting money to spend in the hard currency stores,* he mused. Who knew? Everyone seemed to have some scam going nowadays. Everyone except him, it seemed. Unless you counted his evening job, teaching Math and Physics. It would certainly be hard to survive without that. If only that Algeria deal had come off, he would be living like an *apparatchik* by now with his own car, maybe even a dacha . . . .

His reverie was cut short as he caught sight of a handwritten note pinned to the fading paint of his office door:

"Mels L'vovitch—you are wanted in the director's office."

His throat suddenly seemed parched. The wine had made him light-headed and he felt the need for some strong tea to sober up. He looked at his wristwatch. It had been over a week since he had corrected his military *Kommander* watch. He estimated the time was between 2:15pm and 2:25pm. His tea tray (one cup, no saucer, one sugar cube, and no napkin) would arrive at 2:30pm. Could he risk waiting? No time was indicated on the note. He had been gone for at least two hours. *Damn!* He strode into his office and picked up the telephone. No dial tone. The phones had been getting worse in the last month. People said the security services had installed so many taps because of the Olympics that the system was overloaded. There was no choice. On past experience, he doubted whether the meeting would be pleasurable. *Best to get it over with.*

He retraced his steps along the worn brown linoleum strip to the stairs. A disagreement had clouded his relationship with his boss for several weeks and Mels did not relish going over the same arguments yet again. There were two stories up to the bosses' floor. Here, the faded paintwork gave way to polished wood and a carpet strip replaced the linoleum. The red-and-black Turkmen pattern continued straight past the offices of minor functionaries but sent out feelers at right angles to those of the exalted. He halted before a large padded door with "Director A. M. Ignatiev" on the nameplate.

This presented a problem of protocol. In theory, the door was padded because no one should ever knock on it. If one was summoned, one was expected to arrive at the appointed hour and wait outside the door. Eventually, the secretary would open it and allow one in. Not to the director's office itself, of course, merely to the outer office which was the fiefdom of his secretary, Violeta. A phone call would be made to the man himself who would then apply the "Winter Hare" technique for dealing with his subordinates. This was a method widely used by Soviet bureaucrats, especially those who dealt with the general public. The theory was based on the fact that the big Russian hares that are caught in winter need to be hung out in the cold for a while to age the meat to the required succulence. Officials adopted the same technique, whether with their underlings or the wider populace. Rather than let someone in straight away—which might give him or her a quite misplaced sense of importance (and the risk of table pounding and cursing)—they were left to wait in a cold waiting room for several hours. Eventually, hungry, tired, and cowed, and aware of their impotence in the face of Soviet officialdom, they would be granted admission.

But there had been no time specified on the note. The secretary would not know he was there. Fortunately, the problem was solved for him as a cart bearing a silver samovar bore down towards him. Natasha, the senior *babushka* in charge of tea distribution, placed a lace napkin on a silver tray, then arranged two cups and saucers with a bowl of sugar and a plate of "Sweets of the East" nougat (*hard currency stores*, thought Mels). Without knocking, she strode into the outer office carrying the tray.

Mels followed meekly behind and sat noiselessly on a chair by the door. To his surprise, his presence was immediately acknowledged by Violeta, who called back Natasha.

"Natalya Nikolaevna, another cup for our Senior Geophysical Expert. And, Mels L'vovitch, the Director is expecting you. Please go straight in."

Please? In all the time he had worked at the Institute, it was the first time Mels had heard Violeta use the word. He picked up the tea tray, opened the inner door and walked in. He set the tray down on the director's desk.

"Aleksander Mikhailovitch, you asked to see me?"

The director looked up over a bank of multi-colored telephones and grimaced involuntarily as he saw Mels. With an effort he smiled and gestured towards the chair in front of his desk. If ever there was a mismatch between body type and personality, it was the director. Balding, with a short, roly-poly body and bushy white beard, he looked as though he belonged on a New Year's Card. *Father Frost with the character of Baba Yaga,* thought Mels.

"Sit, please, Katz. It's good to see you. I hope you are well. I have some excellent news for you."

Sure, you do. For some reason there was something about the director's dyspeptic expression that seemed more than usually irritating to Mels. He sat but said nothing.

"I understand you are on good terms with our Vietnamese, ahem, friends?"

"Aleksander Mikhailovitch, I apologize for my late return from lunch. I was the only staff member who accepted their invitation and it would have reflected poorly on the Institute if I had left before the end of the meal."

"That is not why I called you here, Katz. For your information, we are aware that you have gone to extraordinary efforts to make our guests welcome, even to the extent of eating with them. You understand, of course, that most of the senior members of this Institute ate sufficient rats and cats during the Fascist *blokada* and have no wish to repeat the experience. I know you are too young to remember this but your 'heroic' father will no doubt provide details if you wish."

Mels' hackles rose. The snide reference to his father was not the first he had had to bear in this office and was as offensive as the remark about the Vietnamese. With difficulty he tried to make light of the comments but three glasses of *Tsinandali* had affected his discretion.

"I assure you, Aleksander Mikhailovitch, that if this was rat, it was better fed than many of our fellow citizens are at the moment and made for an excellent meal."

"Katz! If you choose to insult the Soviet system you will kindly not do so in my office. I am glad you enjoy Vietnamese cuisine so much because if you cooperate you will be eating a lot more of it in the near future. I asked you here to tell you that the Party Committee has approved your request to accompany our guests on their return to Saigon, that is to say Ho Chi Minh City, as our Senior Liaison. You will be Training Advisor for the upcoming marine seismic survey in Vietnamese waters and will be resident there for a minimum of six months, possibly for a year."

This is Algeria all over again! He stared at the director for a moment before risking an answer.

"Aleksander Mikhailovitch, I am of course honored but you are mistaken. I never applied for this job. Much as I would like to accept, I have a fifteen-year old daughter whom I raise alone. There is also, if I may say so, a familiar ring to this. Without offence, let me remind you of the last occasion on which I was offered an overseas assignment. Much to everyone's surprise, at the last moment it seems to have occurred to the Party Committee that I was both Jewish and *not* a member of the Communist Party."

A pained expression came over the director's normally disdainful face. He walked to the window and peered out through a dusty net curtain at the view. The intense blue of the sky and the fluffy white clouds set off the pastel colors of the buildings along the river. He paused for a moment, apparently surprised by the beautiful weather, before turning back to Mels.

"Katz, Katz, such thoughts on a day like this . . . you know, dwelling on the past is something your people do too much. Besides, as you well know, we have had to pull our people back from Algeria due to misunderstandings concerning our civilizing mission in Afghanistan. Far better for you that we were able to fix up some part-time teaching positions for you to supplement your scientist's pay."

"Nevertheless, Aleksander Mikhailovitch, I sincerely doubt whether the Party Committee will overlook these facts when making their decision again. Who will write a Character Reference for me, you?"

"Perhaps you misheard me, Katz. The Party Committee has *already* unanimously approved your trip."

He walked ponderously over to his office safe and reached inside to produce a manila folder.

"Here is your Character Reference. You will recognize the signature of my nephew, one of our most respected Academicians. Let me see, yes, '. . . Comrade Katz is continually working to expand his political knowledge. He studies party documents and pertinent governmental policy statements. He is able to convincingly defend the Socialist State against its detractors, etc, etc.' Here are your passport and air ticket. And here are your daughter's."

Mels inspected the documents. He had never seen an External Passport before. The few people at the Institute who had been allowed to travel overseas were required to keep their external passports in Ignatiev's safe. The passports were dark red like his Internal Passport, but the gold hammer-and-sickle emblem on the cover was smaller and the pages inside were pink. The photographs inside were very recent. He glanced at the signature; it was indistinguishable from his own. The air tickets were dated July twentieth, a little under three weeks away.

"You will notice the tickets are round-trip. That is, of course, in case anything should happen to your 'heroic' father. You would, of course, want to return."

Mels sat, trying to gather his thoughts. This had obviously been arranged at very high level. *Certainly higher than this oaf sitting in front of me.* He wondered why such important people would be taking an interest in him. He stood up and placed the folder back on the desk.

"What do you want me to do this time, Aleksander Mikhailovitch?"

The director leaned back and smiled.

"Come now, Katz, you are too suspicious. I admit that at the time we offered you the trip to Algeria there was, how should I put it, a certain *quid pro quo*. But I think you are aware of how little choice you had in that matter."

"That's right. I worked for three years on a doctorate only to have you tell me that your nephew was to defend it and I had to coach him what to say."

"Katz, a three year delay was all that entailed. You were young and proved me right to have confidence in your ability to research another topic. Now you have your own doctorate and—if it had been up to me—you would have worked in Algeria and earned enough to buy a car or whatever it was you wanted. This time we are asking for your cooperation in another matter, which will require no effort from you. We simply want you to co-author a paper with one of our distinguished Azerbaijani colleagues and present your joint research at the upcoming Geophysical Convention in Moscow. I can safely predict there will be considerable popular interest in such a topic and you will be required to answer a few questions on television about the techniques involved. The conference is right before the Olympics so there should be many foreign journalists present, also."

"That paper of Kasumov's? I've told you before: it's garbage. There's nothing *I* can do to put that right. It's pure fantasy—making diamonds out of old oilfields by detonating nuclear bombs! It would be comical if it wasn't so pathetic."

"Nobody is asking you to 'put it right,' Katz. I simply want you to co-sign the paper and present it. You have a good reputation amongst your peers and this will attract respect for the technique. Personally I believe the creation of something beautiful and eternal from non-recoverable oil and, in the process, contributing to world peace by destroying nuclear weapons has a certain poetic beauty. Even Sakharov would approve."

"Then why don't you ask him to do it? Because he has too much principle, I'm sure. And if I do it, my 'good reputation' will disappear overnight."

"Due to his anti-Soviet activities, ex-Academician Sakharov is enjoying the delights of the closed city of Gorkiy right now and will not be signing any papers for quite a while. Besides, we need a geophysicist. Yes, or no, Katz?"

"No."

"Very well, Katz. Your unusually belligerent attitude during this interview may have surprised me, but your answer has not."

He leaned across and pressed a button on one of his telephones.

"We have another matter to discuss. This one I believe is a little closer to your heart."

A door at the back of his office opened and a squarely built man of about forty with a broken nose entered. He was carrying a tape recorder that he ostentatiously placed on the desk next to the folder. As he leaned over to plug in the power cable, Mels noted with alarm that the outline of a shoulder holster showed through the jacket of his suit. He pulled up a chair next to Mels and scrutinized him through small suspicious eyes.

"This is Major Radchenko of the First Directorate of the KGB. He is a senior expert on computers and wishes to gather your views."

"Thank you, Comrade Ignatiev. I hope, Katz, that you don't mind us recording this interview."

The major spoke with a slight accent. The vowel sounds were softened—almost musical—giving his speech an unintended ironic tone. *Ukrainian*, thought Mels.

"I was under the impression, Major Radchenko, that all conversations in this office were routinely recorded. However, as a geophysicist, I am also used to the practice of making duplicate copies. You understand that in our case this is necessary because the tape drives on our computers tend to chew up our tapes. I doubt whether the machines used by the Committee for State Security suffer from this problem."

Radchenko and the director exchanged looks.

"Comrade Ignatiev has briefed me on your sense of humor,

Katz. That is good. It is a rare quality in interviews that I conduct. We understand there is some disquiet amongst the scientific community regarding the quality of computers being produced by the ministry concerned. We want you to tell us your ideas for improving the situation."

"You mean which ones to steal next from the West?"

"If you wish to put it so crudely, Katz."

"My point, Major Radchenko, is that I believe these computers are widely available in stores in the West and are also quite cheap. Surely, it would be easier just to buy one?"

Radchenko laughed.

"Your naiveté astonishes me, Katz. The Americans have an embargo against sales to Russia and these computers are far too big to hide in a suitcase. Far better we get the blueprints for these machines and we will build our own. You are aware of our success with IBM's 360 and 370 computers. Progressive forces in the West are providing us with all the equipment and technology we need to make these ourselves. Remember Leskov's story about the dancing mechanical flea that the English King sent to Russia? Send us a flea and we will put shoes on it!"

"If you had read the original of Leskov's story, Major, you would know that the flea was unable to dance once the shoes were put on it and the craftsman who made the shoes died of alcoholism, bureaucratic indifference and police brutality. You are also wrong about the computers. As I told Aleksander Mikhailovitch, I am talking about a computer small enough to fit on one's desktop." He looked at the vast expanse of the director's desk. "Even *my* desktop. A company in America called Apple has been manufacturing these for several years. They came out with the original in 1976 and it cost a mere seven hundred dollars. There have been many improvements since then—"

"This sounds like a mere toy, Katz. What use is a small computer on everyone's desk? Centralization is the key, like Soviet Power. We cannot have people working away on their own computers, unmonitored and uncontrolled."

"No doubt that is why we have such a technological lead on America, Major. Our 'centralized' Soviet computer industry is shared by five separate ministries. When we need spare parts and peripherals we have to contact up to thirty-two additional sub-ministries. Look, this latest Apple computer is code-named 'Sarah.' It will be released this month. It has a 128K of RAM on the motherboard, a 4K ROM, and a built-in floppy drive. IBM is rumored to be coming out with its own 'personal' computer next year. All I'm asking is that you buy one and let us test it."

Radchenko's eyes had glazed over during Mels' technical discourse. He seemed bored. After a moment's silence during which he seemed to be gathering his thoughts, he turned to Mels and spoke in a softer, almost feminine voice.

"And how do you know this, Mels L'vovitch?"

"From the literature. And the radio of course, when it's not jammed."

"Of course. A man in your position would have access to foreign journals I suppose and would naturally need to listen to the Voice of America and the BBC."

"Major, with the exception of our staff of translators—whose excellent English is not matched by any knowledge of technical subjects whatsoever—I am the only person in this building with sufficient command of English to read them. Indeed, Aleksander Mikhailovitch has often asked me to check translations for—"

"Mels L'vovitch," interrupted the director, "you are too modest. I'm sure any 'translation' work you have done has been at your own initiative."

Radchenko continued in his wheedling voice.

"And these foreign journals, I'm sure you're not selfish enough to keep them to yourself. You must show them to your colleagues, perhaps even to your daughter to help her English studies?"

Mels hesitated. He looked at the major's expressionless face. *Why would an agent of the First Directorate have a broken nose?* Militiamen had broken noses as a general rule—arresting drunks made it an occupational hazard. *But KGB men—in the foreign operations branch?* Something was wrong.

"I'm afraid I don't recall, Major. If indeed that is your title. I certainly doubt you work for the First Directorate."

The major seemed again to be lost in thought for a moment. When at length he turned again to Mels his voice had resumed its former timbre.

"You don't recall, Katz. How odd. It seems your mind has no difficulty when it comes to remembering the details of computers with Jewish names. Of course that information would have come from—by your own admission—foreign journals which the Director has told me you have no clearance to read, let alone distribute. And then the matter of illegally listening to propaganda broadcasts by the enemies of the Soviet Union. And, yes, I am a major, though not, as you suggest in the First Directorate. Actually I belong to the Fifth Directorate. It seems you have chosen the path of dissidence. The task of the Fifth Directorate—as you know—is to keep vigilant surveillance of that path."

"So, you're going to execute me in front of a firing squad?"

Radchenko looked horrified.

"No, we're not."

"Then you will rape my daughter?"

"Of course not, we're not animals."

"Then you will kill my father, Hero of the Soviet Union and lifelong Communist Lev Davidovitch Katz?"

"Don't be stupid."

"Well what, then? Some half-wit with no neck is going to follow me around Leningrad and wait patiently for hours while I stand in line for groceries? Or maybe I'll be able to go to the front of the queue so as not to waste the valuable time of the Committee for State Security? Some tough looking hoods will park a gray Volga outside my apartment at night? Great! Perhaps that will stop those teenage brats banging their girlfriends on the benches in the courtyard. Do you have any idea how long I've been trying to get the militia to come and move them on? I've waited six months for my phone to be fixed. Maybe the KGB can repair it?—then I'll actually be able to phone someone so you can listen in. While you're at it, move that drunk Ukrainian from the apartment next to mine so you can put a bug in the wall.

Listen 'Comrade' Secret Policeman, I'm not a dissident and I'm not a *refusenik*. I haven't applied to emigrate. There's no point. My ex-wife will not let me take my daughter with me and my father's heart would break if I left. So I live here in this intellectual prison. You *could* kill me but anything else would probably be an improvement."

Radchenko stood up and walked over to the tape recorder. He switched it off, wound the cable around his hand, and then turned to Mels.

"I'm sorry you feel that way, Katz. Goodbye, then."

He leaned forward with outstretched hand. Mels half rose to shake it. He had just time to notice that Radchenko's watch was on his right wrist when a powerful left-handed punch to the solar plexus took his breath away and sent him to his knees. Moving with surprising speed for such a big man, Radchenko coiled the cable around his neck and tightened it. Before he lost consciousness, he heard Radchenko's parting words.

"You can't even imagine what the KGB can do to you, Katz."

When Mels came to on the carpet of the director's office, Radchenko and the tape recorder were gone. Ignatiev was sitting behind his desk, calmly looking through files. He noticed him stirring.

"Get up, Katz! Fortunately I was able to persuade Major Radchenko that you are still of some utility to this Institute. Indeed I have a task for you this afternoon. Of course, should you continue in your refusal to cooperate, I may not be there to intervene on your behalf next time."

Mels tried to get up. The pains in his stomach and neck made him dizzy. He toppled backwards.

"I don't have all day, Katz. I want you to go and pick up some air tickets for me. I am going to Baku in two days to meet with Professor Kasumov. I hope you will take the rest of the day to reconsider your somewhat hasty decision so that I will have some good news to report to him. And don't worry about your lecture this evening at the Institute of Applied Mathematics. Your pedagogical license has been temporarily suspended."

Mels struggled to his feet.

"Aleksander Mikhailovitch. If you wish to punish me, do so. But I have a child to support. We cannot survive without the salary I get from teaching."

"Don't worry, Katz. I understand there are plenty of positions available in Gorkiy. And you would not have your daughter to support there. On the other hand, you may want to think about our discussion. Violeta will give you my Internal Passport on the way out. You will need it when you pick up my air tickets."

Chapter 2

It was still hot that evening as the number five tram made a slow turn past the Nekrasov museum. Mels paid the tall, youthful Central Asian conductress, then shielded his eyes from the bright midsummer sun coming through the grimy windows. At this time of year it would not set for hours yet. Against the shabby gray and faded colors of his fellow Leningraders' clothes, the bright blue and white plastic bag on his knees seemed to be from another world. Idly, his finger traced the word 'Intourist' printed in large type directly under the Olympic rings logo and a five-pointed star. He poked at the plastic. *Strong.* How was it they were able to make a quality product like this for the Olympics when he had not seen a single plastic bag in the stores for years? Every woman he knew carried an *avoska*, a 'just-in-case' string bag—as he did himself. You never knew when you would see something worth queuing for. Of course, this was an *Intourist* bag and, since Intourist was the Soviet Travel Agency that catered solely to foreigners, it was possible that the Soviet Union exported thousands of these things every year to help pay for—, *well, what exactly?*

He peered through the dirty glass as the tram crossed Nevsky Prospekt, and he made out the elevated dome of the huge 'House of Books' in the distance. *Not books, anyway.* You could search that bookstore from top to bottom and you would find little of value in it. Try to get even a copy of Pushkin! The last time he had attempted to buy a book of poetry for his daughter he was told that he could only have 'Eugene Onegin' if he also bought Leonid Brezhnev's 'Little Land'—the man's completely unreadable ghost-written autobiography. "The book won the Lenin Prize for literature," the officious sales clerk had informed him. "Listen," he had replied, "my daughter is fifteen, she is too old for fairy tales." Then the next man in line had blurted out: "Little Land: Little Truth." From the back of the shop came the suggestion that she file the book under "Fiction." Before long the whole queue was loudly refusing to buy the book. *And what was so amazing*, thought Mels, *was that the sales clerk had backed down.* When the Russian people unite. . . .

The tram stopped suddenly to avoid an official's shark-like, black Zil limousine as it sped by. A slim Asian youth stumbled into Mels. Mels helped him recover his balance and was about to make some remark when he noticed that he was carrying an identical plastic bag. *Foreign tourist.* On any day but this he would have practiced his English but after the events at the Institute he thought it unwise to speak English on a crowded tram. But the bag reminded him of the strange incident at the travel agent. The clerk had glanced at the director's internal passport then addressed Mels as "Aleksander Mikhailovitch." Indeed, the only reason he had been given an Intourist bag for a domestic flight was because the sales clerk had assumed that he *was* Ignatiev, and therefore someone worth "licking up." But Mels was taller than average with dark curly hair. And the only time he had tried growing a beard was on a fieldtrip in Siberia. His young daughter had burst into tears when he got back and would not stop until he had shaved it off.

He took the director's internal passport out of the bag. Actually, the clean-shaven, dark-haired man in the photograph *did* look like him. *Ignatiev must have lost his hair and put on all that weight after he became boss*, thought Mels. He looked at the date of birth—1927—so he was eighteen years older than Mels but he was using an old photograph. It was an official document but Ignatiev must have used his influence to have an old photograph substituted. How typical that a simple thing like vanity could render the passport useless. It was like trying to identify the geriatric members of the Politburo from the airbrushed photographs that appeared in the newspapers. *Take Romanov, for instance.* It was a little over two years since the powerful Leningrad Party boss had come to open the new Geoscience Laboratory. Mels had been surprised at how much smaller and older—not to mention coarser—he had been in the flesh. That was one of the mysteries of life in the Soviet Union. He knew hundreds of intelligent, well-educated scientists who worked in Institutes like his own, but without exception the ones who were promoted were either time-serving hacks or sociopathic egotists; boors devoid of any charisma whatsoever. It was probably the same with politicians. They continued upward in their chosen career, gathering momentum until they collided with an ego even bigger than their own. It was so inevitable there was probably a scientific law involved. If he ever got his teaching job back he could set his students to model it, mathematically. Romanov was a case in point. The most powerful man in Leningrad, destined for great things, and then suddenly some stupid scandal brought him down. Supposedly, he had borrowed Catherine the Great's dinner service from the Hermitage museum for his daughter's wedding. Unfortunately, the wedding had turned out a little more boisterous than expected and the service had been smashed. Much had been made of the coincidence of his family name and Catherine's dynasty in the newspapers, and Romanov's rapid political ascent had apparently stalled. *But who is powerful enough to have done that to him?* he wondered. *No one in Leningrad, that's for sure.*

He turned the page of the Internal Passport. *How about nationality?* "Russian," of course. No surprise to find *that* there. Not that it meant anything. Powerful men had miraculous changes in nationality when promotions were involved. There were even rumors about KGB Director Andropov. Mels' own internal passport had "Jew" written there, a matter of perverse pride in his case since he was a non-believer. There was no premium in being Jewish. A few years ago, during détente, there had been a brief period when ethnic Russians were paying bribes to be re-classified so they could emigrate but the authorities had long since clamped down. Nowadays you could wait years. The authorities would wait until your son was old enough to be conscripted. If he went in the army they would refuse permission to emigrate on account of "possession of military secrets." If he refused to serve he would be imprisoned for evading the draft. For a moment Mels wondered what had been written in the External Passport he had briefly held earlier in the day. *Probably "Soviet citizen,"* he thought. Only outside the Soviet Union did people suddenly stop being Russians, Georgians, Lithuanians, or Jews.

The front page of the newspaper of the man opposite him boasted of record agricultural harvests somewhere in Central Asia. With a sudden pang of guilt he remembered his daughter had asked him to buy something today. *What was it—some agricultural product? Wool? No, cotton wool, that was it—poor Luba.* She had a swimming meet coming up but was due for her period. Sanitary towels had been unobtainable for months and now it seemed that there was some inexplicable shortage of cotton wool. *How can that be,* he wondered, *with all these record crops of cotton being reported from Uzbekistan?* His memory suddenly kicked into gear. *Uzbekistan . . . yes, Uzbek!* The conductress of the tram was speaking to the Asian youth now and he recognized the language. For five years he had had an Uzbek neighbor who worked at one of the Institutes on Vasilyevskiy Island. Their daughters had been inseparable. After they left, that Ukrainian had moved in and his daughter had had to endure drunken anti-Semitic curses and banging on the wall whenever she practiced her violin.

He put the director's passport and tickets in his jacket pocket. He smoothed the thick plastic bag and carefully folded it. He would try at the private market to get cotton wool. Maybe he could barter the bag?

Just then there was a terrible screeching sound. A Zhiguli car had collided with the tram and was being dragged along while the tram braked. Mels saw a gray Volga car pull up and two men get out. They ran to the Zhiguli and dragged out a protesting, thin man with a large bulbous nose and long black curly hair. From the open car door bundles of green vegetables spilled out. A black marketeer, perhaps? Suddenly the Uzbek youth screamed something and pressed the emergency release on the door. A man sitting opposite him immediately sprang up and grabbed the boy's arm, but his path was blocked by the conductress.

"Your fare please, Comrade."

Despite the man's size the conductress stood her ground. But a familiar square figure appeared suddenly in the doorway. Moving with the same speed that had surprised Mels earlier in the day he felled the conductress with a left-handed blow from behind. Radchenko and the other man then took of in pursuit of the young Uzbek youth.

Mels knelt by the side of the unconscious woman. Gently he lifted her up from the floor of the tram and sat her on one of the seats. She came to, slowly.

"They're KGB," he mouthed. "Will you be alright?"

She nodded. He looked up and saw Radchenko punching the Uzbek boy while his colleague held him by his arms. The thin man was being handcuffed. *Where had Radchenko appeared from? Had he been following him? Were they going to try to frame him?* Just a few hours ago he would have sat there woodenly like all the other Leningraders, pretending that what he was witnessing was as natural as a sudden shower of rain. But now panic seized him. He had no desire for another confrontation. He decided to make himself scarce. Quickly he gathered the fallen plastic bag and stuffed it in his pocket. He touched the conductress on the cheek. From a dim memory of his daughter's friend he found the words to say goodbye in Uzbek.

"*Endi ketishim kerak. Xayr.*"

He left the tram hurriedly and ducked into the labyrinthine *Apraksin Dvor* shopping complex. It was late and many of the small stores were closing. He spent a fruitless half-hour trying to find a vendor of cotton wool, but the activity gave him time to calm his jangled nerves. He stood and watched an old man in a World War Two uniform play an accordion while a child with hair the color of wheat danced in front of a small crowd of onlookers. Maybe he was just imagining things? After all, he had not done anything wrong. He decided to risk the open-air private market at the nearby Sennaya Square. Making his way out of the *Dvor*, he caught sight of Radchenko again, apparently briefing a group of about twenty uniformed militiamen. Although he was too far away to hear what was being said, the same fear of being hunted came back. He had the uncomfortable feeling—almost a certainty— that they were looking for him.

Instinctively, he ducked back into the *Dvor* and exited by the back way, near the Fontanka River. What should he do? Adrenaline pumping, he hurried over the bridge. He did not know this district well, where was he? *Didn't somebody infamous live here?* He read the name from a plaque on the wall: Rasputin. *Of course!* This was where the holy man supposedly conducted his orgies. *But, wait a minute, Gorokhovskaya Street . . .* he was sure that was his ex-wife's address, too. Since the divorce he had tried to contact her just once, when he needed her signature on some papers, but she had refused to see him. Instead, the documents had been sent to an address in Gorokhovskaya Street. So her apartment was close to the Choreography School . . . *but why does she live in such a gloomy street when she has a well-paying job and knows so many important people?* He looked for the number and made his way into a bare courtyard. Two prostitutes, on their way out for their evening work gave him appraising looks.

"Be careful out there, my dears, there are more militia than *tarakans* in the market."

"Six legs or two, a cockroach is a cockroach!" said one with a laugh.

"Don't worry, Comrade, in Leningrad we have the best militia money can buy!" said the other.

"Can you tell me, young ladies, where the apartment of Zhanna Borisova is?"

"Borisova? I dunno the name. Oh, you mean Zhanna the ballerina, or whatever she is? She's on the top floor. Classy, if you're into specialty work. But be careful, she's a bit 'soggy,' if you know what I mean!"

Actually, Mels did not know what she meant. Drunk, maybe? *Had she started drinking after the divorce?* It seemed unlikely for someone who always cared so much about her physical appearance. And what work, other than teaching young ballerinas, did his wife specialize in? He was anxious to get out of sight as soon as possible so he left the women to their labors and entered the apartment building.

To his surprise, the interior of the building became progressively more luxurious, floor by floor. The top story was illuminated by a chandelier and had a carpeted floor. He pressed the buzzer of his ex-wife's apartment.

A muffled voice came from inside.

"Asparagus? Let yourself in, it's unlocked."

Asparagus? Was she expecting a . . . well, *what is asparagus, exactly?* He was pretty sure it was some sort of vegetable, but could not recall ever having seen one in the markets he frequented. For some reason his mind briefly flashed back to the accident with the Zhiguli but the thought was soon buried by ocular overload. The apartment he stepped into was the most luxurious he had ever seen. Gilded mirrors and oil paintings covered the purple and gold wallpaper. The carpet was white and so thick that his shoes disappeared in it. The furniture reminded him of the Czar's private quarters at the Winter Palace, but here there was no velvet rope to keep museum visitors from touching the exhibits.

He walked over to a shelving unit containing the only modern items in the room—a wide screen television and stereo system. He recognized most of the components, but *what is this—a VCR?* He had seen one at the Kommissioni store, second-hand, for six thousand rubles, plus the seven-percent commission that the State took. With the cooling of détente, many Soviet diplomats had been recalled from lucrative overseas assignments and had brought with them the booty they had acquired in the decadent West. He made a quick calculation in his head. Even with his teaching jobs, the VCR in front of him represented five years of his salary.

He heard a shower switch off somewhere. There were no footsteps in the thick carpet but his ex-wife's husky voice became louder as she approached.

"So you came after all? The office said something had come up—"

She turned the corner and screamed as she saw him.

"Mels! What the fuck are *you* doing here?!"

"Hello, Zhanna. Welcoming as ever. I'm sorry not to have called. The phones, you know. . . . "

His ex-wife stared at him. She was wearing a scanty bathrobe with a towel wrapped around her wet hair. A few wet blond strands lingered on her flawless forehead. *God, she is still so beautiful!* The only good thing that woman had ever done in her life was to pass her genes on to their daughter. She noticed his gaze and crossed her arms across her breasts.

"Leave. Now."

"Zhanna, I've come to ask a favor—"

"No."

"It's not for me, Zhanna. It's for our daughter."

"What is it? Is she pregnant? She must be old enough by now."

"Zhanna! Of course not. Quite the opposite, as it happens. I came to see you because she needs sanitary towels—or at least cotton wool. She has a swimming meet next weekend and it's her period. I've looked all over, but you know what it's like. . . . "

Zhanna looked puzzled.

"All right, Zhanna. You probably don't know what it's like not to find cotton wool in the shops. And you probably don't know what it's like to wait six months for your phone to be fixed. But the simple fact is that cotton wool is unobtainable in this town—at least on a geophysicist's salary."

She laughed derisively.

"You're probably right about that. So Luba must be what age, now?"

"Fifteen."

"And she's in the swim team? I'm surprised she still *has* periods."

"What do you mean?"

"What with those injections they give them."

"You mean vitamins? She tells me the team doctor gives them shots before practice. But I don't see what that has to do—"

"Mels, you are so naïve. You'll understand in a few years. Just don't show up on my doorstep one day asking for help finding razor blades for her."

It was Mels' turn to look puzzled.

"Never mind, Mels. But, yes, I do have sanitary towels. Which does she need, pads or tampons? Don't look at me like that. You know the difference don't you? Outside or inside?"

"Zhanna, she's only fifteen. I may not know what a tampon is, but I'm fairly sure she's still a virgin, if that makes a difference. If you have pads I'll take those. Otherwise, cotton wool like a hundred million other Soviet women use—when they can get it."

"Sometimes you sound like your father. You'll be giving me his standard lecture on how 'we' survived the Fascist *blokada*, next."

"No. I haven't become a Communist, yet, Zhanna. But he would be unfavorably impressed by your apartment. He usually judges furniture on the basis of how well it would burn in case the heat is shut off. I suppose the Kirov Ballet must be paying its staff well."

"It is not forbidden to live well."

She walked over to an ormolu armoire and pressed a button. A drawer opened and she withdrew a cigarette.

"Hand me that lighter, will you?"

His eyes followed her pointing finger but saw nothing that looked like a cigarette lighter. Impatiently she walked over and picked up a Dresden figurine, flicked the china head and a flame appeared. She took a deep breath on the cigarette.

"So, Mels. How goes your job at the Institute? Have you 'received the napkin' yet?"

"No. I'm still a 'Senior Expert,' whatever that means. But the tea tastes the same whether it comes with a napkin or not."

"Maybe so, but you would get a bigger office."

"And a bigger picture of Lenin. *And* a fur hat every year. Actually, that *would* be worth getting. The rest of it is just garbage. No one respects you in my profession once you get to the top floor. They don't even get paid a lot more, not officially at least."

Zhanna snorted.

"Pay! Money means nothing unless you're a black marketeer and you're outside the system. What matters is influence. Do you suppose your boss has to bribe someone to get good seats at the Kirov? He just calls us and lets us know he's coming."

Mels thought back to the Travel Agent and the sales clerk's ingratiating smile as he passed him the Intourist bag. *She's right, of course*. But the comment about money "meaning nothing" was a little hard to take from Zhanna. No one fitted Oscar Wilde's description of a cynic better. She really did know the price of everything and the value of nothing. He shrugged but made no reply. They stood and looked at each other for a moment, each lost in their separate thoughts. A grandfather clock struck the half-hour somewhere in the apartment. At length, she stubbed out the remains of her cigarette and broke the silence.

"Mels, I'll let you have the sanitary towels but you have to do something for me, OK?"

"Of course, Zhanna, though I don't see what I could do—"

"My boyfriend stood me up tonight. I shouldn't be surprised. He works seven days a week. He was supposed to accompany me to a reception at the Astoria Hotel. I need an escort."

"That seems all right. . . ."

"The thing is, you have to 'be' him. I don't want people thinking I'm with a geophysicist."

"But someone may recognize me—"

She laughed again.

"At the Astoria?! Have you ever been inside that place? Trust me, Mels, no one will have the slightest idea who you are and that's exactly what I need since no one there will ever have seen him, either."

"Zhanna, I'll need to change. I'll have to go home first."

Actually that was the last thing he wanted to do right now. Radchenko and the militia were still out there. Perhaps he was just being paranoid but, in any case, if he could just stall for an hour or two, maybe the militia would get tired and stop looking for him? Fortunately, Zhanna intervened.

"Mels. I am quite certain you have nothing at home suitable. He has some of his clothes here. He is tall like you though not as underweight. You can wear one of his uniforms."

"Uniforms? He's in the military? Look, Zhanna, I don't think this is a good idea."

"Nonsense. Besides, you want those sanitary towels, don't you?"

Zhanna lead him down a corridor to a bedroom about the size of his apartment. She slid back the door of a wall closet and revealed dozens of dresses. From the end of the rack she picked up a teal-colored uniform with royal blue piping.

"So he's in the Navy, eh? Maybe my dad knows him . . . ?"

Zhanna rolled her eyes.

"No. You can wear this with your white shirt. You'll need to polish those shoes. I assume they *are* meant to be black leather? The polish is in the kitchen at the end of the corridor. Now get out of here. I need to change. You can watch a video but don't touch anything else. You know that VCR alone cost eight years of your salary?"

Five, actually, thought Mels. He found a flat circular can of English boot polish and a brush in the kitchen and took it into the living room. He looked at the videocassettes on the shelf. One had a rectangular piece of yellow paper stuck to it that came off when he picked it up. Embarrassed, he was looking around for some glue to stick it back to the cassette when he noticed that it was stuck to his hand. *How typically Soviet—a glue that doesn't dry!* He noticed it had a logo in English on it: "3M." Well, maybe the West had problems in manufacturing, too. There was a handwritten note on the yellow paper in small, neat capitals, quite unlike Zhanna's barely legible scrawl:

"DARTH VADER—HITLER? THE FORCE—COMMUNISM?"

He put it aside. The last thing he wanted to watch was some Marxist-inspired French New Wave film. He found another tape and slotted it into the machine. Laying an old copy of *Pravda* on the floor, he took off his shoes and started to polish them.

The second tape was an amateurish pornographic movie. It started off with a blonde woman in a black leather mask leading some fat middle-age men into a room apparently made to look like a medieval dungeon. After some rather desultory foreplay (. . . *aren't porno stars supposed to look handsome?*) the action started to heat up when a group of very young girls were brought into the room chained together. At this point, Mels switched the VCR off. He was not a prude but the girls were his daughter's age or younger. He wondered where the films were made as he fastened the brass buttons of the tunic. *Sweden, maybe?* Zhanna's boyfriend seemed to have picked up some strange tastes in the Navy. He rummaged through the pockets of the uniform for clues as to the character of the person he was supposed to impersonate. There was not much to go on; in one pocket he found an enamel cigarette lighter, in another a small pistol, no bigger than his palm. He set the gun down gingerly on a glass-topped coffee table. He was not sure if it was loaded and did not trust himself to try to find out. Despite his father's military past and job in the Navy yards, he had had little contact with the armed services. To tell the truth, he was not even sure what kind of uniform he was wearing.

Just then Zhanna entered the room looking, as always, like she had stepped out of the pages of a fashion magazine.

"Here's his cap. You should know his real name is Yevgeny Annichkov. People call him 'Asparagus' but not to his face on account of his rank."

She handed him a peaked cap with a blue band covered with gold braid. Mels was impressed.

"What is he, some kind of admiral?"

"General. Now come, we're late. You can drive my car."

"Now don't tell me, you drive a Chaika?"

"No, it's just a Zhiguli. But Mels, I am serious about your getting a promotion. For you to buy that car you would have two years on a waiting list and it would cost you eight thousand rubles. But if you know the right people you can get one for *fourteen hundred* rubles in a couple of days. Now let's have a look at you. That uniform looks a little loose on you. Put something in your inside pocket to pad it out."

He placed Ignatiev's tickets and passport in an inside pocket. She pulled him back to admire their joint reflection in the mirror by the door.

"That's better. Wait a minute, Mels. Where's your insignia? Stay here."

She went to the bedroom and returned a moment later with a brass badge that she pinned to his right breast.

"That's OK. Now we can go."

"Oh no! Oh, no, no, no! No way, Zhanna. This is not going to work. You are completely insane. . . ."

He stared at the badge on his uniform. It was in the shape of a medieval knight's shield. An unsheathed sword, point down, lay over the shield.

"For god's sake, Zhanna, you didn't tell me he was in the KGB!"

Chapter 3

Half an hour later, a relaxed Mels Katz supported by his ex-wife Zhanna arrived at the Astoria Hotel. She drove, as the sedative she had given him to quell his anxiety attack had rendered him temporarily incapable of doing much more than smile.

"OK, enough smiling," she hissed at him. "You're a general. Try scowling."

He scowled. He found that the pill had the curious effect of making everything seem unimportant except what he was told to do by Zhanna. He noticed that people around them were trying their best to catch his eye and smile obsequiously at him. He felt like shouting at them (*you don't even know me, fools, all you can see is a uniform!*) but checked himself with the thought that Zhanna would disapprove.

A line of people was standing outside the hotel waiting to go in. A doorman at the front was acting the petty Czar, allowing some of them in yet holding others back for arcane reasons. Zhanna walked them to the front of the queue and gave the doorman an imperious glance. He opened the door and bowed ingratiatingly.

Inside, the hotel seemed to be made entirely of marble. He felt a curious urge to get down on all fours and look at it to see what geological formation it came from. He looked at Zhanna and decided against it. A waiter came towards them with a tray of champagne glasses.

"Take one."

"Zhanna, I don't think I should. I'm a little tired—"

"Take one!"

Obediently, he took the glass. It was so cold that frost had formed on the outside. A group of expensively dressed people bore down on them.

"Zhanna, darling!"

In his confused state, he could not follow much of the conversation. It seemed to be mostly theatrical gossip concerning Vladimir Vysotsky's portrayal of "Hamlet" at the Taganka Theater in Moscow. Vysotsky was one of the few people living in the Soviet Union for whom Mels had any respect—an outspoken actor and poet whose life had been made hell by the organization whose uniform he was wearing. He was surprised that the man's health had not broken down under the strain.

"But why is he being allowed to appear on stage in Moscow during the Olympics?"

One of the men laughed in an uninhibited way at Mels' question. Was he drunk or was this how these people always behaved?

"Oh come now, General. I think you are well aware of the relationship his director has with *your* director?"

Mels said nothing. The man's confidence appeared to wane under his scowl.

"Well, forgive me for mentioning it, but I was told that Comrade Andropov's children turned up to audition at the Taganka and were turned down by Lyubimov, the director. Andropov summoned Lyubimov to KGB Headquarters in Dzerzhinsky Square and thanked him 'as a father.' After that, it seems Lyubimov has been allowed more leeway than many of us in the theatrical profession. . . ."

Mels was not sure what to say. Actually the story was fascinating but he was sure that was the wrong response from a KGB general. He stared at the man's sweating face for a moment before replying.

"And who exactly told you that story, Comrade?"

A tense silence followed his question. For a moment he thought the man would actually start crying. His lips quivered and his glasses slid down his nose. Oddly, it was Zhanna who broke the tension.

"Come, come, Zhenya. Even a general in the KGB is allowed a little time off duty. . . ."

She took his arm and moved them on to another knot of admirers. Zhanna kept directing champagne his way as if to compensate for the pill's waning effect. He had not eaten since his lunch with the Vietnamese over ten hours ago and felt rather queasy. Disengaging himself from Zhanna, he sat in an overstuffed armchair and summoned a waiter.

"Bring me some food, would you?"

"Of course, Comrade General. In fact we have a little surprise for you, courtesy of your staff, I believe."

The man left and returned with a silver platter on which strange spear-shaped vegetables gleamed with butter. Zhanna appeared at his side.

"What is this?"

"It's your namesake. You're called 'Asparagus' because you developed a taste for it in France. Eat it."

It had a strange flavor but not unpleasant. Zhanna left him to finish the platter and drink the rest of his champagne. A waiter approached immediately with another tray of *hors d'oeuvres*. As he was helping himself, two men in shabby jackets sidled up to him. One had a camera and flash unit around his neck. The other was bearing a small cardboard folder.

"No photos."

"Comrade General, forgive us. My colleague here is covering this event for *Aurora*. When he heard you were here he called me. I came here at once as I felt—as photo editor—that I should show you these. We will be running these in tomorrow's edition."

He pulled out several sets of glossy photographs. The top two were of Brezhnev. Mels was shocked to see how old he looked in one of the pictures—almost senile. The cameraman had caught him off-balance, perhaps. His eyes were unfocused and a blob of spittle appeared to be dribbling from the corner of his mouth.

The other showed a more youthful Brezhnev with a purposeful expression on his face shaking hands with a cosmonaut. He had the feeling that they would ask him which photograph they should use. *But surely that's obvious, isn't it?* He put the two photos aside and looked at the second two. The two photos were identical—*or are they?* A group of figures in casual dress posing between giant boulders in a mountain resort—presumably somewhere in the Caucasus. One of the boulders had been carved into a massive relief bust of Lenin. On second inspection, he noticed that the figures were standing on a concrete stairway. He recognized the man in the middle as being KGB Chairman Andropov. Next to him stood a short balding man with an ugly birthmark on his head. On the other side, *ah yes!* On one of the pictures there was another figure he did not recognize. In the other the figure had been airbrushed out, leaving a rather obvious gap. The men were obviously waiting for his response. There was no choice but to bluff his way through it.

"I think you know our policies by now, Comrade. But for god's sake, try not to leave gaps"

The editor breathed a sigh of relief.

"Of course, General. But, you know, this *is* Krasnye Kamni—the Chairman's favorite retreat. We, that is, I did not feel we could fill the gap with just anyone. People might jump to the wrong conclusions if we put one of the lesser figures in the foreground. . . ."

"Comrade, I do not wish to tell you your job," Mels saw the man wince at this, "but I am quite sure somewhere in your files you have a photo of a little girl in a white dress or peasant costume holding flowers?"

"Absolutely, General. A brilliant idea."

Mels waved off the compliment.

"As for the other photographs, I fear I must be missing the point?"

"Comrade General, again forgive me. We received this photograph from our usual sources. I, er, realize the policy has changed but we felt that the photograph was a little, well, too realistic . . . You must understand that we have never received any *written* instructions concerning photographs of General Secretary Brezhnev and, naturally, if I may say so, old habits die hard . . .

Mels tried not to look surprised. *Has the man gone out of his mind? Who would issue orders to show Brezhnev as a senile old man?*

"Comrade, you are right. I thought for one moment that you were questioning the new policy. In this case, I suggest a compromise. Of course you should run the unflattering photograph, as these are your instructions, but use your retouching skills to *slightly* rejuvenate the general secretary. Reduce the photograph to one column width instead of the usual two."

"Excellent, Comrade General."

The editor and photographer left as obsequiously as they had arrived. Mels stood up. For the last twenty minutes or so he had been filled with an overwhelming need to urinate. Apparently reading his mind, a waiter pointed down the corridor.

Mels leaned his forehead against the cool marble wall above the urinal as he relieved himself. *What the—?* A strange odor brought him to his senses He looked around but found himself alone. Then he realized the smell was coming from the urinal. His urine was scented with asparagus! As a scientist, he felt he should be able to work out why this was but his brain stalled at the effort. As he buttoned his fly and walked over to the washbasins, two men came into the restroom. He had just time to notice that they had been holding hands when one spoke urgently to the other in English.

"Brantley, no! There's a cop in here!"

The other noticed Mels and replied.

"Wait till he leaves. He probably thinks we came for a piss."

As Mels left, he turned back and commented—again in English.

"Enjoy yourselves, gentlemen."

Why did I say that? God knows, he personally did not give a damn what people did but was it likely a real policeman, let alone a general in the KGB would be so tolerant of homosexuals? He must be drunk. He shook his head to clear it and summoned a waiter.

"Get me some tea."

"Tea, Comrade General?"

"Yes, tea. And bring it to that chair in the corner."

He sat and sipped his tea and watched his ex-wife flit from group to group in the crowded ballroom. An attractive woman in a low-cut dress sat at an adjacent table and produced a long slim cigarette from a silver cigarette holder. She placed it between her lips and waited. From her actions it appeared that she was the kind of woman who rarely had to light her own cigarettes. Amused, he reached into his pocket for the general's cigarette lighter. He leaned over and offered her a light. To his embarrassment, however, the lighter refused to spark. A familiar hand with long red nails appeared in his line of vision, holding a gold lighter.

"Here, dear. Now fuck off."

The woman looked into Zhanna's furious face, picked up her bag and left. Zhanna turned to Mels.

"First, a general does not light cigarettes for other people, least of all a slut like that. Second, that cigarette lighter you have in your hand is actually a miniature tape recorder. Honestly, Mels, I leave you for five minutes and where do I find you—sitting in a corner sipping tea and being polite! It's true what they say, 'no matter how well you feed a wolf, he keeps looking back towards the woods.' You don't change, do you? Look, we have a deal. I want people to think I have a real man for a boyfriend not some shy, tea-drinking nobody. Come with me, I want you to meet someone who works at the American Consulate. You can practice your English."

Zhanna introduced Mels to the two men he had met in the restroom.

"This is Brantley Logan and a mutual friend, Rudolf Bulganin, who recently started with the Kirov."

"We've met. But it's a pleasure to meet you officially."
"Always a pleasure to meet men in uniform. Navy, perhaps?"
"KGB."

The young ballet dancer paled visibly but Logan was completely unfazed, even slightly amused. He made a subconsciously defiant gesture of brushing his thinning hair back over his forehead. As he did so, Mels noticed a purplish birthmark similar to the one he had seen earlier on the photo of Krasnye Kamni. He remembered the short man's name—Gorbachev. *One of Andropov's cronies from the Caucasus, of course.* He wondered who the other man was whose excision he had just approved. His mind drifted back to the present as he realized Logan had made some remark that he had completely ignored. He decided the best way out of the situation was to propose a toast.

"World peace and friendship between our nations!"

Logan seemed a little nonplussed. Evidently he was unused to his remarks going unnoticed. He drank the champagne with a look of distaste on his face.

"Really, General. You should use your influence to get the Astoria to order Californian champagne. Great hotel, poor wine."

"You are not the first Westerner to admire the hotel, Mr. Logan. Did you know Hitler issued invitations for a victory banquet here to celebrate the fall of Leningrad? Invitations that were never taken up, of course. As a teetotaler he too would have taken exception to our fine Soviet champagne. He was wrong about many things. Now if you gentlemen would excuse me, I have some last minute work to do preparing the visit of the Leningrad delegation to the Olympics in Moscow. A shame that your countrymen will not go there, Mr. Logan. Something else they have in common with Hitler."

Later, he sat in the passenger seat of Zhanna's car with his head resting on the glass as Zhanna gave him a running commentary on the evening's events.

"You made a good recovery, Mels, I have to hand it to you.

You certainly knew how to handle that faggot from the Consulate. His face was the color of borscht."

"What does he do?"

"Good question. I believe your real life counterpart would also like to know that."

They pulled up to Zhanna's courtyard. He walked round to her door and opened it for her. She swung her long slender legs round and accepted his proffered hand. Her stiletto heel caught on a piece of loose pavement and she stumbled against him for a moment. Their eyes met.

"You know, Mels. You did well tonight. Perhaps you deserve a reward."

He followed her up to her apartment. He pretended to himself that he had not quite understood Zhanna, that she may have meant something else but the truth was he had not felt so aroused in years. *Why is that?* When they were married they did nothing but argue and the sex had trickled to nothing after the birth of their daughter. Zhanna blamed Luba for that, just as she blamed her for everything; why she had never become a famous ballerina, why she had to teach instead, even why she had been forced to take lovers to maintain her position at the Kirov. None of it made any sense. Luba had not asked to be born and *he* had been the one to persuade Zhanna—just this once—not to abort the child.

Zhanna paused at one of the doors inside the apartment, then shook her head and moved to the next.

"No. I don't think you're ready for that. Come in here and wait. I will be a few minutes."

The bedroom was smaller than he had expected, not much bigger than his own room. The furniture was all made of rattan, or bamboo, he was not sure which. Rough burlap lined the walls and there was a print of a Tahitian scene by Gauguin. There were no windows. The lighting came from two standard lamps that were made of the same material. It was rather tasteful, he thought. He sat on the bed, feeling suddenly shy, uncertain whether to undress. Without his touching the light switch, the lamps gradually dimmed and soft guitar music—*is that Hawaiian?*—came from hidden speakers. The door opened and Zhanna came in. Actually, that was not quite accurate. Mels could not be sure who had come due to the darkness. Indeed he had a creepy feeling that *several* people had just entered the room. His libido evaporated.

"Zhanna . . . ?"

"If you like," came a child's voice.

This is getting too weird, thought Mels. He groped his way to the light and flicked the switch. Lying and sitting in various attitudes around the room were four adolescent girls dressed in grass skirts with flowers in their hair. Their bare breasts swayed in time with the pulse of the hula music. They smiled at him in a dreamy way.

"Hello, Comrade Mels."

He felt sick. He left the room in search of a bathroom. He threw up, washed his face in cold water then stared at himself in the mirror. Even in his disturbed mental state, he had to smile: one advantage of KGB dress uniforms was that they were exactly the color of regurgitated asparagus. He hoped he was not around when Zhanna had to explain *that* stain. Right now, Zhanna had some explaining to do to him. He tried the bedroom she had been in earlier. Her dress lay on the bed but she was not there. He tried next door. This looked familiar. A little smaller than it had appeared in the video but quite recognizable as the dungeon room. He walked back to the living room and found Zhanna in her robe sitting on the sofa with two pubescent girls, smoking cigarettes and watching cartoons.

"That was quick, Mels. Still got the old problem or did the girls not appeal? You can have these two if you prefer. . . ."

Despite himself, Mels felt surprisingly calm. In fact since he vomited, the effects of the drugs and alcohol had abated and his head had started to clear.

"Zhanna, you will go to hell for this."

"Suddenly got religious, Mels? I shall have to give those girls a bonus. And as to whether I go to hell or not at least I won't be going to prison, which is more than can be said for you. I have to say you still have the capacity to surprise me."

"What are you talking about? I never touched the girls!"

"Come on, Mels, you know what I'm talking about."

Why was he wasting time arguing? From his watch he could tell it was probably past midnight and he had a long walk home. He grabbed his jacket and pants off the back of the sofa and made for the door. Zhanna wrinkled her perfect nose.

"What is that awful smell? You can bring that uniform back after you've cleaned it!"

He slammed the door and started down the stairs. *What did she mean about going to prison?* Impersonating a KGB officer was obviously serious but this General "Asparagus" probably would not want it to leak out *how* he happened to be wearing his uniform. Actually that was a good point. Was it safer to make his way home as a civilian, or in uniform? If he was right and they *had* been looking for "Mels Katz" then he was better off in disguise. He looked up at the sky. *Why did this have to happen during White Nights?* At best he had an hour or two of half-light as the sun grazed the horizon before it would be daylight again.

On the other hand, apart from his hat with its gold braid, he looked like any military officer and in normal times about a quarter of the male population of Leningrad was in uniform. The chances were that most of the militia would be as ignorant as he was as to the significance of teal green. Who would ever recognize a KGB dress uniform, anyway? If he could just hide the hat. . . . He checked his own jacket pockets for the Intourist bag. *Not there!— that bitch Zhanna must have taken it.* He patted the pockets of the tunic—at least she had not taken Ignatiev's passport and tickets.

The quickest way home to the Vyborg side of the Neva River was due north, past the Finland Station, but that meant walking right by the infamous "Big House"—KGB headquarters. The area was heavily policed at the best of times. Fearing arrest, he took a circuitous route back via Vasilyevskiy Island, keeping to the back streets. He tucked his hat under his arm with the brim against his tunic to hide the gold braid. In the crepuscular light, he passed small groups of militiamen who gave him little more than a glance (*even in broad daylight they'd only notice the uniform*, he thought). Near Lieutenant Schmidt Bridge, four militiamen were trying to arrest a drunk who had thrown a brick through a window of the Palace of Weddings. A largely inebriated crowd had gathered to jeer and jostle the policemen while the drunk screamed curses about the institution of marriage. *How Russian*, thought Mels. The same people that would walk past with averted gaze as the police broke up an unauthorized art exhibition would rally behind a foul-mouthed drunk.

In the confusion he slipped unnoticed over the bridge and nervously made his way past the University buildings. He knew there was less than an hour before all the bridges over the Neva would be raised to allow river traffic to pass and he still had one more island to leapfrog before he would reach the Vyborg side. He quickened his pace and made it back unchallenged, but as he turned past the shabby apartment blocks on the corner of his own street, he realized that his presence had been noticed by two thuggish-looking men standing outside his building. To his surprise, they both saluted. Obviously KGB, he surmised, replacing his hat and returning the salute.

"Good evening, Comrade General. We weren't expecting you."

"And why, exactly, is that? Do you *listen* to your car radio?"

"Well we, er, had instructions, sir. We were to stay here at the entrance—"

"So if Katz shows up he sees you and takes flight?! He's probably halfway to the Finnish border by now. Whose stupid idea was that?!"

"Major Radchenko, sir."

"Radchenko! That half-wit! Did you leave the daughter alone upstairs?"

"Well, yes, sir . . . the phone is being monitored at the Big House."

"And *that* is where I am going with the daughter. Give me your car keys. One of you will take his car into detention in case he tries to escape in that. The other should stay out of sight."

"His car, sir? We didn't know he had a car."

"And that is why I am a general and you are not. That is his car there. I believe you can start a Zaporozhets with a screwdriver if you don't have a master key."

Heart pounding, Mels left the agents to break into his neighbor's car while he rushed up the stairs to his apartment. He found his daughter sitting on her bed holding a torn photograph of the rock band "Aquarium" in her hands. She had the same determined look on her face he had seen so many times before swimming races. He crossed his lips with his forefinger as she looked up.

"Shhh, Luba. We need to get out of here. Right now. You're going to Grandpa's."

She nodded and gestured to a packed suitcase by the door. *Where does she get her cool nerve?*

"Daddy, they came hours ago. They said they were looking for an Intourist bag. What bag? I didn't tell them anything. I was scared at first but when they started ripping up my things I realized they weren't going to harm me, they were just trying to frighten me."

They started down the stairs. Mels replied in a whisper.

"Lubashka, I don't know why they're doing this. The KGB wants me to do something but I refused. There was a bag but I left it at your mother's place. It was empty anyway. This doesn't make any sense. If I turn myself in now they'll beat the crap out of me. I've had enough of that today. I want to talk to Grandpa first. Maybe his contacts can smooth things out."

A loud noise from his neighbor's apartment indicated that he had noticed the two agents tampering with his car. Mels started the KGB Volga and gunned the ignition. A powerful rumbling noise came from under the hood.

"Daddy, aren't you scared they're going to follow us?"

"In a Zaporozhets? Sewing machines have bigger motors than those things! This car has a Chaika engine in it—they won't even get close!"

Major Radchenko of the Fifth Directorate narrowed his piggy eyes and squinted through the flashing headlights of the oncoming car. An ingrained desire to ingratiate himself with his superiors coupled with his policeman's basic nosiness had quickly spotted the gold braid on the peaked cap of the driver of the Volga. There was something reassuringly familiar but at the same time unsettling about the glimpse of jaw he saw underneath it. And why would a general, without a bodyguard, be driving away the criminal's daughter? As he turned the corner, he saw one of the two agents he had assigned to guard the apartment trying to open the door of a rusty Zaporozhets while another held an intoxicated man dressed in dirty pajamas who was cursing in a language that he recognized immediately as Ukrainian. He swung his car in a wide U-turn and took off after the other Volga.

The first Mels knew that they were being followed was a garbled message on the car's two-way radio. He heard Radchenko's Ukrainian accent shouting his name before it disappeared into static.

"Control. Please repeat your message. Over."

Luba picked up the car microphone and handed it to Mels. He looked surprised.

"Go on, daddy, tell the dispatcher you've been spotted near the Smolniy Institute."

". . . Criminal Katz sighted on foot near Alexander Nevsky monastery, heading towards Smolniy Institute. Request assistance."

"Control. Message received. Agent with bad radio, please cease transmission. You are obstructing radio traffic."

The response was a renewed burst of static through which Mels caught several choice swear words. He laughed.

"That still leaves us with Radchenko to get rid of. I'll try to lose him around Lenin stadium then see if we can get over Tuchkov Bridge before it opens."

"It's too late, daddy. Tuchkov is already open. Try Birzhevoy."

He turned left, away from Tuchkov Bridge and towards the needle-like spire of Peter and Paul Cathedral. The Strelka, the scenic upstream end of Vasilyevskiy Island, was just over the Birzhevoy Bridge. Mels accelerated on the curve towards the Neva, but the roadway was already rising up.

"I love you, Luba. . . ."

He floored the gas pedal and steered for the gap. The Strelka sank below his line of sight for a moment then the overpowered car sailed across the three-meter gap and landed with a squeal of rubber on the other side.

"I think I just wet myself!"

"Me too!"

A loud splash interrupted them. Night fishermen and late night couples on the Strelka started to run towards the embankment. He slowed down. The militia were used to KGB Volgas speeding around Leningrad late at night but there was no point in attracting unnecessary attention to themselves.

"I think Radchenko just wet himself, too. . . ."

For now, and for the next half-hour, Vasilyevskiy Island was isolated. Whatever happened to him after that, it was important not to involve his daughter any more than was necessary. If he had known Radchenko was going to follow them he would never have brought her along. Still, it was best to go through with his plan and drop her at her grandfather's apartment. If she would be safe anywhere in Leningrad it would be with him, a genuine war hero who presumably still had some influence with the military. He turned down Bolshoy Street to the Sea Terminal where his father worked, then slowed as he approached his father's apartment building.

"Luba. If there are any KGB agents, don't lie to them. Just say who you are and say you want to see your grandfather. They won't arrest you, or they would have done it at our apartment. It's me they're after."

He stopped the car. That was odd. No KGB. Just a drunk

lying unconscious on the steps. Luba walked round the outstretched form. Mels was used to the sight of drunks but something about the sprawled figure seemed staged. For one thing, he looked too clean. For another, he could have sworn the man's eyes had been open just now. A small alarm went off in Mels' brain. He wound down the window and called after Luba.

"Lubashka, I'm going to stow away on a ship in the harbor. Don't tell your grandfather."

Before she could respond, he put the car in gear and drove to the gate of the Sea Terminal. He woke up the sentry who saluted sleepily and let him through.

He carefully parked in the space reserved for an admiral and changed back into his own clothes in the car. Abandoning the general's uniform in the trunk, he crept from building to building until he reached the giant loading crane his father operated. He climbed quietly up the ladder until he reached the control cabin then grabbed for the emergency hatch in the ceiling that lead to the corrugated iron roof. He had done this many times as a teenager—at first when he was trying to hide from his father then later when he was trying to find a place to sit and read or just stare across the Gulf of Finland and daydream.

He partially unbuckled his belt and passed a loop of it around the handle of a ventilation grill before refastening it. Then, exhausted, he fell asleep.

Chapter 4

The cooing of pigeons woke Mels at about seven o'clock. Despite the nearly twenty-four hour sunlight, the giant crane's metal roof was cool at that hour of the morning and the side he had slept on felt numb. He unfastened his belt buckle from the ventilation grille, sat up, and gently massaged life back into his stiff limbs, taking care to stay within the shadow cast by a large hammer and sickle that were welded onto the front guttering. From his vantage point on the roof of the crane's cabin he peered over the edge and watched the first shipyard workers making their way through the sentry gates.

A uniformed militiaman stood by the car Mels had abandoned the night before and several dozen more were disembarking from an olive-green bus. They formed themselves into two lines in front of the vehicle. In the quiet of the morning he heard the officer in charge tell them that they were to search the ships and outbuildings for "the criminal, Katz." He gained a certain satisfaction from the description of himself as being "resourceful, cunning, and dangerous" and the fact that the policemen were being told to stick together in teams of two. To his surprise, he found himself quite enjoying his newfound notoriety.

As the trickle of arriving workers became a flood, Mels recognized the unmistakable muscular figure of his father striding purposefully towards the crane. He was not the only one to recognize him. From a second Volga car parked near the entrance emerged the two KGB agents he had last seen at his apartment.

He guessed they had not had much sleep overnight. They called out to his father to stop but were unable to reach him immediately through the crowd.

Mels' father scaled the crane's ladder with the ease of a man half his age. Through the ventilation grille, Mels saw him enter the cabin and look furiously in a small closet by the control panel, muttering under his breath. The two panting agents arrived a moment later.

"Lev Davidovitch Katz? My colleague and I are from the KGB. We want to ask you some questions."

With his back to the door, Mels' father continued to look around the small cabin, apparently unaware of their presence.

"Hey! Are you trying to ignore us?!"

The younger agent grabbed Mels' father by the shoulder and jerked him around. Instinctively, the older man reached for the agent's wrist and in a deft movement that belied his years twisted the man's arm behind his back. With the other he applied a chokehold.

"Who the fuck are you? Quickly, now. Fat boy here has approximately a minute and a half before lack of oxygen will permanently damage what little brain he has. And speak up. I'm deaf thanks to a Fascist shell that landed too close."

That young agent does appear to be changing color rather rapidly, thought Mels, from his overhead viewpoint. The older agent reached into his jacket and pulled out a KGB identification card. He held it close so Mels' father could read it. Immediately, he dropped the other agent who collapsed heavily on the metal floor.

"KGB! Well, Comrades, I'm always at the service of the Soviet State. Here, give me a hand with your young colleague. I'm afraid I'll have to ask your indulgence for just a moment while I get my hearing aid. I must have left it in the shed downstairs."

Between the two of them they managed to balance the younger agent on the only seat in the cabin. Without asking permission, Mels' father opened the door and started down the ladder.

"He's . . . getting . . . away—" gasped the younger agent.

"He'll be back, Misha. Trust me."

"The old yid must take us for fools, Sergei: '. . . always at the service of the Soviet State!'"

"You are too young to remember when many people thought like that. He'll be back. He'll help us, too. His type is easily exploited: 'You can chop your boiled eggs on him.' Not because he's afraid of us but because he thinks it's the right thing to do."

"Like roughing up an agent of the KGB? You saw him, Sergei. I should beat the shit out of him just for that."

"Maybe you'll have your chance before this is over, Misha. For now we have business to attend to."

"Why exactly *are* we here? What did Mels Katz do? Is this still the ballerina business?"

"What did Katz *do*? Misha, the probability is that, originally, he *did* nothing. Of course, now Radchenko is dead and someone will have to pay for it. But that is not why we are here. We are here to find Katz and make sure he does what *we* want. And yes, everything we do these days has something to do with tripping the ballerina."

"I don't understand this. We'll never be able to get through the ballerina's guard. . . . "

"Don't be so sure. Remember two things: (a) the spouse is Jewish and (b) the weak link is the daughter. He doesn't know it but Katz himself is going to be our leverage. As I said, trust me, Misha, I know you would like to frighten his father into submission but you will find that some of the old men of his generation have seen things many times more frightening than the knuckle-duster you have in your pocket. Far better we get his willing cooperation. The phones are bugged. We have informers everywhere. Eventually Mels Katz will attempt to contact his daughter. Then we will have him. And, one more thing: don't talk to anyone about this—even at the Big House. I'm serious, Misha, Asparagus will skin you alive if you say anything about the ballerina."

The door opened and Mels' father reappeared. He placed a

plastic box about the size of a small transistor radio on the control panel and plugged a cable into one side. He placed the headsets at the other end over his head. Mels heard the device whistle as it was turned on.

"Continue, Comrades."

"Lev Davidovitch, a missing KGB car was found around here. We know that this car was used by your son to deliver your granddaughter to your apartment last night. We have reason to believe that your son has stowed away on one of the ships in port. Our agents are conducting a ship-by-ship search but in the meantime we ask for your cooperation. As your granddaughter has no doubt told you, some misguided agents of the KGB arrived at your son's apartment yesterday evening. In fact, a regrettable error was made due to a quite unforgivable mix-up at headquarters. Your son's name is unfortunately very close to that of a known anti-Soviet agent. Although we were prepared to forgive this man's activities against the State, it has recently come to light that he was involved in black marketeering of an egregious nature, stealing penicillin from a Children's Hospital.

Naturally, we moved against what we thought was his base but the agents were sent to the wrong apartment. Sadly, one of best agents was tragically killed last night while speeding after your son to try to explain the misunderstanding. We hope that you can be of assistance to us in locating Mels L'vovitch. If he does contact you, please ask him to telephone us at his earliest opportunity. We would like him to come down to the Big House where we will of course reimburse him for any property damage that has been caused."

Throughout this, Mels' father had nodded vigorously and made occasional notes with a blunt pencil on the back of an envelope.

"Well, Comrade. I am pleased that you have come to me and that you have attempted to hide nothing. My granddaughter woke me last night with a strange tale of 'agents' breaking into my son's apartment and wrecking the place. I confess I felt I thought I'd misunderstood her—my hearing not being all it could be. I tried to telephone my old colleague, General Gureyvitch, last night and demand an explanation but the telephone was out of order. Now you have saved me the trouble. As I told Luba, I was sure there was a reasonable explanation. Even in Stalin's time—though mistakes were made—there was generally no smoke without fire. Mels is a good boy but sometimes naïve with his head in the clouds. For someone with his education, his understanding of the class struggle is somewhat lacking. I was worried his attitude may have unintentionally offended someone but you have reassured me. We are not capitalists—though mistakes are made we are not ashamed to admit them—"

"So you will inform us as soon as you hear from your son?"

"Of course, of course! Now if you will excuse me, I have a daily quota of work to fulfill."

The two KGB agents returned to their car. Misha, the younger, could not restrain a laugh as they went down the stairs but by that time Mels' father had switched off his hearing aid to conserve batteries. As Mels jumped down from the safety hatch into the cabin he reflected on whether his father's beliefs and deafness were related. His ideas and ideology had frozen in time in 1943 when a shell had exploded a few meters from where he and his men had fought, hand-to-hand against the Germans. He had inhabited a world of black and white, with honest Communists and demon Fascists, ever since. Born in 1920, he had actually been called Lev by his father—a Red Army colonel—in honor of Trotsky. How he had survived Stalin's time with a Jewish last name and the forename and patronymic of Trotsky was beyond belief. He'd even spent three weeks in Peter-and-Paul fortress, not knowing if he would end up in the Gulag, on a trumped-up charge. Anyone else would have learned from this and called his own son something neutral; "Ivan," or "Sasha." Not Lev Davidovitch. Against his wife's wishes, he called his son "Mels" after *M*arx-*E*ngels-*L*enin-*S*talin.

After his mother's untimely death when he was still a child, Mels had found himself increasingly alienated from his father, particularly when he chose a life in Academia instead of the military. That said, family was family and—unlike the USSR in 1943—right now he did not have many powerful allies on his side.

He waited patiently in the cabin for his father to turn round. The incident with Misha had not been the first he had witnessed where his father's reflexes had got the better of him and he had no desire to experience one of his father's chokeholds.

"Mels! Where did you appear from?! You just missed two Comrades from the KGB who came to apologize for last night."

Mels mimed for his father to put his headphones on.

"Father. I heard what they said very well. I spent the night on the roof. Perhaps you should hear what they really said, too."

From his pocket he produced the cigarette lighter recorder and set it down next to the hearing aid. Though the acoustics were somewhat poor, Lev Davidovitch Katz listened silently to the entire conversation as recorded by his son, including the part that had taken place between the two agents in his absence.

"The ballerina? Do they mean that slut ex-wife of yours?"

"Who else? Look father, I was at her apartment last night. She seems to be running some sort of high-class brothel for important people who like young girls. She obviously has powerful protection. This 'Asparagus' guy is a general. But that's not the only problem I have with the KGB. The agent that died came to my office earlier in the day. He wanted me to cooperate on writing a technical paper that has no merit whatsoever. He followed me around all afternoon. Then there was a tram accident. They arrested someone—a black marketeer, I think—and an Uzbek boy...."

He paused.

"Well, what about the Uzbek boy?"

"He was carrying a bag. I think I may have picked up *his* bag by mistake. The KGB want it."

"Well give it back, then."

"I can't, father. I left it at Zhanna's. That must be what she meant about me going to prison—"

A whistling noise came from the hearing aid. Lev Davidovitch turned it off for a moment.

"It's the batteries. You'll just have to listen to me for a minute while they recover. Look, son, this all sounds very complicated but I'm sure I can make some calls and sort it out. Gureyvitch is retired now but he'll remember our time in the trenches while our wives subsisted on nothing but linseed oil and wallpaper paste. Did I tell you about the time he saved my life by throwing himself on a Fascist hand grenade?"

Many times, thought Mels. Actually, the story had never made any sense. Gureyvitch survived the Great Patriotic War completely unscathed whereas his father had been wounded four times. Perhaps he made a habit of throwing himself on dud grenades. And, although both he and his father had been awarded Hero of the Soviet Union and the Stalin medal, Gureyvitch was the one who was living on a general's pension while his father was still doing hard manual work for a living.

His father switched the hearing aid back on.

"I saw your friend Gureyvitch coming out of the special store last week. Why don't you ask him to get you new batteries for this antique? And how is it that he shops in a store that is only open to people who have been members of the Party since 1930? He's younger than you, father."

Lev Davidovitch's back stiffened.

"That's the kind of slander I would expect from you, Mels. You spend too much of your time listening to western propaganda. Gureyvitch will be at the Anti Zionist Committee meeting tonight at the Palace of Culture. I could talk to him then."

That's probably why the man gets special treatment. He was not sure he wanted help from someone who would sell out his fellow Jews, but for Luba's sake he would have to swallow his pride.

"All right, father. Gureyvitch is 'a goose with big feet'. He knows how to work the system. But I don't want Luba to go to this meeting. She has enough to contend with without sitting through a lecture about how Zionists were in league with Hitler. In the meantime I will try to locate that Uzbek boy, if he isn't in the Big House. Right now, though, I need to get out of the Yard to find somewhere to lie low. When does the beer wagon get here?"

"About ten. Why? It's unlike you to drink, Mels."

"It's not for me, father. It's a warm day and my guess is those two agents down there in that car are starting to get a little thirsty. They've been on duty all night so a little beer and the hot sun should do the trick."

At ten o'clock a trailer resembling a military water wagon was towed to the front gates. A line of hung-over workers seeking the hair of the dog soon formed. The woman in charge filled liter plastic jugs with beer from a hose. The queue was slow moving as there was a shortage of jugs and those waiting at the back of the line enjoined those at the front to drink faster. Mels' father walked to the front of the line and silenced the chorus of grumbles from his fellow workers by insisting on being served next "in solidarity with our colleagues in the KGB." He took the jug to the Volga and handed it through the window to a sweating Misha.

"We really shouldn't. On duty and all that. . . ."

As Mels anticipated, he did not need much persuasion. Half an hour later, Mels—dressed in overalls over his clothes and wearing welder's goggles—walked nonchalantly past the snoring agents, and turned north on Sredniy Street. As he went past the Kirov Palace of Culture, a team of workmen was putting up a banner that advertised the Anti Zionist Committee meeting. The huge red and white banner covered at least half of the ugly Soviet Constructivist facade. As the banner drifted slowly in the breeze, Mels noted that the Palace of Culture would be honored by the presence of the Chief Rabbi—no doubt justifying his State salary. He smiled as he remembered the old joke about how hard it was for the Politburo to find someone acceptable for that job—the only candidates being a non-Communist and a Jew.

He stopped at a kiosk and bought a small loaf and a bottle of mineral water then sat on a bench at a tram stop and chewed the bread slowly while he considered his options. The best course of action was to get off the streets for the rest of the day to give his father time to talk to his old army pal. Maybe some strings could be pulled on his behalf. If they were just trying to "get" his ex-wife he certainly was not going to defend her, not after what he had seen last night. *But what about the plastic bag? What was in it—drugs?* There was no point asking Zhanna, even if he could contact her now. She would want something in return. He could warn her she was being targeted but then he would be on "her" side, against the KGB! *And the Uzbek bo . . . ?* How did one locate someone in a city the size of Leningrad? Even if he was out of jail, Mels did not even know his name. A tram pulled up at the stop and disgorged its passengers. He saw the conductor inside trying to wake an inebriated passenger and throw him off the tram. *Of course . . . that pretty conductress!* She seemed to know the boy. Maybe he could track her down?

Still hungry after he finished the loaf, he pondered the wisdom of getting something to eat in one of the cheap local eateries frequented by students. Actually, wasn't there an Uzbek restaurant somewhere near the Fontanka district? It was too up-market for him ever to have eaten there but maybe some of the staff would know the conductress. There were not all that many Uzbeks in Leningrad and it was worth a shot. He walked up to the Vasileostrovskaya metro station, intending to take the subway across the Neva. But standing outside the entrance were half a dozen militiamen, checking identity papers. He turned—too quickly—towards the bridge that would have taken him to the Fontanka. One of the cops called after him to stop. He ducked into St Andrews Cathedral.

Inside the darkened church, a guide was misinforming his tour group about the rites of the Russian Orthodox Church to the evident discomfort of a nearby priest. When the priest saw Mels he called him over.

"About time! The lights have been out all day. You took your time getting here."

He showed him into a back room where an antiquated fuse box was illuminated by a votive candle.

As soon as the priest left him, Mels stripped off his overalls and dumped them with the goggles in a closet containing surplices. He slipped out of a side door and strode quickly away, right into the path of the militiaman who had beckoned him earlier. Resignedly, he took the Internal Passport from his pocket and placed it in the man's outstretched palm. To his amazement, the man merely glanced at it, then waved him away. Mels could not believe his luck. Not daring to look back in case he was being followed, he hid himself in the midday crowd thronging the Strelka. As he walked past the Academy of Sciences, a thought came to him. He looked at the Internal Passport, still in his hand. *It's Academician Ignatiev's!* Elated, he laughed out loud to the surprise of a crowd of students standing outside the Kunstkammer Museum. How easy it was to become someone else in a country where people put symbolism above reality. Nevertheless, it would be foolish to assume that the KGB would be as easy to fool as their lowly cousins in the militia. Presumably some time today Ignatiev would be informed about his disappearance and tell the KGB that he had his Internal Passport—or would he? It was an offence to loan one's Passport to anyone, let alone a wanted "criminal." Ignatiev would be pissing his pants worrying about it . . . which reminded him, he needed to change his clothes.

He followed the line of students into the Kunstkammer. At least it was cool in there amongst the glass cases full of freaks and curiosities. He stared at the pickled Siamese twins and two-headed cows with a gaggle of fascinated schoolgirls his daughter's age.

"Peter the Great gave rewards to his countrymen for finding these 'monsters.' He was intensely proud of his collection but worried that Russians would not understand the concept of a 'museum' so he gave visitors a glass of vodka to encourage them to visit."

The girls nodded. Why was he telling them this? He was supposed to be making himself inconspicuous.

"Are you Professor Suslov? We waited outside for you for an hour."

"No. I'm, er, Professor Ignatiev. Comrade Suslov couldn't make it today. How many of you are there?"

"There are supposed to be twenty of us but most of the boys took off when Professor Suslov didn't show up."

"Well, I don't blame them! Have you seen Lomonsov's Globe, yet?"

The girls smiled. He spent the rest of the afternoon in their company, delighted to show them around the dusty halls filled with ethnographic exhibits from all over the world. It was no hardship to him. It was a museum he had loved since childhood. And, whoever Suslov was, he never showed up. Much to their regret, Mels eventually bade the girls farewell, telling them he had an appointment in the Fontanka district. Two of the more precocious girls came with him, happily chattering away about their studies as they approached a group of militiamen checking identity papers. Mels' rumpled, unshaven appearance awakened the suspicions of one observant policeman who seemed unconvinced of Mels' resemblance to his passport photo. One of the girls, a freckle-faced redhead, immediately leapt to his defense.

"This is Professor *Ignatiev*. Can you read?"

The cop shrugged and handed back Ignatiev's passport.

The girls left him in front of the Uzbek restaurant. As they departed, the redhead impulsively put her arms around his neck, pulled his face level with hers and kissed him on the cheek. Before she pulled away, she whispered in his ear.

"Give my love to Luba, Mels L'vovitch."

She gave him a knowing smile, then left with her friend.

"Your charm doesn't work so well with me, friend."

Mels came to with a start. He turned to find himself being addressed by the doorman of the Uzbek restaurant.

"You're not coming in here dressed like that. You look like a bum."

Mels looked at his reflection in the mirrored surface of the door. The doorman was not entirely accurate but he had a point. His jacket still had the marks left by the corrugated iron roof, there was a suspicious stain on his pants and the smooth contours of his face were obscured by a day's stubble.

Mels felt in his jacket for a bribe then checked himself. He still had a pocketful of rubles—the change for Ignatiev's tickets—but how long would they have to last? The tip that would be required to get into such a classy restaurant would be more than the cost of a bath at a public bathhouse.

"Can you tell me, Comrade, where the nearest *banya* is?"

"Well, there's one at the big hotel next to the Russian Museum. You could try your charms there. . . ."

A weary Mels presented himself at the *banya* and paid the attendant for a towel, soap and a razor blade.

"Look, I had an accident. Do you suppose you could get these clothes cleaned in an hour? I'll make it worthwhile. The man sized him up with a conspiratorial look.

"That could be possible. But frankly, Comrade, I think you might want to stay out of Tepidarium B. And don't use the changing rooms at the back."

Strange, thought Mels. He undressed in a cubicle at the front and took his clothes to the attendant who summoned an ancient *babushka* to see to his clothes. Shaving himself with a firm grip on the razor blade, he wondered what the man had meant about Tepidarium B. He had an hour to kill, however, so he ventured into the first tiled room and sat on a bench.

Around him, men were scrubbing themselves or their companions, pouring water over each other's heads and soaping each other. Attendants handed out bundles of birch twigs with which men flailed at each other's bodies; a whirring sound followed by a satisfying "thwack" as the birch made contact with pink flesh. Despite the sign forbidding the consumption of alcoholic beverages, the sweet smell of spilled beer pervaded the place and the floor was awash in abandoned rubber shoes, birch twigs, and drunken flies.

A fat man swathed in towels with several bottles under his arms walked towards Mels' bench. He opened the first by holding the cap against the edge of the bench and striking the bottle top with a chubby hand. He stemmed the flow of foam gushing out of the opened bottle with his lips, then tipped his head back and finished the beer in two or three gulps. Mels was impressed.

"That's quite a thirst you have there, Comrade."

"I've been here three hours. You have to replace the sweat."

Well, you've certainly done that, thought Mels, looking at the folds of the man's stomach. He declined a proffered bottle of beer and got up to go into the Steam Room.

"Be careful where you step, Comrade. . . ."

Careful? Did he really look so out of place? Admittedly it had been a few years since he had been to a *banya* but he had been regularly when he was doing fieldwork in Siberia. That was how they would end their day. There was nothing more exhilarating than the contrast between outside temperatures of -30° C and a sauna set to +50° C.

The Steam Room was nearly empty. He sat on a lower bench and closed his eyes. He was in pretty good physical shape for a man in his mid thirties, though that was more due to the fact that he had no car and walked everywhere rather than any conscious effort on his part. Still, it was best not to fall asleep here. Like most things in life, heat like this was best taken in moderation. He was rudely awakened by a voice in English.

"General! So, have we got over our little snit last night, hmm?! I'm surprised to see *you* here. . . ."

Brantley Logan, of course. He was sitting on an upper bench, wearing a tailored bathrobe that did not quite hide several more purplish-brown birthmarks on his skinny body. Aware that the KGB was probably routinely following Logan, Mels looked around before risking a reply. The room had emptied except for the two of them.

"How are you, Mr. Logan? Rudolf not with you?"

"Rudolf is practicing his pirouettes like a good boy. He's

terribly nice, you know, but a bit boring for my tastes. I really prefer something a little more exotic, if you know what I mean. Maybe you could ask your colleagues to arrange that?"

"*My* colleagues?"

"Oh come on, General, I know they work for you. And I'm sure you have some excellent photos for your files by now. The trouble is, I don't care. And I don't think my bosses in the State Department really care, either. They knew what I did back in San Francisco and they know what I do here. So save your videos for training purposes."

Mels shook his head. He poured water over the clay tiles of the boiler. All the air in the room seemed to disappear. He waited to catch his breath before replying.

"Thank you for the tip, Mr. Logan."

"Brantley."

"Brantley. However, I have some business to attend to, so I hope you will excuse me."

"Pity. We were just getting friendly."

"Some other time, perhaps."

"Well, I'm here every day at this time. I haven't been able to get rid of a chest cold and the steam helps. I must be getting old."

Logan smiled coquettishly. *If you were a woman I'd think you were fishing for a compliment.* He stood up to leave. He noticed there was a door on the other side of the room with a painted letter "B" on it. Well, that would have to stay a mystery for now. He needed to find the young Uzbek woman.

He returned to the front desk the way he had come in. His clothes were hanging on a hangar. They smelled slightly of some chemical.

"Don't worry. The smell will disappear in the open air. They've been 'dry cleaned.'"

He showered, dressed and retrieved his belongings from a locker. As he left the fat man was negotiating with the assistant to fetch more beer.

Chapter 5

It must be a slow night, thought Mels, as the doorman let him in after a token ten-minute wait. Sure enough, most of the tables were empty. He seated himself near the stage at the front of the restaurant, which was decorated with sabers, camel saddles, and over-sized brassware to evoke a Central Asian flavor. An Uzbek-costumed waitress handed him a multi-page menu and awaited his order. He pondered what to choose. The restaurant fare seemed to be based on lamb and horseflesh. He had never had horse but was sure it tasted no worse than some of the things he had eaten in Siberia, including his own dog at one stage—though that had not been by choice. The waitress gave an unsubtle cough to indicate that she was still waiting.

"I'm sorry. I don't know much about Uzbek food. What do you recommend?"

Disarmed by his politeness, the normally surly waitress smiled. She whispered her answer.

"We're not supposed to tell you this, but all we have is horse sausage and borscht."

He laughed.

"Supposing I'd ordered something else?"

"I'm supposed to go into the kitchen, then return and tell you we just ran out of it."

"Well horse sausage and borscht sounds just fine. And mineral water."

"No vodka? We always have vodka. You know they say that everything tastes better with vodka—even vodka."

"Thank you, no. I don't usually drink."

The waitress looked puzzled; a polite customer was strange enough, but one who didn't drink?

"Are you a foreigner?"

He laughed.

"No. Look I'll have a beer if it will please you."

She departed to the kitchen with his order and he looked around the restaurant. A loud-mouthed red-haired man was arguing with a waiter about the bill. His hair color reminded him of the teenager from the museum. A friend of his daughter's obviously, but from where? Not school, he was sure of that. Swimming perhaps? The restaurant manager was summoned to the table to settle the dispute. He brought with him the cashier's abacus. The argument abated somewhat when the red-haired man realized his arithmetic was off. Could the girl have been in one of his lectures? Surely she was too young? Then he remembered. He knew it had something to do with mathematics! Boris Grebenschikov, the lead singer of Aquarium, worked as a computer programmer when he was not composing songs. Mels had casually remarked to his daughter one evening a few months ago that Boris had been in one of his lectures at the Institute of Applied Mathematics. Luba had insisted on coming to the Institute herself for his next lecture, ostensibly to hear him speak but really—he knew—to get Boris's autograph. She had come with another Aquarium fan— the redhead. Well, she was quite a sport to have played along with his little charade, but was she discreet?

The waitress arrived with his food and a bottle of beer. He ate slowly and sipped at the beer, hoping either the restaurant would fill up or the entertainment would begin so he could ask questions about the conductress without attracting too much attention. Unfortunately, both occurred at once and no sooner had the music begun than he found himself having to share his table in the crowded restaurant with a uniformed major and his wife. Shy at first, the man started to loosen up as the vodka bottle in front of him started to empty. A chance remark by Mels about the man's unusually detailed knowledge of Uzbek cuisine lead to a diatribe about the unreliability of the moslem troops in the Fortieth Army against their brethren in Afghanistan. He seemed eager to explain to Mels the tactics his unit had used against *'dushmans'* on the southern front, using the condiments on the table to demonstrate troop movements from Termez to Qandahar.

Mels might ordinarily have been interested in the man's account, contradicting as it did everything he had read in the Soviet press. He had never heard of "Black Tulips" before—the grim transport planes sent to pick up the Russian casualties—and had no idea there were so many in use in Afghanistan. But right now he had a mission of his own to complete and he was at a loss as to how he would get the major to shut up. A troupe of folk dancers in national costume came on stage. *Excellent.* Now was his chance to talk to the waitress as the man's attention was distracted. He raised his hand then checked it halfway as his eye caught who had just appeared from the wings. It was her—the conductress.

What a dancer she was! *How could someone so graceful work on the trams*? If there was any doubt in his mind about her identity it was stifled when she executed an elegant twist in mid-air. From his seat at the front of the restaurant he could see an ugly bruise across the back of her neck where Radchenko had hit her.

He sat hypnotized. He had not been to the Kirov—on principle—since his divorce but he had sat through hundreds of ballets in his time. He knew he was watching a natural, against whom the other dancers in the troupe looked clumsy and earth-bound.

At the end of the dance, he leapt to his feet and shouted "Bravo!" He clapped his hands for what must have been a full minute before he realized he was the only one standing and that most of the other diners were looking at him, aghast. He sat in confused embarrassment.

After the second show, he paid his bill, left the restaurant and waited by the side door. She exited with a group of dancers and performers. She caught his eye as she passed but made no outward sign of recognition. After a few meters she stopped and searched the bag she was carrying.

"Shit! I left my keys. You guys go ahead."

She turned back to the restaurant then paused for a moment in front of the door, pretending to tie her shoelace. As soon as her companions had turned the corner she said one word out of the corner of her mouth to Mels.

"Follow."

He obeyed, switching from one side of the street to another and trying to keep at least half a block behind her, just in case. Eventually she stopped in front of a shabby communal apartment building in the southern suburbs. She waited while he caught up then issued another one word command before entering.

"Wait."

A few minutes later she re-emerged and beckoned him to follow her. The apartment was up five floors. Her room was down a corridor with creaking floorboards that lead from the stairway to the kitchen. A whining sound from a leaking water heater emanated from the bathroom next door.

"You are in luck, Mels Katz. I share this apartment with three other families. Inevitably in a place like this one or two of them are 'soggy.' Two of them are on vacation and the couple in the other room are out."

"'Soggy'? You're the second person to use that expression in two days. You mean they're KGB?"

"Not full-time agents of the KGB. Just assholes who like to inform on their fellow citizens in return for some petty favors. Maybe just a chance to buy chocolate in the special stores or the opportunity to jump ahead in the housing queue. But don't worry, they can't listen in with that noise. All they can do is report if I have a visitor. To tell the truth, I think most of them are too stupid to know the trouble their snooping causes. I think even the KGB despise them."

"You sound like an expert, young lady. Look, you know my name and I don't know yours."

"It's Tanya. A very Russian name for an Uzbek, but my father is a great believer in the art of merging in. I guess your father was a Communist?"

"*Is* a Communist. A name like 'Mels' is a bit of a giveaway, isn't it? Actually I think he's the last Communist in Russia. How *do* you know my name, by the way?"

"The big man with the broken nose who hit me came back to the tram. He thought I was still unconscious. I think he was following you and the other one—the one I thought was trying to get off without paying—was following Timor, the Uzbek boy. They started looking for Timor's Intourist bag. You know, the one you picked up. Apparently it has something in it they want. One of the passengers told them you had grabbed it and got off the bus with it, then 'Broken Nose' told a militiaman to radio for back-up to look for you. I pretended to come round at that point and they started in on me. Broken Nose would have hit me again if the other one hadn't stopped him. I hope that man rots in hell."

"He may be doing that right now. He's dead, apparently. He drove off a bridge while he was following me last night."

"Good. One less of them. Though I don't suppose that improves *your* position?"

"You know, Tanya, you haven't asked me what I've done yet. I could be an American spy."

She laughed.

"Mels, you asked me if I was an expert in the ways of the KGB. Not really. But I've brushed shoulders with them before now. Like me, I suspect you hadn't done very much or you wouldn't still have been walking the streets."

"Actually I have no idea what I'm supposed to have done. Radchenko—'Broken Nose'—was pressuring me to do something I didn't want to do, but I never even got a chance to look in that bag. My wife took it."

"Your wife?"

"Ex-wife. That's a long story. Look, tell me about this Timor. How well do you know him?"

"Everyone in the Uzbek community knows him. He's a sad case. Uzbek society is even less tolerant of his kind than Russian—"

"His 'kind'?"

"He's gay. Homosexual. He works for one of the big paint factories. I believe he helps in their design section. You know, where they put together displays for trade shows and the like. I don't think he was very good at it but the KGB pulled strings because he was more useful to them that way."

"So *he* works for the KGB, too?"

"Mels, I don't believe in making excuses for people. The KGB tried to get me to work for them and I refused. But in Timor's case I have a certain amount of sympathy. Were you born in Leningrad?"

"Yes."

"Then you're probably like all the other Russians who complain about how few things there are to buy in the shops and how long you have to stand in line. You probably don't know what it's like to come from a place where the clothes are always ugly and out-of-date and the shops *never* have foreign shoes for sale. Timor was arrested back home in bed with some man. He says the other man propositioned him then set him up with the police. Anyway, they let him off with a warning but after that the KGB came round and told him they were going to need his services some time. He didn't want to, so he left and came here. The same week that he arrived he did a really stupid thing. He saw some shoes in a window display. He stood in line for three hours but when he got to the front of the line they didn't have his size. He bought the shoes anyway. Then, when he was leaving the shop, he asked someone at the back of the line if he wanted to buy them. A militiaman heard him and arrested him for 'professional speculation.' When they found out he'd been arrested for a homosexual offence and he had no residency papers they handed him over to the KGB. This time he had no choice. They told him he'd get two years on the profiteering charge alone. This way, he was told, you get to do what you like doing *and* get paid for it. They got him the job with the paint company so he'd meet people. Foreign businessmen, that sort of thing."

"So why were they following their own employee? Seems a bit odd doesn't it? It's not like he's going to do anything on a crowded tram."

"That I don't know. You'll have to ask him that yourself when he gets out. He's 'sitting' on the other side of the Neva right now."

"'Sitting'?"

"In the Kresty prison. You remember that old joke? 'Under Stalin we were all passengers on a tram. Some standing, some 'sitting' but all of us shaking'. . . ."

"I know very well about Stalin. My father is a Hero of the Soviet Union but it didn't prevent him from falling foul of the old bastard. He ended up in Peter-and-Paul Fortress after the war basically just because he had an argument with one of our neighbors."

"What happened?"

"The next thing he knew he was having his belt and laces removed and being thrown in a cell. After a couple of days they hauled him before someone from the NKVD. On the desk in front of him was a smelly brown paper bag. He was told to identify the contents."

"What was in it?"

"Shit. Specifically a page from Pravda with Stalin's photo that someone had used to wipe his ass. The interrogator asked him whether he denied that he'd done it."

"What did he say?"

"What *could* he say? They had 'witnesses'—this neighbor and her brother—who claimed they'd *seen* him do it. As if he took a dump with the door open! He told them it was hard to find a page of Pravda that didn't have Stalin's photo on it. I should also tell you that my father's hearing is pretty bad so he couldn't follow everything that was going on. They threw him back in the cell for another week and then he was freed."

"On what grounds? People died for less."

"Oh, if this had happened fifteen years earlier he would have got a bullet in the back of the neck. But two other people died. One was my mother, whose nerves never recovered from the *blokada*, when she saw her parents die from the cold and hunger. She'd go to pieces whenever my father had to be out of town, even for a night. One time I woke up to find her chopping up the kitchen table—'for fuel,' she said.

She locked me in a small closet then threw herself out the window. Even today I can't bear to be in enclosed spaces. God knows why she killed herself. Maybe she thought it might make them more sympathetic to my father, what with me being a young kid with no one to bring me up. Who knows, maybe she would have been right. She didn't know who else was going to die that week."

"Stalin?"

"That's right. My father was released overnight. He still believes it was his military 'connections' that got him out. But you know the weirdest thing?"

"What?"

"To him the whole thing was just an administrative error. He never blamed anyone for it—not Stalin; not the neighbors. And the neighbors themselves acted the same way. As if what had happened was a train wreck or a natural disaster. They even sent flowers for my mother. Apparently they'd hoped to get our apartment if we'd had to move out.

There, I haven't told that story to anyone except my daughter. Isn't it funny the way we censor ourselves? After all, the KGB already know about it."

She smiled.

"But what about you, Tanya? I know a little bit about dancing. How come you work on the trams if you can dance like that?"

"I'll tell you later."

"Later? Why not now?"

"Now we have something else to do...."

She unbuttoned her blouse and drew it slowly over her head. The brown nipples under her white nylon bra were already hard. They kissed. It had been so long since Mels had kissed a woman he had almost forgotten how sweet it was. He fumbled with the bra but she pulled his hand away and undid it herself. His hand reached up her smooth thighs to the top. He was surprised to find how wet she was. He slowly pulled the panties down over her legs and kissed her knees and then between her thighs. She shivered. He undressed under her fascinated gaze. He looked down at his circumcised penis.

"I'm Jewish."

She giggled, then lay back on the bed and said something under her breath in Uzbek. He recognized the word.

"Of course I'll be careful."

She half raised herself and looked at him as if about to say something but then lay back again and beckoned for him to come to her.

Afterwards, a troubled Mels lay next to a radiant Tanya. He reflected on the fact that—much as he loved women—he always had complex feelings about sex.

Accomplished as he seemed to be as a lover, his own enjoyment was always tempered by practicalities—was the woman enjoying this, was he going to be able to pull out in time, why were they doing this, was this going to lead to misunderstandings from either party, could anyone hear them (particularly his daughter)? Now, this new complication . . . .

Tanya's face suddenly clouded with concern.

"What is it, Mels? Was I no good?"

"Tanya, you were wonderful. Really wonderful. It's just that I've never had sex with a virgin before."

She shrugged.

"Oh that. Well it didn't hurt much and I hardly bled at all, did I?"

"But you're always going to remember your first time—"

"And what? You're not worthy or something? Mels Katz, international spy, licensed to kill. . . ."

He laughed.

"But not licensed to teach any more, unfortunately. I'm really just a geophysicist. That's someone who uses physical methods like seismic waves or gravity to work out the structure of the earth."

"I know what a geophysicist is. My father is an engineer. It's strange to think after all the worrying my father did about my choice of suitors that I would find happiness with a Jew."

"What with you being an Uzbek, you mean?"

"I'm not Uzbek. I *come* from Uzbekistan. I look Uzbek. I speak Uzbek. Even my passport says my nationality is 'Uzbek.' But I'm a Sephardic Jew from Bokhara. My family has lived there for, well, who knows, certainly hundreds of years, maybe a thousand."

"So why does your passport say 'Uzbek'?"

"I nagged and nagged my father until he paid someone to have it changed. You see, I never wanted to emigrate. I always wanted to be a ballet dancer. And where else is better than the Soviet Union for that? In Bokhara, the Jews are discriminated against by the Uzbeks. I knew I would never pass for a Russian but I was naïve enough to believe that—as an Uzbek—maybe I could get into the Academic Choreography school in Leningrad."

"That's ironic. You're Jewish and your passport says 'Uzbek.' My daughter's says 'Jewish' even though her mother is Russian. For the last two days I have been walking round Leningrad using a fifty-three year-old Russian's passport and nobody batted an eyelid. But go on with your story about the school."

"I applied there when I was twelve. There are fifteen hundred applicants a year but they only accept eighty of which maybe fifty stay the course. You have to have a long, sturdy body and natural grace or they won't even look at you. And they won't take you if you've had any prior ballet tuition because they say you can't undo bad training. I got through to the last hundred then I was told I was 'too ugly' to be a dancer; no one would accept a Central Asian dancing the part of Odetta in Swan Lake. I was so devastated I couldn't even cry. Then this beautiful blonde woman spoke up and said she would accept me in her class. She took all the minority kids plus some that had been rejected because they were a little too 'developed' physically, but we were treated differently from the other girls and put in a separate dormitory.

The ballerinas' dormitory had a *dezurnaya*—the usual combination head maid and paid informer. If you did something wrong, your first infractions were reported by her to the Young Communist League and you'd have to go to a boring meeting after class. If you were a persistent offender you'd be turned over to the 'operatives'—the Peoples' Guard for Preservation of Social Order. They're young thugs in their teens under the direct supervision of the KGB. You've got to remember that we were just kids. It was like throwing lambs to wolves.

After a while some of my classmates girls started wearing cosmetics, smoking cigarettes and acting up. From somewhere they got money to buy nice clothes, the kind you never see in the shops. This kind of behavior was tolerated—maybe even encouraged—for a while, then one day we'd come in and some particular girl would be missing. We were told whoever it was had gone 'back home.' All this time we were studying ballet, though we were kept separate from the other girls. I trained for three years then one day I got a message from our teacher that she wanted to see me. I was told to come to her apartment—"

"On Gorokhovskaya Street."

"Yes, on Gorokhovskaya Street. How did you know?"

"Never mind. Go on."

"There were six or seven girls there. Two of us were new but the others were old-timers and told us the best thing to do was not to put up a fight. Our teacher would give us some pills and after that nothing would hurt very much. If we did as we were told, we would get presents from some of the men that we could keep.

The men were often foreigners and they had dollars to spend. If we didn't cooperate, well, the teacher was going to make some sort of film which would be shown to our families. Most of the girls were younger than I. I guess I was a slow developer.

Then the teacher herself showed up but she had on some strange looking costume made of black leather. She told us that on that particular night we would be entertaining some high up officials so the camera would be turned off but that didn't mean we shouldn't do everything we'd been taught. If the men asked any personal questions we were on no account to give our real names. I told her that I'd been taught to be a ballet dancer, not a whore. She got angry at that and slapped me. She told me she'd tolerated me for three years because I would be a 'variety act.' If I wanted to dance I could go back to my village in Kazakhstan or wherever I came from and join a local folk dancing troupe. I said that was fine with me."

"What did she do then?"

"Oh, I got beaten and locked in a closet for the night. It was frightening at the time but they didn't kill me. The next morning they let me out. A tall soft-spoken man even drove me back to the student hostel. He didn't say anything about what had happened, not directly. First he made a few hints about me going home. He said my best bet was to go home to Bokhara where my sister, Irina, was waiting for me. He said that it wasn't good to be away from home too long because things could happen to one's relatives when one was away.

I knew what he meant, but I didn't think he'd risk hurting my family because then I'd have nothing to lose if I told people what had happened, so I told him that I wasn't planning on leaving Leningrad. He was quiet for a while. Then he surprised me by saying I was probably right, because Leningrad was a beautiful city."

"Really?"

"Yes. But then he told me that that beauty had not come without sacrifice. Leningrad was a city built on bones. He said a hundred thousand of Peter the Great's laborers had died building

St Petersburg from the marshes. And then another half million died in the Fascist *blokada*. Even today we all had to make some sacrifices. Sometimes we had to do things we didn't like and for reasons we didn't understand but that people like him knew that it was necessary because the same enemies were still out there.

If only those people who'd died to build St Petersburg and defend Communism were alive they could tell such stories! But dead people couldn't tell stories. He said he was telling me this because he knew that I was a clever girl and wouldn't be influenced by a few toys and trinkets like the other girls.

All the 'operatives' saluted when we got to the hostel. They'd trashed my room, of course. All my personal letters had been ripped up. That was the only time I saw him upset. He went back to the operatives and started shouting at the leader that he should *never* rip up letters or diaries—that the information in them was priceless. The chief operative was trembling.

I took what was left in a small suitcase and walked out. The man told me that he would be checking up on me from time to time. He also said that I should remember that dead people couldn't tell stories. Then he smiled and got in his car."

"What did you do? Where did you go?"

"Oh, I got a job at the Uzbek restaurant, dancing, but it doesn't pay enough to live on. So I got this job as a conductress. I was lucky because they were rehiring conductors after the great Socialist experiment failed."

"Oh you mean the honor system where passengers were supposed to drop in five kopecks?"

"That's right. They thought they could get rid of tickets. The older conductors said that under capitalism we had conductors and drivers. Under Socialism we had got rid of the conductors. When Communism finally arrived they would get rid of the drivers, too."

"It's a living, but it's a bit different from ballet, isn't it?"

"In some ways. But the strange thing about ballet is how much of it is actually ugly. The fixed smiles for example. And splayed legs are unnatural yet most of the *pas* are built upon it—the *glissade*, the *assemble*, the *echappe*, all the *entrechats*—what makes it beautiful is the grace of the ballerinas. So it comes down to the individual in the end. And that's no different when you're dancing on a stage or selling people tickets."

"Still, it's no way to spend your life. What are you going to do next?"

"If I can get enough money together I'll pay someone to get my nationality changed back and then I'll emigrate."

"That's a nice dream. Israel?"

"America. That's where I always wanted to go."

"Me too. Where would you go?"

"Detroit."

Mels laughed.

"Detroit?! That's just a big industrial town where they make cars. Like Togliatti."

"Not just cars. They make music there. You know. Mo'town. The Supremes, The Jackson Five. Anyway, where would you go?"

"California. They have sunshine and beaches and mountains and rivers. And earthquakes and oil, so there's always jobs for geophysicists! The earth is very fertile and all kinds of fruits and vegetables grow there."

"It sounds like Georgia."

"But instead of the Black Sea there's the Pacific Ocean. I'd live in Malibu and learn to surf. And you can come, too."

"Right!"

They both laughed. She traced circles on his chest with her forefinger.

"Well, Mels, if we're going to live in Malibu together we'd better make sure we're sexually compatible, hadn't we . . . ?"

Chapter 6

Tanya had already left for her early shift when a tapping noise from next door woke Mels the next morning. The whine had stopped. Someone had evidently come in to fix the water heater. Mels wondered whether that had anything to do with his presence in Tanya's room but decided he was being paranoid. No one had seen him enter the apartment building so his presence would remain undetected until he left. Was there a fire escape he could use? He walked over to the window and looked through the thin net curtains to the interior courtyard. In common with most buildings in Leningrad, it had no fire escape. A rusting construction crane obscured most of the view. Like many sites all over the Soviet Union, it had simply been abandoned when the majority of the building workers had been mobilized to Moscow for the Olympics construction work. Actually, if he stretched, he could just reach the crane with his fingers. The rust crumbled in his hands. He watched the flakes fall to the ground, six stories beneath him. He was not actually afraid of heights—a youth spent climbing loading cranes at the docks had seen to that—but he did not relish climbing down in his clean clothes if he could avoid it.

He looked around the small room. *Not much here.* A travel poster of Bokhara's "Tower of Death" was the only decoration. A wardrobe with a few old-fashioned dresses and Tanya's dancing costume took up what little wall space remained. A few books were arranged tidily on the window shelf. Another was open on a chair by the bed. It was in English and she had annotated notes in the margin in Russian. He assumed Tanya was trying to learn English as part of her plan to emigrate, though—despite his comments the previous night—he knew her chances of being allowed to leave after butting heads with the KGB were as slim as his.

He picked it up and read, "The Heather Ale—A Galloway Legend" by Robert Louis Stevenson. He had read it as a boy. It was strange what English classics were available in Russia. They always had to have a heroic quasi-Marxist message. In this one a wicked Scottish king captures a father and son who are the last surviving 'workers' possessing the secret of heather ale. The father tells the king to kill his son because his own life would be at risk from him once he betrayed the secret. After the son is killed the father laughs and tells the king that the secret is now safe as the son was the weak link but he—the father—would *never* give it away. *What kind of message is that to be teaching?* thought Mels; that a beer recipe is more important than a son's life?

He heard someone in high heels approaching along the corridor outside. A clinking noise indicated that the person was carrying some bottles in a bag. Whoever it was stopped outside the bathroom. Through the thin walls he heard a woman's voice talking to the plumber.

"*Three* buses I had to take to get here!"

"Elena! You came. And I see you brought a little light refreshment. . . ."

"There's some bread and cucumbers as well as the vodka. Honestly, I didn't think I'd ever get here. Whose place is this?"

"It's a friend's. We help each other out. I fix his heater and he doesn't mind if I borrow his room. He won't be back for a couple of days."

"You should have said, you idiot. I told my husband I'd be back tonight."

"Well we haven't much time, have we? His room is the second door after the kitchen. I just need to wash up and I'll be there."

About twenty minutes later, a squeaky mattress was competing with Elena's moans as Mels left a note for Tanya that he hoped was not too cryptic:

"Let no one forget. Let nothing be forgotten. 6pm."

On his way out he first looked into the bathroom. The man's tools were scattered on the floor. He picked up a pair of carborundum-tipped plumber's gloves and put them in his pocket. If he did have to climb that construction crane he wanted to be prepared.

On the wall by the kitchen was the communal telephone. He wrote down the number on the dial, switching around the first and last numbers so as not to compromise Tanya if he was stopped and searched. The activity in the bedroom appeared to be reaching a climax. He stepped quickly past the door and let himself out of the communal apartment.

He bought an apple, tomatoes, and some bread then suffered a moment of panic when he saw militiamen rushing down the street towards him. Fortunately, they were just harassing the Georgian fruit vendor ("Blackass" they called him) from whom he had bought his breakfast.

He sat on a bench ruminating both on the food and his most pressing problem—how to get in touch with his father or daughter to find out what Gureyvitch had told them. Both their apartments were watched and the phones were tapped. He could go to his father's place of work again but that would be a lot harder to get away with during the day than at night. If only he had an intermediary he could trust. There was always Tanya, though he hated to ask her.

He stared at the graffiti-covered wall on the other side of the street. Apparently Natasha was a whore and someone had thoughtfully provided her telephone number. Zenit soccer club was—against all evidence—the best in the world. And Volodya allegedly sucked dick. All very inspiring and uplifting. Then something else caught his eye:

"So long, Aquarium! Good luck in Tbilisi!"

His knowledge of rock music was just about zero but Aquarium was a band that everyone in Leningrad had heard of—at least everyone with a teenage daughter. As a result, he actually knew why they were being wished good luck in Tbilisi. There was an officially sanctioned rock concert there this month and Aquarium was being allowed to participate. His daughter had planned to see the group off at the train station (or was it airport? What kind of father was he that didn't listen to his daughter?). He knew she had said it was sometime this week, but he could not recall when.

He passed several public phones until he found one by a tram stop that he felt he was far enough away from Tanya's place to safely use. Folklore had it that the KGB could trace a call within three minutes. He waited until he saw a tram approaching at the other end of the long straight boulevard. He estimated he had at least five minutes before it would arrive. That gave him two minutes exposure. Hopefully, the KGB did not maintain mobile units in this distant suburb. He picked up the phone and dialed the Institute of Applied Mathematics. A bored receptionist was only too pleased to tell him that Boris Grebenschikov had not been in all week and was not taking any computer programming commissions due to his departure for Tbilisi . . . yesterday. He cursed.

"You must be a fan."

"Well, kind of. I was hoping to see them before they left."

"They had to leave early. There was a big send-off party planned. The authorities got wind of it though so they moved their departure forward for them. Yulia was really pissed about it."

"Mmm. Yeah. Who? Yulia?"

"The little redhead. She organized half the teenage girls in Leningrad, I think. She was in here this morning complaining about having to be in a museum yesterday when they left."

"Yulia. Yes, of course; Yulia. The redhead! Do you happen to know where she is now?"

"Now?"

"Yes, now."

"Well, she's here. Look, you're not from her school are you? She's very upset. I think she's washing her face right now. She's been crying all morning so I said she could use the phone here and call her friends."

"Can I talk to her? Tell her it's Professor Ignatiev."

A precious minute of silence went by before Yulia's voice came on the line. The tram was almost at the stop. Her voice had lost its exuberance of yesterday.

"Hello?"

"Yulia, it's me. It's very important I speak to you. Can you get to the Victory Monument in an hour?"

"What's this about?"

"I can't talk. Just be there. By the violin. Please?"

"OK."

He hung up and jumped on the tram. It had been an unbelievable stroke of luck for him to have contacted this Yulia girl but he could hardly say he knew her well. If she did not show, he had no choice but to risk contacting his father at the Sea Terminal. He took a seat at the back and watched the public phone slowly disappear from sight. After several minutes no Volga cars had appeared. At least that call had been unmonitored.

The Victory Monument, in the center of Moscow Prospect in the south of the city, was built in the massive inhuman scale beloved by Soviet architects. An eternal flame burned within a vast ring of steel lined with giant medals. Above it towered a fifty-meter red granite obelisk. Underneath was a gloomy marble hall with several relics of the *blokada*, including the violin that was used to play Shostakovitch's Seventh ("Leningrad") Symphony. It was there, hiding amongst the crowds of schoolchildren being shown around by their teachers, that Mels waited for Yulia. After an hour's wait, he was about to give up when she strode purposefully towards him, wearing dark glasses despite the dim light.

"Mels L'vovitch, I'm sorry I'm late. This is not a good place. I'm supposed to be in school today and there was a party from my school here! I had to wait outside for half an hour until they left."

"Sorry, Yulia. I wasn't thinking. Do you want to leave?"

"It's OK. They're gone now. Why did you want to see me? How did you know I was at the Institute today? Did Luba tell you?"

"No. Actually I haven't seen Luba for a day. But before I explain I wanted to know why you played along with my little charade yesterday?"

"You looked a little rough. Like you'd slept out or something. But you were really interesting and school is usually so dull. Plus Luba is my friend and she says you're a really cool dad."

"'Cool,' eh? I'm flattered. Look Yulia, I guess we're both trying not be seen today. I, I'm in a bit of trouble right now and I need to contact Luba. I'd explain it to you but it would get you into serious trouble if you got caught."

"So you want me to contact Luba? Sounds great. And I thought I'd have to go to boring school this afternoon. . . ."

"Yulia! This isn't a game. I really need your help but you must understand that you could get hurt so if you don't want to do it please just say so."

"Of course I'll help. But I won't do it for free."

"Yulia. I'm not a rich man—"

"I don't want money. I want you to help me with my Math."

He laughed.

"No, I'm serious. I hate school but I need to get to college if I'm going to do anything with my life and I have to pass Math if I'm going to go to Moscow State University. Will you help me, please?"

"What do you want to study?"

"Geography. But you know M.S.U. You have to have perfect grades in everything in the entrance exams."

"Why geography?"

"I want to learn about places that aren't like . . . this. Mountains and deserts and tropical islands! Places where people aren't gray and dull...."

"Yulia, when all this is over I'll tutor you day and night if you like. And if you're serious about Moscow State, I'd do that anyway, regardless of whether you help me or not. What I want *you* to do is go to my father's apartment on Vasilyevskiy Island after school. Luba should be there after four o'clock. There will be some policemen there who will ask you questions. Don't lie to them, just say you're a friend of Luba's and you wanted to talk to her about Aquarium having left already. Go for a walk with her. Get an ice cream or something. Ask her if her grandfather has smoothed things out. That's all—'are things smoothed out?' But don't ask in the apartment, it's probably bugged. How late does your friend at the Institute work?"

"Natasha, the secretary? Oh five o'clock, I guess. Actually things are really slow at the moment. That's why she let me hang around all morning."

"Well call Natasha after you speak to Luba and tell her Professor Ignatiev will call her before 5pm. I'm pretty sure that phone line is safe. Tell her 'things are smooth' or 'things are rough.' That's all. Can you manage that?"

She nodded.

"Now, let's get out of here. I'll leave by a different exit."

He gave her a five-minute start then walked briefly back up into the sunlight of Moscow plaza before descending into the Metro station. Even with a change en route, the journey to the Piskarovsky Cemetery took less than half an hour. He had several hours to kill before he met Tanya there. He bought an ice cream and sat on a bench in a secluded part of the cemetery. He looked around him. Young girls in summer dresses played among the bright flowerbeds and threw small coins into the ponds for luck. Tearful old ladies walked along the central avenue and laid flowers on the mass graves. Tchiakovsky's *adagio lamentoso* was playing softly through loudspeakers. After all the excitement of the last few days, it was a peaceful, touching scene.

Strange to think that if General Gureyvitch has managed to pull the right strings, I could be back at work tomorrow. Hopefully that would mean he could still avoid presenting the controversial paper in Moscow. Ignatiev was scheduled to fly to Baku in the morning but he might be able to meet him at the airport to talk to him first. And surely the KGB would realize that whatever this Timor character was up to, he had blundered into it purely by accident? As for his ex-wife's activities, much as he despised what she was doing, it was in his interests to try to smooth things out with her. He did not trust her to do the right thing, but the chances were that whatever was in that bag had no value to her. She might even have already handed it straight over to this "Asparagus" character, and if she had not—out of malice—perhaps he could persuade her to? Maybe she would cooperate if he gave her a friendly warning about the "ballerina" business? In any case, there were advantages to be gained from staying on good terms. There was always the remote possibility that at some time she would have a change of heart and let Luba emigrate with him.

He looked up and read the inscription on the statue of Mother Russia,

"Let no one forget

Let nothing be forgotten."

Who am I kidding? Did he really think the KGB would just *forget* that one of their agents had been killed? Or that he knew what went on at Rasputin's old street? *Yeah, right.* There was about as much chance that Zhanna would ever stop punishing Luba and let her leave the country. He may have been smart—or lucky—enough to stay on the run for two days (and no mean achievement, that) but the fact was that he was living on borrowed time. His only trump card was that they had approached *him* to give the talk in Moscow. He was no Sakharov, but he prided himself on the fact that he did have a reputation among his peers for ethical behavior. No one had ever chided him for his one lapse—handing over three year's research to his boss's nephew—because the people he respected realized he had no choice in the matter. Maybe they would be equally understanding about this? Whatever happened, he should contact Ignatiev and offer to give the talk in return for, well, what? A return to the *status quo ante*, perhaps? A chance to change his clothes and sleep in his own bed? *Not that there was anything wrong with the bed I slept in last night.* Or at least the occupant thereof. His mind drifted to the events of last night. The only good thing that had come out of this so far had been meeting Tanya.

He looked at his watch. *Time to start looking for a phone to call the Institute.*

He walked a kilometer or so out of the cemetery before he found a public phone with a plausible escape route. He dialed the Applied Mathematics Institute and got through to the receptionist.

"Professor Ignatiev? Yulia just called."

"What did she say?"

"She said things are very, very rough. That's all. 'Things are very, very rough.' Does that make sense?"

"Yes, thank you."

"Can I be any help?"

"No, no. You've been a great help already."

He hung up and quickly crossed the road to stand in line in a butcher's shop where he could observe the phone through the window. Ten minutes passed. No KGB appeared so he left the shop and walked straight into two militiamen.

"What's your problem, Comrade?"

"Problem? What's a hundred meters long and eats potatoes? A queue for meat in Leningrad. . . ."

The policemen were not amused but they did not detain him.

Tanya was already standing by Mother Russia when he returned to the cemetery. She was carrying a bulging *avoska* string bag.

"Good evening, Mr. Bond!"

"Shhh! Let's get out of public view so we can talk. I'm sorry to have dragged so you so far out of your way."

"Not at all. My shift finishes at Finland Station so I was halfway here. In fact, I just had a conversation with a mutual friend en route."

"Who?"

"Timor! Kresty prison is just around the corner from the tram stop."

"Tanya! You didn't actually go into the prison, did you?"

"Of course not! There's a building on the corner with a courtyard that is overlooked by the cellblocks. The prisoners communicate with their wives and girlfriends by gesturing with their arms. They spell each letter in the air. Of course, the guards are watching through binoculars but I doubt whether any of them understood Timor's and my conversation. Not unless they speak Uzbek!"

"Tanya, you are a genius! But didn't they challenge you to find out who you were?"

"I think they would have done. But there was a big fuss going on inside. Timor said one of their oldest prisoners had just died and was being buried. Apparently he was the last of the cannibals."

"The *blokada* cannibals! I thought they'd executed them all. How did he survive so long?"

"All Timor said was that he was a cook. Maybe he was more useful alive. I guess he worked in the prison kitchen."

They both laughed.

"Only in Leningrad! What else did Timor say?"

"We couldn't 'talk' for long, but I gather that Timor has a foreign client at the moment. He works at the American Consulate. His name is 'Lagonde'—"

"Logan."

"You *know* him?! Goodness, maybe you *are* James Bond! Anyway, this Logan promised Timor he'd buy him a car. At least that's what Timor says. He says that afterwards he backtracked and kept procrastinating. So Timor 'borrowed' some money from his Trade Union vacation fund to buy the car himself. He says he was going to pay it back after Logan gave him the money but obviously he never had the chance. It was that car that hit the tram. The other man that was arrested was the man who was going to sell it. Unfortunately, you—or your ex-wife—went off with the money!"

"How much was in the bag?"

"About five thousand rubles. Large denomination bills, apparently, which is why you may not have noticed them."

"Shit! I'm screwed, then. No way will Zhanna give that much money back—"

"Zhanna? Not . . . you mean your ex-wife is Zhanna Borisova? I knew her married name was Katz . . . . So *that's* how you knew about Gorokhovskaya Street."

"I found out about it on Tuesday night. I thought perhaps the bag had a secret document or a smuggled icon or something she has no use for. But she'll never part with money, the greedy bitch. She has connections—powerful connections—but maybe I could tell the KGB that *she* took it—they know I was at her apartment—then I can shift the blame for the missing money on her. That just leaves the misunderstanding with Ignatiev. That's my boss. If I can straighten things out with him. . . ."

"I gather your other lead didn't pan out?"

"My father's 'friend'? No. I'm not surprised. I shouldn't have got my hopes up there. It's not the first time the man has left my father 'sitting on beans.'"

"They're still going to want that money back, for Timor's sake as much as yours. If it's just your word against Zhanna's, who will they believe?"

"You're right. The only person I know who could easily lay his hands on five thousand rubles is Logan. Maybe I should talk to him."

"Are you mad? How are you going to get into the American Consulate unobserved? And they watch their apartments like hawks."

"That's probably true, but I happen to know precisely where Mr. Logan is right now. I'll have a quiet word with him then meet you back at your apartment. Make sure you leave your window open tonight. Now what have you got in that *avoska*?"

"It's a present. It's nothing special. I saw them on the way. The line was just forming so I didn't have to wait long. I bought you some new clothes."

"You sweetheart. I don't have time to look through them now. I have an appointment near the Russian Museum."

He took the metro back to Nevsky Prospekt and walked to the *banya* through the back streets amongst the throng of rush hour commuters. The attendant greeted him like an old friend.

"Any cleaning to be done today? Anything I can get you? Beer, perhaps?"

"Thank you, no. But I would like an extra towel if you have one."

He undressed, then walked through the Tepidarium to the Steam Room. The heat stung his eyes at first and he blinked as he peered through the steam. But to his dismay there was no Brantley Logan among the men sitting there. His eyes traveled to the door marked "B." Well, nothing ventured, nothing gained. A voice from the steam wished him luck as he reached for the handle.

Mels was not so innocent that he did not have a vague idea about what was behind the door. Nevertheless, the scale of what was going on was, frankly, rather shocking. The Tepidarium was identical to the one on the other side of the Steam Room except for the activities of about two dozen naked men who were sitting, lying, kneeling or bending over the benches, performing sexual acts on each other in a frenzied orgy. Though one or two looked up as he came in, the majority seemed oblivious to his presence.

He saw Logan on the other side of the room, watching his friend Rudolf perform oral sex on a middle-aged man of Middle Eastern appearance. Mels walked past his field of view to the changing cubicles at the back of the room. He pulled the thin plastic curtain closed behind him, unwrapped what he had brought with him in the extra towel, and waited for Logan to follow. But instead, to Mels' surprise, he heard the curtain being pulled in the next door cubicle.

He was just wondering what he would do next when a loose tile at about waist height in the intervening wall was removed and an erect penis appeared through the hole. It appeared to have a nasty sore near the tip. Mels said nothing, waiting for an American voice to confirm the identity of his tumescent neighbor.

"General?"

Mels grabbed Logan's phallus with one of the carborundum-tipped gloves and yanked it towards him. A loud yelp came from next door coupled with a thud as Logan's forehead hit the tiled wall. Mels slipped out of his cubicle and into Logan's.

"I'm a US consular official and have diplomatic immunity. You can't touch me—!"

"I know who you are, Mr. Logan. And I can assure you, you can 'scream like a beluga' but your diplomatic immunity will not protect you here. Let us not beat about the bush, as you say. I know you're aware of what happened to your friend Timor. He tells us you were going to buy him a car."

"A car for Timor?! There's no way I'd buy that little bitch a car! He whined and whined about it so I said I'd think about it. Look, Rudolf told me what happened. I had nothing to do with it either officially or unofficially."

"Well Timor lost the money he stole for the car. It would get him out of trouble if you could help him out—"

"Get *him* out of trouble? Help *him* out? What do *you* care about that? Really General, if this is just a crude shakedown attempt to get money out of me I'm surprised at how low the KGB had fallen!"

Mels looked at Logan, slumped on the floor. Maybe there was more light in the cubicle than there had been in the Steam room but his skinny body appeared to have even more purplish birthmarks than yesterday. Tiny spots of blood had appeared in his groin where Mels had grabbed him and a red mark had appeared on his forehead that portended a colorful bruise. Despite that, he had kept his dignity and—overall—he had a good point. Why *should* Logan be expected to bail Timor, a KGB employee, out of jail? He held out his hand to help him to his feet but Logan misunderstood the gesture and cowered in the corner.

"It's all right, Brantley. I won't hurt you again."

He made his way back through the orgy to the Steam Room. The pace of activity seemed to have slackened somewhat and some of the participants had changed places, but no one seemed aware of, or cared about, what had just transpired in the cubicle. He changed quickly and left the *banya*.

On his way back to Tanya's apartment, Mels felt remorse for what he had done. Those who lie down with dogs get up with fleas, he reflected. *But that doesn't mean I have to adopt the bullyboy methods of the KGB on innocent people.*

The evening sun was shining on the street-side of Tanya's apartment building. That left her room and the construction crane in the shadows. The low sun would be in the eyes of anyone on the other side of the courtyard that was watching him. He stripped down to his underwear, tied his pants and jacket together with his belt and clenched it between his teeth, then climbed up to her window. She laughed as she helped him in.

"If anyone's looking they'll think you're a rapist! The snitches are back but I doubt if they'll hear anything. There's a guy down the corridor who's been banging his girlfriend like a rabbit since I got back. The water heater was fixed when I arrived but a couple of blows with a wrench seem to have restored it to its former state!"

"I don't think the plumber will mind. I believe he planned on staying for a few days, anyway."

Tanya had cooked some dumplings that they washed down with apple cider from a private market. Mels told her what had occurred at the *banya*.

"I felt really sorry afterwards. It's not his problem and he seemed really sick."

"What are you going to do, then?"

"I don't have any other bargaining chips. I'll meet Ignatiev at the airport and tell him I'll present his and Kasumov's paper if they'll just leave my family alone. I can't put my scientific reputation above the safety of my daughter. I only wish I knew what this is really about. God knows, Ignatiev is a wily political animal and it won't be the first time our Institute has published incomplete or misleading results. We spend half our time re-writing technical papers on his orders to make the diagrams smaller and more confusing, or replacing clear Russian words in the text with scientific jargon that obscures the meaning. But it's not like him to court publicity with a high-profile paper that will fool no one. At least no one in the scientific community."

"You haven't really told me what it's about."

"Well, to the layman it might sound plausible. You know that diamonds are pure carbon?"

"Of course!"

"OK, Tanya. A lot of people don't. Then you probably also know that you can produce them in the laboratory by subjecting coal to extremely high pressure. The problem is that the diamonds that are produced are not gem quality—they're just used in industry.

Years ago when people starting drilling for oil they thought it was a volcanic fluid, like lava. It isn't really. It's made up of lots of miniscule dead animals that have slowly decomposed over millions of years to make simple hydrocarbons. But sometimes all the lighter hydrocarbons leak away through geologic faults or by migrating through the porous rocks. When that happens, all you're left with is a lot of heavy tar, rich in carbon. Some people have speculated that the diamond fields in Siberia are the result of enormous pressure being exerted by the overlying rocks on the oil that's left in old oilfields."

"Sounds reasonable so far."

"That's the trouble—bad science always sounds plausible. In fact the diamonds are produced by a completely different process but that's not the end of it."

"So what else?"

"Well, Kasumov—he's the guy who came up with the original idea—said you could do this artificially by detonating thermonuclear bombs underground and then just mine the diamonds."

"Can you?"

"Tanya, even if it were true, can you imagine how dangerous it would be to explode a hydrogen bomb in an oilfield, shallow enough that you could mine it? No one in their right mind would do it!"

"But they obviously believe they can do it in Baku? Is there anyone there you trust?"

"Actually, there is. An old college friend, Elmar Shahtahtinsky. But I couldn't risk a phone call."

"It's a shame there's no way to get there."

"Such is life. Do you have an early shift tomorrow?"

"No, why?"

"After I leave, make sure there is no trace of me left here, and get rid of that note I wrote. If things go badly with Ignatiev, the KGB are not going to believe I evaded them without help. I won't mention your name but they may come snooping."

Tanya looked suddenly tearful. He put his arms around her and held her close.

"Don't be upset, Tanya. Just remember the old joke about the five rules of Socialism."

It was evidently before her time. She looked puzzled.

"Don't think. If you think, don't speak. If you think and speak, don't write. If you think, speak, and write, don't sign. And if you think, speak, write, and sign, don't be surprised."

She smiled weakly.

"I'm not worried about me. I'm worried about you. Promise me you'll be careful."

He kissed her.

"Of course I will, " he lied.

Chapter 7

The next morning it was Mels' turn to leave early. Asleep, Tanya looked much younger than her nineteen years. Struck with the sudden thought that she was the first person he had loved since the birth of his daughter, he wanted to leave her a note but feared compromising her. He tiptoed down the creaking corridor and let himself out of the apartment block. In these blighted suburbs few taxis were about at this time of the morning. According to the tickets in his pocket, Ignatiev's plane did not leave for nearly three hours but he knew the man's habits well enough to know he would be at the airport early and he wanted time to talk to him before he left. He thought about taking the Metro back into Leningrad to look for a taxi there but decided not to risk it. He walked three blocks to a busier road and finally flagged down a taxi going towards the airport. Seeing his lack of baggage, the driver asked him if he was meeting somebody.

"Only my boss."

"Arriving or leaving?"

"Leaving, why?"

"I have a lot of people in this cab, Comrade. You look like some sort of white-collar worker, am I right? If you don't mind me saying this, you don't act like a boss. I mean, I couldn't help noticing that you got into the front of the cab instead of sitting there in the back with your nose in the air, so I assume you're just a working stiff like me, eh? The thing is this; there's this asshole cop on the way to the airport. Every time I drive by when he's on duty I have to give him something—a pack of cigarettes, some foreign postcards (you know the type)—he's always on the take."

"Can't you turn him in?"

The cab driver laughed.

"A friend of mine did just that. You know why? He told him he wouldn't let him drive on the airport road again unless he bought him a drink. A *drink*! Can you believe it? So they go to a Georgian café and, of course, my pal's on his shift so he doesn't want to drink. So he orders tea while the cop orders vodka—and he has three glasses. No sooner does my pal get to the airport than he reports the policeman to our boss. And that was when the shit really hit the fan."

"What happened?"

"Well, believe it or not, the cop *was* arrested (they had no choice. I mean, how often does anyone turn in an official complaint against a cop?) but they tested his blood and the test came back negative?"

"How come?"

"Well, some of the cabbies think he paid off someone at the lab. Me, I think the café owner was in on the scam, too. He must have been serving just water and splitting the charge for the vodka with the cop. My friend ended up 'sitting' himself for defaming the cop's reputation. Fucking blackasses!"

Mels smiled. How typical that the cab driver's real anger was directed at the Georgian café owner rather than the militiaman. Policemen represented authority that was despised, resented and avoided where possible, but the Georgian was a class traitor for collaborating. Ironic, too, that in English "Caucasian" was synonymous with "white" when the peoples of the Caucasus were universally referred to by Russians as '*black*asses.'

"This sounds terrible, my friend, but I'm not sure how I can help."

"Oh, I wouldn't expect anything from you. If you have to go all the way to the airport to see off your boss then he's probably a worse asshole than that cop. But if you were going to meet him then I'd offer to wait for you—no charge—in case we get stopped on the way back. I know his type. That cop would shit his pants if he got a mouthful from someone who had influence."

Influence . . . , thought Mels, *it always comes down to that in the end.* A social hierarchy based on a complex web of strings that one either could—or could not—pull.

"Fuck!"

The driver banged his fist against the steering wheel, then slowed to a halt at the side of the road. A fat traffic policeman carrying a striped baton sauntered arrogantly up to the driver's window and leaned into the taxi. He gave Mels a supercilious glance then turned to the driver.

"Documents. Or have you something else for me?!"

Mels' movements in the next two minutes could best be described as reflexive. His defiance was part fueled by adrenaline and part by his apparent invulnerability over the last two and a half days. The driver's hand was already in his pocket. Mels reached across and held his arm.

"What's your name, Comrade Militiaman?"

"What?"

"I said *give me your name*! Mine is Professor Suslov. I am on my way to the airport to see off the Minister of Education. If I am made late I will need your name for my report to your superior officer."

"Well there's no need for that—"

"I disagree. You obviously feel you have some reason to stop this cab. If I felt that you were doing this arbitrarily I would have to make very, very sure that you are in no position to do it again."

The policeman stared incredulously at Mels' steely expression. Gradually the bafflement gave way to doubt, then fear. It was a look Mels recognized from the party at the Astoria. It pleased him to notice that a KGB general's uniform was not necessary to produce it.

"Really no need—"

"Cab driver, I will give you my telephone number at the

Ministry. If this man stops you again, do not hesitate to call me. Now drive on, I have ministerial duties to fulfill."

They drove on for a full minute before the cab driver spoke. His tone of voice had changed from the conspiratorial to the respectful.

"I am deeply sorry, Comrade Professor, for my remarks just now. Please accept my humble apologies and my thanks for what you just did. . . ."

"No problem."

Mels was reminded of a guard dog that used to roam his father's Yard. He was terrified of it when he was a young boy until one day he saw a naval sentry throw sticks for it to fetch and then tickle its belly. The next time it had come loping up towards him, bearing its canine fangs, he had walked towards it with a purposeful stride and instructed it to sit in a firm voice. The dog had obeyed. *Maybe influence isn't everything. You need attitude, too.*

The taxi pulled up near the old airport terminal, a two story building built like a Greek temple, with Ionic columns and a balustrade along the roof. Typically for Soviet buildings of its vintage, it had completely inadequate parking. Mels had to work his way through a mass of badly parked cars and taxis to get to the entrance. The terminal was modeled on a railway station with no individual departure gates, just a set of parallel benches on which to wait and watch for the flickering board to announce flight departures. After about half an hour, Mels went in search of an Aeroflot official to confirm that Ignatiev's reservation had not been cancelled and to inquire whether there was a VIP lounge. It was out of character for his boss not to be there by now. To Mels' surprise, although the reservation was still valid there was no sign of him in the VIP lounge, either. An hour passed as Mels sat patiently waiting and pondering his options. Without any idea of *why* the paper he was supposed to present was so important, he felt he really had little choice but to try to negotiate some sort of closure with Ignatiev. Unpleasant as it would be, it was certainly preferable to talking with the KGB.

A Jewish family, obviously en route to Moscow to emigrate, stood in line for their flight. Customs officers appeared and made them open their bags on the floor of the terminal in full view of everyone. There did not seem to be much there. Just a few clothes and some personal mementos. One of the officers found a set of army medals—which were confiscated—but there were no books or papers. Mels knew well what the Customs officers were really looking for—not gold or money or drugs but documents, particularly University diplomas. Technically, these were the property of the Soviet state but without proof of qualifications most emigrants worried that they would be forced to take menial jobs in Tel Aviv or New York when they got there, so they tried to take their degree certificates with them. The very public search was not just to humiliate those departing. It was an obvious way of sending a message to anyone observing and thinking of doing the same thing.

Another half-hour passed. Mels wondered if something had happened to Ignatiev. A stroke was always likely, *what with all that extra weight the man carries around—the man's blood pressure must be astronomical.* Bored, he walked to the newspaper stand and bought a bar of chocolate and a newsmagazine.

The front page was devoted to photographs of Politburo members and a denunciation of Chancellor Schmidt of West Germany who had evidently failed to see the Soviet Union's point of view over Afghanistan on his recent trip to Moscow. The West Germans were accused of using "Nazi methods" to foment labor unrest in Poland. That was interesting. That must mean there were more strikes in Poland. Mels had not been able to listen to the Voice of America in days. He was amused to discover the photograph of Andropov and Gorbachev that he himself had approved on an inside page. The sports page speculated on how many gold medals the Soviet Union would win in the Olympics, with an explanation for the Americans' absence based on their apparent poor showing in recent competitions due to disaffection amongst "negro" athletes over their lack of civil rights. *Why bother to print this stuff?* thought Mels, it all seemed too convoluted, as though someone had been trying a little too hard. Better just to say the Americans were simply trying to spoil people's fun—that would get the average Russian far more heated.

He paged through the paper without much interest until he saw a headline that caught his breath.

"Untimely Death of Prominent Scientist at Geophysical Institute."

So he was right—Ignatiev had died! He folded the page open to read the details then his hands started to shake so violently he had to prop the magazine against the bench in front of him to continue reading.

"The death has been announced of Doctor Mels L'vovitch Katz—a geophysicist of international standing—at the premature age of thirty-five. Doctor Katz was found drowned on the night of July 1st at the mouth of the Neva River in Leningrad. He had just finished work on the revolutionary concept of producing diamonds from abandoned low pressure oilfields using a new technique involving nuclear explosions and was to have presented his results later this month in Moscow. . . ."

There followed a list of his various publications and eulogies from his colleagues.

For a moment he had difficulty catching his breath. *Why are they doing this?* Was it a message to him? That his time was up if he did not turn himself in? One thing was clear. They no longer needed his presence to present the paper in Moscow. And yet they specifically tied his name to the work. *Why?* Surely, no scientist worthy of the name was going to be fooled by something so patently bogus? Surely even the ignorant, the timeserving Ignatiev clones that existed in all the Soviet Institutes, would be too cynical to accept such a technique at face value.

He heard Ignatiev's name being paged. The other passengers were already in the bus waiting to drive to the aircraft. Suddenly the fog cleared from Mels' brain. Ignatiev was not coming because he had no reason to know that the reservation had ever been made. Mels certainly had not told him and the chances were that Ignatiev had not had had the intestinal fortitude to admit to his friends at the KGB that he had voluntarily handed over his internal passport to Mels. He heard the bus engine start up. Quickly he sprinted to the departure gate and handed over Ignatiev's ticket and passport. Despite the forced politeness, the attendant's annoyed expression indicated her real attitude towards people who kept airplanes waiting—even Academicians, and even Aeroflot airplanes.

The flight was a long one though Mels spent most of it asleep in his comfortable seat at the front of the aircraft. As he waited to disembark down the tail stairway, a sickly tar-like odor wafted into the plane. One of his fellow luxury class passengers sniffed nervously. Mels explained.

"Black gold."

The man still looked puzzled.

"It's crude oil. That's the smell from the oilfields. The whole topsoil is saturated."

"It smells disgusting."

"Wait till you see it. There's nothing worse than an old oilfield."

Mels left the horrified passenger to pick up his checked bags. En route from Leningrad, he had formulated a plan of action of sorts that anticipated meeting with Kasumov in late afternoon. That left him with several hours to kill. He bought all the local newspapers on sale in the terminal then boarded a Baku-bound bus. After scanning the obituary columns, he watched the scenery pass by on the way into town. Several long rusting pipelines paralleled the road, occasionally looping up and over to the other side, then returning several hundreds of meters later with no apparent reason for the detour. Gnarled, dusty trees had been planted by a town planner with over-ambitious dreams of a French-style avenue at some time in the distant past, but these had failed to thrive in the polluted soil and were dwarfed, like large bonsai.

There were fewer private cars and many fewer military vehicles than in Leningrad. The bus slowed to pass ambling horse-drawn peasant carts laden with vegetables and twice had to come to a complete stop, as sheep wandered into the road from the almost barren fields in search of tufts of camel thorn on which to graze. Everywhere there were old-fashioned steel derricks and pump units that slowly rose and fell like nodding donkeys.

Mels looked around at his fellow passengers. Not so different from Leningrad, really. He had expected a more homogenous crowd. It was true that the majority of the people on the bus were stereotypical dark-haired Caucasian types with gold teeth and moustaches. But there were also Russians, Jews, a few colorfully dressed ethnic types in regional garb—probably hill people— even two African students. A babble of different languages rose and fell around him.

He got off at a village called Surakhany and bought *shashlik* and *lavash*, barbecued lamb and flat Georgian bread from a vendor outside one of the oilfields, while living relatives of his lunch wandered through the derricks, pulling at resilient grass growing near iridescent pools. *No wonder this lamb is so greasy*. Still, it was more meat than he had eaten in months and the bread was delicious. His stomach filled, he walked through the oilfield. It was a hot, humid day. Few people were about and no one seemed to be working. Well, it was Friday—wasn't that the moslem Sabbath? Maybe they were all at the mosque. Crude oil dripped from leaking joints in the pipelines. Eventually he met a group of oil workers, dozing in the shade of a concrete shed by the side of the road. A thickset man in his forties eyed him suspiciously.

"Good day!"

"Salaam."

"Can you tell me where this road leads?"

"Possibly. I *could* tell you many things my friend."

The man's accent was terrible. Mels was not in the mood for playing games but continued, politely.

"Where *does* it lead?"

"It leads to its destination. Why do you need to know?"

This was ridiculous. Was the man simple? This was Mels' first visit to the Caucasus and he was unfamiliar with the regional pastime of verbal arm-wrestling. In contrast with the terse, matter-of-fact speech patterns of most Russians (when sober), even the most mundane conversation in the Caucasus would always go through a stage of verbal intimidation and exaggeration.

The other oil workers were gradually starting to stir and take an interest in Mels. He decided to address his questions to the whole group.

"I need to know because I am lost. Is there anyone here who can give me a straight answer?"

The others all looked to the heavy-set man to answer.

"I answer questions around here. . . ."

"Then listen to me, Comrade oil-worker! Give me a straight answer or I'll report your lack of cooperation to your superior along with the fact that you were sleeping on the job. There are leaking pumps all around, wasting the property of the State. Or is this the time you set aside to visit a mosque in this republic?"

The man's attitude perceptibly changed, though not to indecision or fear. Instead, a smile came to his face and he nodded affably. Mels' response in the verbal battle of wills had evidently been appreciated. He seemed particularly to like the comment about the mosque. He laughed.

"I've never been in a mosque in my life! And pumps always leak. That's why they need us, to stop them leaking. Just for your information Comrade, *we* fulfilled our weekly quota on Tuesday. As far as where this road leads, it will take you to Ateshgah, the fire-worshippers' temple. Taxis wait there for the tourists, or there's a bus from there that goes into Baku."

Mels continued up the road until he reached a tourist complex consisting of a stand selling faded postcards and a small modern teahouse built next to a tall wall made of blocks of yellow limestone. After paying a nominal sum to a cashier, he entered through an archway into a pentagonal inner courtyard, designed like an ancient caravansari.

The inner walls of the courtyard had a number of archways that lead, in their turn, to small low-ceilinged rooms once used for eating and sleeping. Now, they were filled with extremely unlifelike mannequins, painted black, which were intended to represent ancient Zoroastrian pilgrims who had traveled from India to visit the eternal flames of Baku. The stylized pilgrims had been equipped with sacks that were supposed to suggest trade goods but were rather unromantically filled with chunks of styrofoam. Next to the mannequins were much more life-like figures of donkeys and horses. The Azeri artist who had produced them was obviously more familiar with these than the concept of an Indian pilgrim.

In the middle of the courtyard was a vaulted structure in which the eternal flame burned. Mels knew that the existence of this in the middle of the Surakhany oilfield was no coincidence and that the flame was nothing more mystical than a natural gas seep. Even he, however, was surprised by the exposed pipeline that lay above ground, leading from the oilfield to the flame. *Couldn't they have laid that in a trench?* It was as though some unknown Soviet architect had been at pains to demonstrate the prosaic nature of the phenomenon and to deny the supernatural. Nearby, a harassed teacher tried to explain what had happened to her disappointed class of elementary schoolchildren.

"'Azerbaijan' means the 'Land of Fire' and the flames burned for thousands of years. But the 'eternal' flames went out, proving the non-existence of god."

The children looked tearful.

"*Why*, Miss? If there are no more flames does that mean we don't live in 'Azerbaijan' any more?"

"You live in the Azerbaijan *Soviet Socialist Republic*. The flames went out when they started to produce the oil in the oilfield we drove through."

"*Why* did they produce the oil, Miss?"

"The oil was needed to build Communism."

The class was unimpressed by the explanation.

"Miss, does that mean Communism will make the flame at the Olympics go out, too?"

Dig yourself out of that, thought Mels, as he left the teacher to stutter a reply.

At the kiosk selling postcards he asked where the nearest public telephone was. For a few kopecks the sales clerk allowed him to use the one in the concession stand. He dialed the number of Kasumov's Institute and asked to speak with his secretary.

"Hello. This is Ignatiev. I have arrived in Baku."

"Doctor Ignatiev! I am terribly sorry. We were not expecting you. Frankly, I spoke with your secretary, Violeta, and understood from her that your trip had been postponed. Would you like to speak with Doctor Kasumov?"

"No, that won't be necessary. And there won't be any need to contact Violeta. I will speak with her myself on my return. I would like to meet with Director Kasumov, though, if he is free this evening."

"Well, it is Friday. He normally goes to his dacha—"

"Excellent! If you could just remind me of the address I will meet him there at 7pm."

"Well I really should ask Doctor Kasumov first. . . ."

"Nonsense. I'm sure he'd be delighted."

He bullied the address out of her. It was in a village on the north coast of the Apsheron peninsula called Mashtagah, about ten kilometers from central Baku. The name meant nothing to him but when he climbed into a taxi and explained where he was going, the cabdriver laughed.

"You'd have to be nuts to go there."

"Nuts? Why?"

"It's a joke, Comrade. Mashtagah is where the nuthouse is. You know, the mental hospital."

The ride was a short one through a sun-baked brown landscape of oil derricks and rounded hills with scrubby vegetation. The sun was starting to get low in the sky to the west—much earlier at this latitude than in Leningrad—and the light was reddening as its rays were diffracted through the haze coming from a small industrial town visible in the distance.

"Where's that?"

"Sumgait. You know why so many Armenians live there?"

Mels said nothing. Experience had taught him that the only funny ethnic jokes were ones that made fun of the narrator's own ethnicity.

"Because that's the only place that smells worse than their *basturma*."

Mels looked blank. The driver scanned his face in the rearview mirror for a response.

"*Basturma*. You know, the spiced meat they eat."

"Enough 'jokes.' Just drive."

Up ahead he could see the Caspian Sea. On this side of the Apsheron peninsula there was no offshore drilling to leave trails of oil on the surface, and the blue of the water was so intense in contrast to the brown of the land that it seemed unnatural.

The town of Mashtagah itself was unremarkable. The dachas were as far different from the Russian ideal of a wooden cottage set in a forest as could be imagined. Instead there were single-story terraced blockhouses partially hidden behind high whitewashed stone walls covered with grape vines. Kasumov's was situated on a corner where the main road intersected with a long narrow alleyway, barely wide enough for a single car to pass. A flock of sheep, tended by a young shepherd boy, grazed on the grass verge in front of the dachas. On the other side of the street was an even higher wall topped with looped barbed wire. There was no traffic about. Mels paid the driver and surveyed his options.

His first concern was to make sure Kasumov could not telephone anyone after he discovered that Mels—rather than

Ignatiev—was in town. Although his obituary had not made it into the local press in Baku, the geophysical community was a small one and word of mouth could have reached the Institute. He had a cover story ready. His internal passport had been stolen, he had been out of town when the militia made inquiries after a drowned body had been found. But he did not know Kasumov's role in the affair and was uncertain how much he knew. In any event, it was important that Kasumov should not call to verify any part of it until he had had a chance to make his escape.

A utility pole stood outside Kasumov's neighbor's house. Telephone wires snaked from the pole to six or seven adjacent dachas. He stood at the base, looking up, wondering whether he could scale the pole before a car came along. As he stood there, the neighbor's door was roughly pushed open from inside. A tousle-haired Russian with a collapsed stomach and sagging shoulders staggered out of the house. He regarded Mels with an unfocused gaze—he was extremely drunk—then flicked a forefinger against his throat and clicked his tongue in the traditional Russian invitation to drink. Mels looked at the bleary face of dissolute fleshiness and shook his head.

"C'mon, ya bastard . . . give me a drink!"

He took a swing at Mels, lost his balance, and fell over, cursing.

Mels left him laying on the ground, struggling like an upturned beetle to regain his feet. His eyes returned to the utility pole, then followed the path of the telephone wire to the back of the dacha. He walked round to the deserted alley and threw a stone over the wall into Kasumov's property. Hearing no response, he quickly climbed over. The back yard was empty. A small herb garden in the center thrived under the shade of a giant fig tree growing in the next dacha. At the far end was a huge barbecue pit with skewers like swords dangling from a spit. At the other end was a water well with a powerful pump modeled on the ones Mels had seen in the oilfields. The telephone wire entered Kasumov's dacha from a junction box half way up the wall on the other side.

He pressed himself against the back wall of the house, listening for sounds from within. All was quiet. He looked through a back window but saw no signs of life. Satisfied that he was unobserved, he reached up to the telephone wire and yanked it away from the junction box then retraced his path back to the alleyway.

Chapter 8

    Mels picked himself up after landing awkwardly from the high wall surrounding Kasumov's dacha. The formerly deserted lane in which he landed was now full of bleating sheep pulled as if by a magnetic force after one determined individual that was making its way down the alleyway. The shepherd boy was nowhere to be seen. Mels clapped his hands and drove the lead sheep back onto the grass verge at the front of the dacha. The others followed.

    He was brushing whitewash from his clothes when he heard a muffled child's scream coming from the dacha next door. The entranceway was locked but the wood was rotten with the sea air and he kicked it open easily. Whoever owned the dacha had long since abandoned it to squatters and the elements. The place was empty of furniture and even some of the floorboards had been ripped up for firewood. A sour odor like rotten apples pervaded the building. Another cry came from a room to his right. He rushed in and discovered the shepherd boy—his clothes torn—struggling with the drunk who was now dressed only in briefs and a soiled undershirt.

    "C'mon boy, I said I'll give you some candy—"

    Mels grabbed the man's arm and twisted it behind his back in a move his father had tried in vain to teach him throughout his childhood. With his other arm applying a chokehold, he spoke with a calm but firm voice in the drunk's ear.

    "You lay a finger on this boy again and I'll break your damn neck. Understand?"

The man nodded. Mels released his arm, expecting the drunk to turn round and start swinging at him but instead the man ran unsteadily out of the house, still dressed only in his underwear. Mels took the tearful boy's hands.

"It's OK. He's gone. You're OK."

Between sobs, the boy tried to explain in Azeri what had happened. The singsong Azerbaijani language meant nothing to Mels but he nodded and smiled and dried the boy's tears. He tried again, in Russian.

"He's gone now. Can you speak Russian? Can you understand me?"

It was clear that he did not, but he seemed calmer. Mels cleared a space on the floor and crouched down next to him. He found the remains of the chocolate bar he had bought at the airport and gave it to the boy. It was not an ideal place to have a conversation, the sour smell in the house was coming from numerous abandoned bottles of *bormotukha*, or babbling juice, the cheap fortified wine favored by Russian alcoholics. A dirty plastic container and rubber hose with a vaguely soapy smell lay nearby. Strangely enough, Mels knew exactly what that piece of apparatus was for as he had witnessed its illicit use many times when he returned late to his apartment. Soviet motorists added vodka to their windscreen wiper fluid to prevent freezing in wintertime but then added liquid detergent to deter drunks from siphoning off the fluid. The trick was to add enough soap to the cocktail to render it unpalatable without clogging the washers.

The shepherd boy suddenly started to panic and ran to the door.

"*Goyunlar!*"

Goyunlar? Mels followed him and realized the boy was worried about the sheep he was supposed to have been watching. He mimed a story about how he had rounded up the flock. The boy smiled. Mels pointed at himself.

"Mels."

The boy repeated his name then pointed at himself.

"Kasoum."

They both smiled. *Communication*! Actually, Mels was surprised. Even in Siberia only the oldest of the native people still spoke their mother tongue. He had never come across a child of seven or eight years old who could not speak Russian. Inexplicably, it cheered him up. To think of all the propaganda his daughter had had to endure by the time *she* was eight from government-sanctioned television and radio! He pointed at the sheep, grazing determinedly nearby.

"*Goyonlar?*"

"*Goy-un-lar!*"

OK, my accent isn't so hot, thought Mels. He looked around for something else to play language games with. He pointed to the utility pole.

"Pole."

But Kasoum's response was way too involved to have anything to do with a utility pole. He pointed down the street and excitedly repeated a phrase.

"*Bu gachan adama bah!*"

Mels followed his finger to see the figure of a tall curly-haired middle-aged man with a long nose. Though he was now wearing some sort of striped pajamas, it was unmistakably the same man he had taken to be a black marketeer at the site of the streetcar accident in Leningrad. He was running in their direction. From some distance behind him came the sound of a siren.

"Over here!" yelled Mels.

The man spotted them and ran breathlessly towards them, looking over his shoulder.

"Hide me, please!"

"In there—in the dacha—quickly!"

The unmistakable sound of the type of police wagon known throughout the Soviet Union as a "Black Crow," grew louder as it turned a distant corner and hurtled towards them. The Black Crow screeched to a halt and a militiaman leaned out of the window.

"Hey you! Did you see a man running this way?"

"There *was* a man. I wasn't paying attention. He turned down that alley. I didn't see it but if I'm not mistaken, I think there must have been a car waiting for him because I heard an engine start and a car move off."

The militiaman did not bother to reply. He threw the Black Crow into reverse and backed up, then sped off down the alleyway. The high walls echoed its siren as it dopplered away. After a few minutes, Mels got up and went into the dacha. He gestured to Kasoum to stay put.

"Hello? The police are gone. Hello?"

He found the man in a back bathroom, standing on the commode, ready to flee through an open window.

When he saw Mels he relaxed and stepped down. He held out his hand.

"I suppose I owe you my gratitude for what you did."

They shook hands. The man had a curious habit of grasping Mels' hand in both of his, as though they were long lost friends.

"Your gratitude you can keep. But I would like an explanation. My name is, er, Ivanov. What's yours?"

"You don't need to tell me your name. But I don't mind if you know mine, in fact I'd like you to know it in case they catch me. Maybe you can tell my relatives where I've been. My name is Hamlet Sirounian."

"Gamlet? Is that a real name?"

"It's Hhh-amlet. What is it with you Russians and the letter H?"

"I'm not. . . ."

Mels stopped, embarrassed.

"No, you don't *look* Russian. But take my advice, friend, if you're going to give a false name at least make it believable."

"Like *H*amlet?"

"Actually Hamlet *is* my real name. It's very popular with Armenians here."

"But not in Leningrad."

Hamlet looked suspiciously at Mels.

"Do I know you?"

"No. But I saw you in Leningrad earlier this week. You were in a car accident."

Hamlet laughed.

"Yes! One of the worst business deals of my life, that one. If I'd known what would happen I never have got into that damn car."

"So why are you here? You'll forgive me asking but it seems something of a coincidence."

"I could ask you the same question, Comrade 'Ivanov.' I don't know what sort of trouble *you* are in but I just broke out of Mashtagah."

"I thought Mashtagah was a mental hospital."

Hamlet snorted derisively.

"Mental Hospital! Oh yeah, it's a mental hospital all right. And they have real nutcases in there. Real *screaming* cases. But they've also got a lot of people in there who are classified as 'Intellectual Deviants.' You know, 'paranoid delusions of reforming society, moralizes and overestimates his own personality.' That sort of thing. KGB psychiatrists can incarcerate someone in a psychiatric hospital for as long as they choose."

"I guess that didn't work in your case?"

"They know well they're not going to change me. I'm no dissident. That's not why they locked me up. They did it to frighten me and make me more cooperative. If you maintain too independent an attitude you find yourself sharing a room with some psychotic. It only takes a pillow over your face while you're asleep. . . ."

He looked at the watch on his wrist, shook it, and held it to his ear. It looked familiar to Mels.

"Here, you can have this back. Where did you get that piece of junk—the army? I can get you a good Japanese watch if you like—imitation Rolex."

Mels was not sure whether to be angry or grateful. Hamlet continued.

"Oh, sorry about that. It's just force of habit. They took mine away when they put me in Mashtagah, about four or five hours ago."

Mels reattached the watch to his own wrist.

"How did you get out?"

"They don't usually put people like me in there. Most of the inmates are dissidents or nutcases. The first group is too traumatized to escape and the second doesn't care."

"And you?"

"Let's just say I've always believed in taking advantage of opportunities as they arise. Unfortunately, one occurred at the wrong time of day. I must have run two kilometers without seeing a single car. Another half an hour and these streets will be packed with cars as people start arriving at their dachas for the weekend."

"And you'd steal one?"

"You know, Comrade, *stealing* is rather a moralistic description, isn't it? I prefer to call it 'using.' *Stealing* implies taking something for a profit. You *steal* a car in Mashtagah, you drive it to Rostov or Odessa and you sell it to some gorilla with a gold chain around his neck. I just need a car to get me out of Mashtagah. When I get where I need to go, I'll leave the car for someone else to 'use.' That's not stealing, that's Communism! In the present circumstances, you think I should just wait for a bus?"

"You make 'using' a car sound easy."

"Do you know how many different car locks there are on a Volga?"

"No, why would I?"

Hamlet produced a car key from his sock.

"Well, if it's of no interest to you I won't tell you. But thanks to our unimaginative central planners at the Ministry of Automotive Production in Moscow, I only need this and about half an hour in an untended parking lot and I have transportation for the night!"

"Where did you get *that* key?"

"This was from the KGB car that brought me here this morning. I was hoping it would still be parked outside but they must have had a duplicate key."

"So will you be safe now? I mean, once the cars start arriving?"

"I wish I could say yes but the police are like bears. You know, if you want to catch a bear in the Caucasus you smear honey on a rock. The bear will come and lick the rock then come back the next day to the same rock and sniff it and then keep coming back every day for months. It never thinks why the honey was there in the first place. All bulk and no brains. You try that with a wolf—you can fool it once but then it learns. But the bear never learns."

"So you're saying the police are going to come back and sniff this rock?"

"Oh yes. Plus thanks to you they'll be stopping every car leaving Mashtagah."

As they spoke a car pulled up outside. Mels put his fingers to his lips and tiptoed to the front room. Through a dirt-smeared window he saw Kasoum speaking with his old friend Elmar Shahtahtinsky and a tastelessly dressed woman with butter-colored dyed hair. Kasoum was shaking his head in a convincing fashion.

"Listen, Hamlet, I need to talk to you but this isn't the time. I can help you out but I'll need your help, too."

"OK."

"You're right, my name isn't Ivanov, and I have no particular desire to rub up against the police myself at the moment. We can talk about that later. For now, I'm going to call upon a small but powerful ally of mine—that little boy outside."

"But he's an Azerbaijani—"

"So?"

"I'm an Armenian."

"He's not doing it for you. He's doing it for me, and he knows he can trust me. Just before you appeared on the scene I saved him from some unpleasantness involving a drunk pervert that was squatting here."

"That would explain the smell of *samogon* in here."

"*Samogon?*"

"Moonshine. Home-distilled liquor."

"Well, I think he was drinking *bormotukha*, judging by the bottles in the other room."

Hamlet wrinkled his long nose in disgust.

"Russian, then? No class, Russians. Pity. I could have got him some good *samogon*. Like liquid gold."

"So he can get drunk and molest some other child . . . ?"

Hamlet looked shocked.

"There we go with the moralizing again, Comrade 'Ivanov.' I'm sorry, is this child a relative of yours? Look, the man is a drunk. That means he's going to drink *somebody's* product. If he were an *Armenian* drunk he'd have a nice still set up here. Nothing fancy, a hundred-liter drum, some copper pipe. Switch it off at the weekend so the neighbors don't smell it. Get drunk yourself and sell the rest to your drunk friends. Use the rubles to buy a woman instead of messing with little boys. Before you know it you're drinking good Armenian brandy. But he's Russian, so he buys *bormotukha* when he can scrounge the money and—being Russian—he may not have two kopecks to rub together but as soon as he has a bottle, he shares it with his friends.

You know the story about the Russian Czar and the tax collector? The Czar sends his tax collector to tax his subjects. When he returns with all the gold he could find, the Czar asks him 'How are my people?' And the tax collector replies 'Your majesty, the people are crying and they're drinking in despair. They say we took their last kopeck.' But the Czar replies that he knows they've got more gold so he sends the tax collector back. Next time the tax collector returns with all the silver he could find and the Czar asks him the same question again. The tax collector replies that the people are in despair, selling their last shirts and drinking even more heavily and saying that they've given all they have.

But the Czar says 'I know my people and I know this is not all!' So the tax collector goes one more time and this time he returns with all the copper coins he could find. He tells the Czar 'Your Majesty, the people do nothing but drink and have parties like there's no tomorrow . . . . ' And the Czar finally smiles and says 'Now I know you've brought me everything!'"

"So what's the point of this story?"

"So we know we have a market. I was just thinking of the business opportunity."

Mels shook his head in amazement.

"You're totally amoral, aren't you?"

"Just call me an independent businessman, my friend."

"Well, be that as it may, right now that boy, Kasoum, is your lifeline out of here. There's a pair of pants and a jacket in the other room. Put those on over those pajamas of yours. There are some boots in there, too, but they may not fit so you may be walking a long way in those hospital slippers. You're going to be a shepherd. I'll tell the boy you're my friend and that he's to look after you. Go with him and the sheep to wherever they pasture them at night. I assume it's one of those hills I saw on the way here. Keep a low profile for a couple of days. If you go past any police roadblocks keep your face covered with a cloth or something. Is there some way I can contact you tomorrow?"

They walked into the room with the bottles where the drunk had left his clothes.

"Go to the cobbler's shop in Zavokzalnyi Rayon, behind the Sabuchinskiy railway station in Baku. If you get lost, ask for the *Armanikand*—the Armenian quarter. When you get there, speak to Rapik. I'll get word to him somehow. He will know where I am. Phew—these clothes stink!"

"Wait till you've been around sheep for a couple of days. Stay here and I'll see if those people are still out front."

Shahtahtinsky and the woman were standing in the long shadow cast by Kasumov's dacha, smoking cigarettes, and exchanging a desultory conversation in Azeri-accented Russian.

Kasoum sat on the front step of the empty dacha to prevent anyone entering. Mels touched him on the shoulder and gestured for him to come inside. He started to mime what he wanted him to do but was swiftly interrupted by Hamlet who explained the whole thing in rapid-fire Azeri.

"I didn't know you spoke Azeri."

"I'm Armenian. That doesn't mean I come from Armenia. Actually I was born a long, long way from Armenia. But I grew up in Baku. This kid's a country hick; that's why he only speaks Azeri. If he was from Baku he'd speak Russian, Azeri, Armenian, maybe a few words of Farsi, even Yiddish. Hey, that's Baku."

"One big melting pot, eh?"

"Nah. More like one big pressure cooker with the lid held down by our friends in the Black Crows."

"OK. We'll have this talk later. Now let's look at you. Do you look like an Azerbaijani shepherd?"

Hamlet mimed the role of an Azerbaijani shepherd looking desperately for his sheep. He uttered a few anxious words in Azeri. (Mels caught the word *goyunlar*). Kasoum said something that made Hamlet laugh.

"He says I may sound like an Azerbaijani shepherd but I still *walk* like an Armenian!"

Mels sighed. It occurred to him that the reason the Caucasus was famous in the Soviet Union for its tolerance towards Jews was because the locals were too busy hating one another.

"Just tell the boy to drive the sheep round to the alley then follow me."

Mels led the way through to the back yard of the house. An ancient fig tree grew there that he had seen from Kasumov's side of the wall. They climbed the thick branches easily, dropped down into Kasumov's yard, and then scaled the wall on the alley side. Kasoum was waiting for them in the alley.

"All right. I'll see you sometime tomorrow. Take care."

They parted. Mels walked up to the junction with the main road and hailed Shahtahtinsky.

"Elmar Shahtahtinsky! How are you?!"

"Mels Katz?! What the hell are you doing here? Is Ignatiev with you? How did you get here?"

"A taxi. He dropped me down the alley. He couldn't get through because of the sheep. Ignatiev was detained on business in Leningrad."

"That's strange. The story I heard from Kasumov was that he'd called from the airport to say he was already here. Kasumov's gone off to buy enough food for a feast in his honor!" He lowered his voice. "He even got Mehri to come along."

The blonde woman had been standing hopefully up to this point on the periphery of the conversation, waiting to be introduced. At Shahtahtinsky's summons, she stepped forward.

"Doctor Katz, let me introduce Mehri Gajieva, Director Kasumov's personal translator."

Shahtahtinsky winked behind the woman's back as she shook hands rather formally with Mels.

"And you were going to, er, 'translate' for Aleksander Mikhailovitch?"

"I have a degree in foreign languages from the Maurice Therese Institute in Moscow."

In contrast to a few minutes earlier, she had now assumed a strong Moscow accent. It struck Mels that whatever her linguistic or other skills, she was not particularly bright. His own Institute in Leningrad also had its share of translators trained at the same language school. It was common knowledge that they all held honorary ranks of lieutenant in the Red Army, since the school was sponsored by Military Intelligence. Mehri's anxiousness to boost her own standing in Mels' eyes had somewhat detracted from her usefulness. Still, it was useful to know. If Kasumov had planned on Mehri's "translation" skills being used on Ignatiev, there was still a degree of mistrust between them.

The speculation was cut short, however, by the arrival of an older model Zhiguli. Two sad-looking women—evidently mother and daughter from their appearance—disembarked, laden with groceries. They smiled meekly at the visitors and let themselves into the dacha.

"Kasumov's wife and daughter," explained Shahtahtinsky. "My guess is that you won't see much more of them this evening until dinner."

The front door was left open. Uncertain whether to enter, uninvited, they lingered a little longer in the driveway then went in. Inside, the dacha was identical in shape to the next door dwelling. Rich red carpets hung on the walls next to a dusty photo of Geidar Aliyev, the Azerbaijani Communist leader, and the obligatory picture of Lenin. Then the blaring of a car horn outside announced the arrival of Kasumov himself.

Chapter 9

Mels went to the door of the dacha to greet Kasumov. To his surprise, the man grasped his proffered handshake and pulled him roughly over the threshold. Fortunately, Shahtahtinsky was at his side to explain his *faux pas*.

"Never shake hands in a doorway. It encourages the Evil Eye."

He pointed at a blue glass disk hanging on a wall facing the doorway—evidently some sort of talisman against whatever the evil eye might be.

"Comrade Director, may I introduce Mels L'vovitch Katz, one of the foremost experts in Director Ignatiev's Institute. Mels, this is Adil Narimanovitch Kasumov, whom I have the honor of serving as Director of our Institute."

Kasumov said nothing for a moment, as if expecting more flattery. He was a small, portly man, like Ignatiev, but brimming over with nervous energy. He stood fidgeting with coins in his pockets—his eyes flashing from Mels to Shahtahtinsky then back again—while nervously rocking on the balls of his feet. When he realized Shahtahtinsky was not going to add anything he deigned to speak.

"Katz? I was expecting Ignatiev."

"Director Ignatiev sends his apologies, Adil Narimanovitch. I hope that I will be able to answer any questions you may have on our joint paper."

Kasumov looked puzzled.

"To be frank with you, Katz, I understood the paper was

finished. In fact my secretary handed me a finalized copy she had received from Leningrad just before I left the office—though I haven't had an opportunity to glance at it yet. Perhaps we can do that before dinner?"

"An excellen-"

Although he had not realized it, Mels' insistence on talking business before social niceties had been dealt with had skirted the edge of a major social gaffe since Kasumov's arrival. Once over the threshold of his own house, Kasumov's personality had been in the transitional state between autocratic boss and his traditional responsibilities as a host. Mels' answer was drowned out by a bellow from Kasumov, summoning his wife.

"Nig-yar! Why have you not offered tea to my guests?!"

The woman came scurrying from the kitchen with a tray of tulip-shaped glasses and a saucer of sugar cubes. As she brushed past Mels, he noticed her fingers were aromatic and stained green with the herbs she had been preparing for the evening meal. Kasumov's daughter followed a pace behind with a silver samovar. To the women's evident surprise, Mels started to clear a space on a low coffee table for them to arrange the tea paraphernalia. Kasumov disapproved.

"Nig-yar! Naza! So now our guests have to do housework for you?"

Embarrassed, Mels left the women to their work. Meanwhile, Shahtahtinsky had quietly exited the dacha and returned with a large bouquet of flowers from his car, which he presented to Nigyar Kasumova with a few words in Azeri. She blushed and mumbled a few words of thanks before disappearing back into the kitchen.

They sat down around the coffee table, waiting for Kasumov to choose a topic of conversation. Despite Mels' anxiety to see the finalized paper, in truth his overwhelming emotion for the time being was simply relief. Although it was evening in Mashtagah, Ignatiev was probably still at his desk in Leningrad. Mels had gambled that the senior staff in Baku was as unquestioning of authority as those in his own Institute, and he had been right. No one had bothered to call Leningrad—as the absence of a Black Crow outside the dacha proved.

In keeping with her standing as the only female in the room, Mehri poured glasses of tea for all present. Shahtahtinsky lit himself a cigarette. Mehri then sat and stared at Shahtahtinsky, hoping he would offer one but not wanting to lose face by asking. Although Kasumov himself did not smoke, this afforded him the opportunity to shout again—for his daughter this time—to fetch an ashtray. While this was being retrieved, Kasumov reached into his leather briefcase and pulled out a sealed envelope which he opened with an ornamental dagger.

He sat abstractedly leafing through the contents for a minute or two then snorted contemptuously and passed the entire package to Mels.

"Comrade Katz, please send my condolences to your, er, widow...."

Mels froze. Had Kasumov been toying with him? Did he know?

"I'm sorry, Mels L'vovitch, a joke in poor taste. I noticed they have mistakenly put a black rectangle around your name on the contents list."

A black rectangle, as Mels knew, meant that the author was deceased. He noticed that the author's list had also increased by one—Ignatiev's nephew—since he had last seen the abstract. A note from Ignatiev himself, handwritten on the front cover, said simply:

"Adil Narimanovitch, we will meet to discuss these changes. Do not phone me.—AMI."

Although the note was undated, given the state of the Soviet postal service it was obvious that a decision to declare him officially dead had been taken days ago—perhaps immediately after his meeting in Ignatiev's office. Kasumov seemed to be wrestling with another problem.

"One more thing puzzles me, Mels L'vovitch. Has there been a practical test of this technique? The methodology I described in my original abstract to Ignatiev merely proposed this as a theoretical technique but Ignatiev not only states that the technique has been proven but that diamonds produced by the method will be shown at the conference this month. I am surprised that there has been time to conduct such a test given the need to use nuclear technology."

"Adil Narimanovitch, I am sure Aleksander Mikhailovitch would not state such a thing if it were not true."

Kasumov rapped his knuckles twice on the table in front of him. It was a reflex among Soviet citizens and its meaning was clear to all present: "Let us not discuss that here." A twinkle in Kasumov's eye indicated that he was as doubtful of Ignatiev's honesty as Mels was, but he was not prepared to talk about it— either because of the presence of his employees or because he thought his own dacha was bugged by a device too sophisticated for a blue glass disk to exorcise. Mels took the hint.

"Adil Narimanovitch, I wonder if I might glance at this overnight? I seem to have mislaid my copy."

"Of course, of course, but let us not discuss it now. I think if you will excuse me I need to prepare the *shashlik*."

The greasy *shashlik* that Mels had consumed at lunchtime was sitting rather heavily on his stomach but he felt it would be ungracious to mention it. Besides, eating meat twice in one day was a luxury he had not enjoyed for years. Shahtahtinsky quickly offered his assistance to Kasumov and gestured to Mels that he should follow. However when Mehri attempted to bring up the rear, Kasumov himself intervened.

"I'm sure my wife would welcome your assistance in the kitchen, Mehri *hanum*."

Cooking of meat is evidently a masculine preserve, thought Mels.

It was good to be out in the open air. He had rationalized his flight from Leningrad as essential fact-finding but in truth it was driven by fear—of walls closing in on him. Ever since Kasumov's reluctance to discuss Ignatiev, Mels' initial relief had given way to acute claustrophobia inside the house. This was not completely rational, of course. Hamlet had informed him there was a KGB presence just the other side of the high hospital wall on the other side of the street. If the house was bugged and was being monitored, they would have arrived within minutes of Shahtahtinsky's introduction. He looked at the wall he had climbed twice already this evening. In an emergency he could get over that in a hurry, but there was a long straight alleyway to negotiate without cover. If they came for him, he would not be able to escape as Hamlet had done. *And what, actually, have I learned so far?* Only that the wily Kasumov did not appear to be the instigator of this particular nefarious scheme. Hopefully he would get the chance to question Shakhtakhtinsky to find out what he knew before the evening was out.

In practice, most of the preparation of the kebabs had already been done. The fire in the *shashlik* pit was already glowing and a table had been placed in the back yard next to it. Fresh lamb had been cut into large chunks that were sitting in a large bowl half-filled with blood. Another bowl had minced lamb, mixed with herbs, and yet another contained raw onions and tomatoes. With evident satisfaction, Kasumov and Shahtahtinsky set to work threading chunks of meat onto huge skewers interspersed with the vegetables. Mels looked around for something to do. Kasumov gestured towards another table set with a white tablecloth next to the herb garden. On it were several bottles of wine and six glasses.

"Katz, I see my wife has neglected to open the wine to let it breathe. Perhaps you wouldn't mind?"

The choice of wines was astounding to Mels—*Tsinandali*, of course, but also a pale straw colored *Gurdzhaani*, a ruby-red *Teliani*, and a dark amber *Sameba*. The labels were in both Georgian and Russian script. Inexpertly, since he was unused to the task, he uncorked the bottles and sniffed the contents.

Kasumov was quick to notice his curiosity.

"A poor selection but I hope you will excuse it. I hope you don't mind Georgian wine?"

Mels knew Kasumov was fishing for compliments. It was not difficult to oblige.

"Really, Adil Narimanovitch, I have never seen such a selection!"

"Then we must make sure you sample each before you leave. Pour us a glass, this is thirsty work!"

Unlike most Russians, the two Azeris sipped their wine instead of gulping it back as though it was vodka. A huge fig leaf fell as the three of them stood under the branches. Kasumov pointed up at the tree.

"There should be a good crop this year. It's a shame our neighbor left. He would bring us round a basket of figs in August—delicious!"

"What happened to him?"

"He left. For Israel."

Mels inwardly cringed, waiting for the disparaging remark that inevitably followed this statement in Russia. Instead, Kasumov sighed and shook his head.

"Shame, he was a good man."

To his surprise, Mels discovered the glass he held in his hand was empty. It had gone down remarkably smoothly and he did not put his customary hand over the top when Shahtahtinsky came round with a refill. Perhaps he should propose a toast? He cleared his throat.

"Adil Narimanovitch, a toast to your good health."

Kasumov smiled and held his glass in front of him, rocking on his feet expectedly. After a pause, Mels realized this would not suffice.

"And to your house and hospitality."

Kasumov still stood there, glass frozen in space.

"And to your family. And this excellent food we are preparing. And to this fine evening."

Kasumov had started to lick his lips in anticipation. Mels was evidently getting close, if he could just think of a good closing line.

"And to our friendship."

"Our friendship"

Kasumov drank with evident satisfaction. As toasts went, it was a satisfactory opening round from Mels. All three of them knew that Kasumov's duty was to trump Mels' little speech with a response but the second toast of the evening was reserved for women—'a toast to the flowers not *on* our table, but *at* our table,' for example. Not that a woman would ever propose a toast herself, of course. Indeed women did not need to be physically present for this particular toast, though their absence inevitably meant that the talk became more risqué. As Mels predicted, Kasumov passed this duty on to his subordinate. Elmar made the best of the opportunity.

"When I was a boy there was a secluded lake where the women of the village would bathe. We had a donkey that would choose that time of day to go to there, watching the women as he drank. Of course, being a donkey, that was all he could do. I propose a toast to the women, of course, and to all the women in our lives, and to ourselves. May we never be like that donkey!"

The toast made no sense and Kasumov had probably heard it a hundred times but he laughed good-humoredly.

"Katz, has Elmar ever told you his story about how he convinced his enemy at the University that he was being drafted into the army? He showed up at his apartment one night with two soldiers and a jeep and drove the poor kid into the countryside for over an hour before telling him the truth—it nearly broke his poor mother's heart!"

Apart from their college days together, Mels also had shared a native hut with Shahtahtinsky for two successive winters in Siberia while attached to a seismic crew. There were few aspects of Shahtahtinsky's early life with which Mels was not intimately familiar. Nevertheless, the bottles of Georgian wine—they were now on their second—had induced a genial feeling of goodwill between the three in which old stories were greeted like old friends. They stood there, exchanging jokes, toasts and stories and occasionally turning the *shashlik* until Kasumov's wife—now dressed in her best dress—came out of the house with a tray of food and started arranging plates on the table. This time Mels stood his ground and left her to it. Kasumov's daughter and Mehri followed and waited patiently at the table until Kasumov was prepared to accept that the kebabs had been cooked to perfection.

The first course was a salad course of fresh tarragon, basil, and other herbs. Bowls of black caviar and butter were placed in front of Mels in the guest of honor's seat at the end of the table. Kasumov tore off a large piece of Azerbaijani *choerek* bread, reached across Mels, and liberally buttered the bread. He then piled it high with caviar and handed it to Mels. Though Mels had eaten red salmon caviar in Siberia, he had never eaten this, the most famous of the Caspian's products. He took a small nibble and felt the fat melt in his mouth. Maybe it was the effect of the wine but the taste was sublime. He rose to his feet, protocol be damned, and proposed a toast.

"Adil Narimanovitch, ladies. As your guest here I have much to be grateful for, but one thing I must mention. I have never tasted sturgeon caviar before and so would like to propose a toast to the Caspian's other black gold . . . !"

A look of delight came over Kasumov. He looked across at his wife and cocked one eyebrow. She seemed instinctively to know what this vague gesture meant and disappeared back into the house, reappearing a minute later with two bottles of clear fluid on which a light frost was forming in the humid seaside air. Mels looked at them with dread—vodka! He had been hoping that the presence of wine on the table and his hosts' Middle Eastern names and appearance had somehow signified that he had flown south of the vodka zone. He sighed. *So along with Communism we have taught you to drink vodka*, he thought; perhaps one was an escape from the other. The first bottle was opened and poured into cut crystal shot glasses. Straight from the freezer, it had the viscosity of glycerin. Mels stuffed his mouth with *choerek* and goat cheese. If he was going to have to drink vodka he wanted to have something more in his stomach than wine and caviar.

While a second course of lamb kebabs was being served by his daughter, Kasumov rose unsteadily to his feet and lifted his glass of vodka. The toast he proposed touched upon world peace, children, the triumph of scientific socialism over ignorance, the role of Azerbaijani scientists in most of the Soviet Union's major discoveries, the hardships he himself had overcome in attaining his present position of wise leadership, and diverse other topics in a random stream of consciousness-like discourse that lasted several minutes but felt like hours. Mels played with the slab of butter on his plate. He felt he had misjudged Kasumov. In truth, the man was a pompous windbag like all the rest and he had automatically slipped into his public persona with the same ease that Mels' knife went through the butter. He tried to follow what was being said, but soon found his attention wandering. He looked at the others sitting there, each lost in their own separate thoughts. Elmar was smoking and trying not to look bored. Mehri passed him the plate of kebabs and surreptitiously stole one of his cigarettes while he was distracted with the food. The two Kasumovas, mother and daughter, were stuffing their faces with the leftovers from the first course. It appeared to be their function to eat slightly out of phase with the others so that there would always be enough of any one course for the guests. Now, Mehri's look of triumph was replaced by annoyance as Elmar noticed that she had taken a cigarette and put both the pack and his cigarette lighter in his pocket out of her reach. She sat there, twirling the unlit cigarette in her fingers.

At length, Kasumov's rambling toast came to an end. He had started in Russian but in mid discourse the glass in his hand had started to tilt and vodka spilled over his wrist. Distracted, Kasumov had finished his speech in Azeri. Shahtahtinsky started to translate the punchline but Mels—who had long since lost track of whatever Kasumov was talking about—silenced him with a gesture. He was interested to notice that although he and

Shahtahtinsky were both expected to follow Kasumov's lead and toss back the vodka, the two Kasumovas merely sipped theirs. Mehri took an intermediate course, at first sipping the drink then knocking it back, making a satisfied smacking noise with her lips.

The next course was sturgeon, served with a pomegranate sauce and lightly fried potatoes. While Kasumov refilled the vodka glasses, Shahtahtinsky rose to tell a story which started off being about the relative strengths of the Leningrad and Baku soccer teams and then devolved into a joke about a Siberian hunter and a female polar bear. The story ended with the inevitable toast but, as all eyes were on Shahtahtinsky, Mels threw his vodka over his shoulder. Part of it hit the open shashlik pit and ignited with a blue flame that Mels hoped no one noticed. When Kasumov returned with the vodka bottle, Mels poured the contents out under the table and replaced it with mineral water.

The main course—rice pilaf—came next. In truth, no one was hungry but that was not really the point. The two Kasumovas exchanged contented looks, happy that they had avoided the shame of having guests wanting for anything at the end of the meal. Another two toasts were proposed—one by Mels in which he congratulated the cooks, which Kasumov interpreted to mean himself. Mels tried to find some topic other than food with which to engage the Kasumovas in conversation. He had some limited success on the subject of pest control—cockroaches being an apparent nuisance in Mashtagah. The younger Kasumova explained that the only way to deal with *tarakans* was with borax mixed with mashed potato—whereupon the thirst-maddened insects would throw themselves into the Caspian. The elder Kasumova gravely intoned that the problem had originated when Armenian families had started building dachas in the area in the nineteen-sixties. Mels had heard a variant on that one before. The equivalent urban myth in Leningrad blamed African students who had started to appear at the various institutes in town at around the same time. The conversation soon lapsed and, after removing the dirty dishes, the Kasumovas returned to their stronghold in the kitchen. Kasumov waited until they had disappeared from sight then tottered towards the house himself. He turned towards Mels.

"I hope you will excuse me, Katz. I have some important telephone calls to make."

Mels stiffened, but as Kasumov went past Mehri's chair he tapped her on the shoulder in an unsubtle way. She blushed, then followed, after quickly throwing the remains of her glass of vodka down her throat. Shahtahtinsky exchanged his seat for one next to Mels.

"You look troubled, my friend. You can talk here. The house isn't bugged or we'd all have ended up on the other side of the street by now."

He gestured in the direction of the mental hospital.

"Mehri is a snitch, as I'm sure you realize. She's supposed to report *to* Kasumov but he's not as stupid as he looks. He knows she also reports *about* him. Bear in mind the local satrap here—Aliyev—was a KGB general before he became Party Leader. There isn't much that goes on here that he doesn't get to hear about sooner or later."

"That's what worries me, Elmar. I can't tell you all the details or you will be compromised but that box around my name on the paper was no accident. They offered me a bribe—an overseas assignment—but I was foolish enough to refuse. For some reason they are determined to publish that paper with my name on it and they're frightened I'll cry 'Foul!' "

"You are too modest, Mels. That 'some reason' is glaringly obvious. I've worked for Kasumov for more years than I care to remember and I know well the standard of work that passes for original research in this place. Kasumov needs to get your name on the paper or people will dismiss it as another of his pseudo-scientific ramblings. Don't get me wrong. He's not a bad guy, in his own way. But he knows the art of survival according to the rules of the five-year plan. We get our maximum bonus at, oh, I don't know, 105% or so of the plan, so that's how much work we do. It's easy enough—the quotas are set so low. And our work is measured in quantity, not quality. He does favors to the editors of scientific journals—a case of caviar at New Year's, for example—and he makes sure this Institute gets its 'fair share' of published papers each year. You think I'm exaggerating? You know that two-thirds of the world's mud volcanoes are in Azerbaijan? Of course not! Nobody outside of Azerbaijan gives a damn about mud volcanoes. Now I have nothing against mud volcanoes—in fact I'd go so far as to say that no one should leave this life without seeing one up close. But I ask you, how many special issues of scientific journals devoted to mud volcanoes does the world need?"

Mels laughed.

"But, Elmar, this paper on diamonds—is Kasumov serious about it? Surely no one is going to be fooled?"

"Except for the presence of your name I think the entire scientific community would smile and turn the page. Even then, frankly, I think most geoscientists would read the abstract and assume you were forced into it. Where was this bribe, by the way?"

"Vietnam. But if the scientific community isn't going to be fooled, then who is all this aimed at? And why are the KGB involved?"

"Who knows? The Americans? The Chinese? I guess not the Vietnamese or they wouldn't send you there. Funny you mention Vietnam. I saw a map of the place in Kasumov's office. I assumed he was going to pull strings to send one of our guys there. I'll say this for him—he knows how to buy loyalty among his staff. You know that I got to go to Algeria in your place the last time?"

"Yes, I know. It's OK, Elmar. No hard feelings. What was it like, anyway?"

"Horrible. Most of the others chosen were Kasumov's age. You need money and connections to get on the list to go there so most of them had senior positions to start with. All of them were Party members, too. The problem is that the Algerians didn't *want* a bunch of administrators and Candidates of Science. They wanted someone who could show them how to conduct a seismic survey. I guess that's why they chose me when they decided not to let you go. They knew I wouldn't defect—with my family being here in Baku.

The biggest problem was the wives. Most of them were nuts before they even got on the plane. Then living packed together in one apartment block in Algiers meant they were always getting on each other's nerves. They were all Russians, of course. All trying not to spend a kopeck of their salaries so they could buy a car when they got back home. The Algerians hated them but I don't think they even noticed. They reminded me of dogs. You know how it is when you take a dog for a walk? Of course you do. You had that dog in Siberia until we ate it! All the dog is interested in is other dogs. And when they meet another one they try to intimidate it to see who's boss. The Russians were like that—a pack of two-legged dogs. Territorial, too. Most of them never even left the suburb where we lived until Russians were banned from the local bazaar because they kept stealing from the locals!

I was glad to get out in the field. The desert is beautiful and it's surprisingly cold at night. But the problems didn't end there. We had one idiot who came straight from a Moscow Institute with a folder full of drawings. A young kid—a general's son, actually. He started telling the locals that they were building the temporary camps wrong. So the next time we moved it had to be done his way. He disappeared that week."

"What happened?"

"Oh, it turned out that the planners in Moscow had designed the toilets so that the crew all had their backs to Mecca when they took a dump. They'd also provided him with some Communist literature in Arabic. God knows what it said. Actually, most of the guys out there couldn't even read so they were easy enough to stir up when the rumor went round that it insulted Islam.

We found his body a couple of days later. The vultures had torn it up pretty badly by then but it was pretty obvious that his pants were missing. I think they had a bit of fun with him before they killed him. I had to fly back to Algiers with the remains. His poor father was there to meet me. By the time I got back to the camp our goodwill ambassadors from the embassy's KGB staff had gone to work on my seismic crew. The place was deserted. I think they thought *I* knew too much, too. They were going through one of their periodic panics about the loyalty of the 'Islamic southern republics' so I was sent back to Baku."

They sat in silence for a while, looking at the glowing embers in the *shashlik* pit. Suddenly Elmar laughed.

"Mehri jumped a mile when you threw your vodka into the barbecue!"

"Really? I was hoping no one noticed!"

"Only her. And me. I'm sure it awakened some nasty memories in her. She's a bit fond of a tipple, as I'm sure you noticed. About six months ago we had some guests here—and she was on duty of course. She'd had one too many and she was leaning over the barbecue pit with vodka in one hand while trying to light a cigarette. She leaned too far and spilled the vodka. There was a big blue fireball and the next thing we noticed there was Mehri wandering around the back yard with a cigarette stub in her mouth and no eyebrows! She was lucky she didn't get seriously burned—which in her profession could be disastrous."

"So does she translate, too?"

Elmar's eyes twinkled.

"I'm told she has various specialized lingual skills. You should consider yourself honored, Mels. Moscow-trained and foreign-traveled, and all that."

"If she's so good at her profession, why isn't she still in Moscow?"

"The call of the Azerbaijani homeland, Mels! No, seriously, I believe there was some unpleasantness regarding freelance work she was doing while on a foreign trip. I'm told she tried to pick someone up in a hotel bar and discovered he was a plain-clothes cop. All part of an imperialist conspiracy, of course."

"Of course. Those evil capitalists framing a poor Soviet working girl. She seems to be taking a long time with Kasumov. Does his wife know what he's up to?"

"Oh I should imagine she's quite relieved not to have that weight rolling on top of her. Kasumov is fond of dipping his hand in the honey-pot but he's not stupid enough to go to some bugged hotel with Mehri. If you're wise, you won't, either, unless you want your ass on some private movie being shown at KGB headquarters. Try to get to stay at her place. Chances are it's not bugged or she wouldn't usually take clients to hotels. In any case, she's here to keep an eye on Ignatiev, not you. Her apartment is in the city center. I'll give you a ride there. I don't know what you'll do tomorrow (and I don't *want* to know!) but that way you can slip out early in the morning while she sleeps off her hangover. Who knows—you might enjoy it?"

"Thanks for the tip, Elmar. But, getting back to Kasumov and this paper. Do you honestly think he believes what's in it?"

"With him, it's hard to tell. He's about as honest as a *Pravda* editorial but he's not mad. I ask you, nuclear bombs to convert oil to diamonds! All I know is that it started after he was summoned to KGB headquarters here. It was just after a bunch of other department heads had been canned by Aliyev for corruption. He was literally shaking when he got in his car to go there. When he came back he put me to work at compiling statistics on pressure waves from nuclear explosions and estimating the amount of oil left in some of the old oilfields around Baku. Not that they mean anything. The only statistic that matters is that the price of oil doubled last year. And this year our brothers to the south of here in Iran are selling their crude seventy-five percent higher than last year. We have the highest production rates in the world and ten percent of the reserves. The Americans had to drop their embargo on oilfield equipment because they're shitting their pants that the oil price is going even higher. They get three tons of oil a day out of their wells; we get twenty. On top of that, the price of diamonds depends on *low* production levels. If we start mass producing the damn things, that's going to destroy the Soviet diamond industry.

With oil so valuable, why would we want to mess things up with some crazy scheme to make diamonds?"

Mels shrugged. He had come to Baku for answers, not questions. If Shahtahtinsky was right, the genesis of this paper came from a higher level than Kasumov—one with access to the very highest levels of the KGB. *But why?* He was still searching for an answer when Mehri and Kasumov reappeared.

"Adil Narimanovitch, was your connection satisfactory?"

Kasumov looked blank.

"The phone connection."

"Ah yes. Of course—"

But Kasumov's response was interrupted by the wail of a police siren and the screech of brakes on the other side of the wall. A flashing blue light illuminated the night sky as Mels heard voices and the sound of Kasumov's front door bell ringing.

Chapter 10

Two uniformed and one plain clothes policemen pushed their way into the back yard, ignoring the attempts by the Kasumovas to ascertain their business. The one in plain clothes appeared to know Kasumov and—from his disdainful look—Mehri.

"Adil Narimanovitch. We are sorry to disturb you but this afternoon a dangerous criminal escaped from our custody. He was last seen near your dacha here. Have you seen anyone suspicious?"

Kasumov's eyes darted from side to side with excitement, though whether this was caused by the vicarious thrill of proximity to danger or the opportunity to puff himself up and seem important was hard to tell.

"It's Lieutenant Babayev, right? Well, Babayev, no criminal has dared to penetrate my property while I have been here. As you can see, those present are all my guests, and they have been under my protection all evening."

"Did anyone else see anything suspicious?"

Mehri spoke up.

"As a matter of fact, when we arrived, the next door was open. I thought I heard adult voices inside but all we saw was a young boy with his sheep."

"Sheep, eh?"

Mels moved quickly to derail the train of thought before it went anywhere.

"Unless he left the scene disguised as a ewe, Lieutenant, I don't think the sheep are very relevant. Director Kasumov here was telling us the next-door apartment is abandoned. Perhaps the criminal is still there."

Babayev looked skeptically at Mels for a moment then ordered his men next door. Within minutes they heard cursing as they dragged away the drunk Mels had encountered earlier in the day. Mels decided it was time he left, too.

"Director Kasumov, it's been a pleasure but it has been a long day. I wonder if I might call for a taxi to take me to my hotel?"

"I wouldn't hear of it, Katz. Shahtahtinsky here can give you a ride."

After protracted farewells—which involved a final toast from Kasumov—Shahtahtinsky drove the three of them out of town on the Baku road. Mels had attempted to avoid Mehri's clutches by sitting in the back of Shahtahtinsky's Zhiguli but Mehri had ignored the more comfortable front seat and climbed in the rear with him. He noticed that her skirt had ridden up when she got in, exposing a long length of white thigh that she pointedly failed to cover. One of her arms rested on the back of his seat and she took advantage of each time Shahtahtinsky turned a corner by edging towards Mels. Up close, she smelled of expensive perfume, vodka, and cigarettes with a meaty undertone that Mels speculated was from Kasumov. He tried to move away from her but the springs in the back seat had collapsed and the two of them kept sliding together. So intent was he on evading Mehri that he did not notice that the car was slowing down until it had nearly stopped.

"What's going on, Elmar?"

"Roadblock."

Even Mehri was surprised at the speed at which Mels' defenses crumbled before her charms. He put his arm around her and pulled her towards him, kissing her full on her musky-tasting lips, just as a militiaman came up to the car and shone his flashlight through the glass. Shahtahtinsky rolled down his window.

"Lieutenant Babayev. So did you find your suspect?"

"Only some drunk. But don't worry. We may not be as successful as Mehri here at catching men but when we do we usually keep them for more than a night!"

Mehri responded with an oath in Azeri.

"Temper, temper, Mehri *hanum*, let's be professional, shall we?"

Mehri sat and sulked silently all the rest of the way into town. But when Shahtahtinsky stopped the car opposite a building housing the Committee of People's Control she remonstrated with him in Azeri. After a heated exchange, Shahtahtinsky turned to Mels.

"Mehri objects that I drop you both halfway between the Azerbaijan Hotel and her apartment. I have explained that you can escort her safely home. Now you must excuse me. I have a long drive to my home."

Shahtahtinsky winked at Mels as Mehri got out of the car.

"God be with you, old friend."

Mehri's temper tantrum soon faded. As it turned out, her apartment building was only a ten-minute walk from where they had been dropped. Mels followed her upstairs without asking and deflected her attempts at conversation with monosyllables. Despite Shahtahtinsky's assurances about the lack of listening devices in the one-bedroom apartment, he was only too aware of the fact that evading the KGB thus far had been more a matter of luck than judgement. Mehri was trained to get information from people and anything he said would be passed on in the morning. *Better say nothing than concoct some involved fabrication and get caught out*, just in case Mehri got suspicious. Who knew if she had a panic button in her apartment that could summon her handlers at a moment's notice? In his pocket he had the enamel badge of Lenin he had been given to wear on May Day. When Mehri excused herself to go to the bathroom he stuck the heavy brass pin of the cloisonné medallion through the wire of her telephone then tucked it under the receiver. He lifted the handset and listened. If the KGB were monitoring through the phone line, all they would now hear was static.

He heard the toilet flush and Mehri leave the bathroom to go into her bedroom. *Should I follow her?* Presumably sometime in the next hour he would be expected to have sex with this woman. While he did not exactly dread the prospect—Mehri was an attractive woman in her way—he was conscious of the fact that only this morning had he shared his bed with Tanya, who was not only infinitely more alluring but also the woman he knew he loved.

"Mels? Could you give me a hand with this?"

Mehri's muffled voice came from the bedroom. He went in and found her struggling to get her dress off. She had managed to pull it over her head until it was held only by the neck. Her arms waved helplessly, entangled in the material of the upside-down garment. He was surprised to find that the underwear on her overripe body had a picture of a large shark about to consume a swimmer and the cryptic initials "J.A.W.S" in English.

"The zipper got stuck. This is very embarrassing."

Well, at least this breaks the ice, thought Mels. A small piece of dress fabric had jammed in the zipper. He pulled it free then unzipped the dress. Mehri's blushing face came into view. The mascara smeared over her eyes made her look like a red panda.

"Mels, I don't know anything about you. I mean, we didn't have time to talk, did we? Do you like showers?"

"Showers?"

"Yes. I just need to know so I can put a rubber sheet on the bed."

He kissed her on the forehead.

"Mehri, I'm going to pretend I have no idea what you're talking about. I think we've both had a little too much to drink. Let's get some sleep."

She protested mechanically but seemed relieved. He undressed and slid into bed while she went back to the bathroom to remove her make-up. He was asleep before she returned.

Some hours later he was having a vivid dream about cockroaches, driven mad with thirst, licking the sweat from his body. In his dream the cockroaches became larger and somehow metamorphosed into Laika, the dog he had had in Siberia. Laika was licking him quite furiously, down his back, between his buttocks, then his . . . .

"Hey!"

He woke with a start to find himself lying on his face with Mehri kneeling over him, licking him in a *very* personal place.

"What the hell are you doing?!"

"You don't like this? I thought all men did. It's called 'Going round the World.'"

"I don't care what it's called. You know, if you'd been around thirty years ago you could have saved my father a trip to Peter and Paul Fortress. . . ."

Mehri looked blank.

"Never mind. Look Mehri, you're a lovely woman but I'm a little tired. Why don't we try to get some sleep?"

Mehri looked crushed. Seeing her cow-like, brown eyes cloud with tears, Mels felt remorseful but not enough to consider having sex with her. *How many men has this woman performed anilingus on in the last month?* He shuddered inwardly at the thought. An idea came to him.

"Unless maybe you have a little vodka we could sip . . . ?"

Mehri's eyes brightened. She jumped out of bed, still in her attack shark underwear, and hurried to the refrigerator in the kitchen. Within a minute she had returned with a bottle and two glasses. Within half an hour most of its contents was inside her (*better it than me*, thought Mels) and she was snoring softly next to him.

He woke again just as it was getting light. A glance at Mehri showed that she was still out for the count. Her blonde hair flopped over her face, showing dark roots. Nevertheless, he knew it would only be a few hours before she would report his presence to her superiors and he no longer had the home advantage of knowing the town in which he was going to try to evade them. His only hope now was that Hamlet would feel sufficiently indebted to him to help.

He dressed silently. His clothes smelt unwashed. In the bathroom he found a magnificent array of perfumes and colognes but he felt the smoky smell from the *shashlik* pit would be less likely to draw attention to himself in Baku. He washed his face and hands as quietly as he could and dried himself on a facecloth embroidered with the words "Hilton Hotel" in English.

He blinked as he walked out into the road. It was already hot in the sun. The apartment blocks were partly covered by ancient grapevines that grew from small holes in the paved sidewalk. The vines extended right up the sides of the buildings and had been cultivated to spread their branches over each balcony. From below, bunches of nascent purple-gray and light green grapes could be seen among the leaves. A gang of women who looked like gypsies were sweeping the street with long besoms. He called to one to ask directions but she shook her head uncomprehendingly. A Russian woman who had been sheltering from the sun in the shade of a grape vine stepped forward, broom in hand, and explained that the women were Talysh from the southern mountains who spoke little Russian. She laughed when Mels asked the way to an Armenian cobbler's shop in Zavokzalnyi Rayon.

"Comrade, all the cobblers in Baku are Armenian! And most of them live in the *Armenikand*. I can tell you how to get to the Sabuchinskiy railway station. You just walk north on Lenin Prospekt, but after that you are on your own."

The sinking feeling that came over Mels was not helped when he reached the station and walked into the first cobbler's shop. Half a dozen Armenians were sitting inside smoking, reading newspapers, and conversing in Armenian while one—evidently the owner of the shop—tapped nails into the heel of a work boot he was repairing.

"Is Rapik here?"

Three of the men responded to Mels' question in the affirmative.

"Er, does anyone know Hamlet?"

The three shook their heads. One of them made a remark in Armenian that provoked laughter from the others. They returned to their conversation, ignoring Mels.

Nor did he have much success in the next two shoemakers' shops. Convinced that he had been deceived, he started to feel he was being followed, too. He crossed the street to a large park and started to run across the grass. After a few minutes he ducked behind a tree in a wooded area and waited. Within seconds, one of the men from the first shop passed by the tree. Mels tripped him and jumped on his back, twisting his arms behind him.

"OK, OK. You think I'm going to admit I know a man who's wanted by the militia in a crowded shop?! Let me go and I'll take you to him."

Mels released the man and helped him to his feet. He was not grateful.

"Look what you did to my suit, asshole. This is imported Italian cloth. How am I going to get grass stains out of this?"

The complaints continued as they walked towards *Icheri Shekher*, the old city where Mels was informed he could meet up with Hamlet. It was a long walk but Mels did not want to risk losing his escort in a crowded Metro station. En route, they passed a massive Soviet Realist monument consisting of a circular white marble ring enclosing a giant stone statue of a man with bowed head. Music was playing from loudspeakers embedded in the stone and baskets of red flowers had been left as offerings to whoever this secular saint might be.

"That's Shaumian. He's the leader of the Twenty-six Baku Commissars."

"What did they do?"

"They got executed."

"Any particular reason?"

"The British did it because he was an Armenian."

"Not because he was a Communist?"

"Well he was a Communist, too. But they killed him because he was Armenian."

"Were the others Armenian?"

"Yes, of course!"

"All of them?"

"No, there were some Communists. But the Armenians were killed because they were Armenians. The British were allies with the Turks."

"When did this happen?"

"Nineteen-eighteen."

"Weren't the British fighting the Turks in nineteen-eighteen?"

"Then why would they kill Armenians?"

They passed a mock Greek temple whose façade announced that it was the V. I. Lenin museum. Mels thought it would be wise to change the subject.

"I didn't know Lenin had visited Baku?"

"Who?"

"Never mind."

They were within sight of a high medieval city wall made of yellow-gray limestone that marked the entrance to the *Icheri Shekher*, the old citadel of Baku. They entered through a castellated gateway surmounted by a coat of arms of a bull and two lions. They walked down an old street lined with fine old buildings whose facades had crumbled over the years. Some were ancient caravansaries, which had been converted into restaurants. Others housed small industries like carpet making or silversmiths, presumably aimed at however many tourists a place like Baku could attract. Ahead, Mels saw an impressive medieval tower some thirty meters tall but they turned abruptly down a narrow passageway before they reached it.

For the next thirty minutes, Mels unnamed companion lead him at a breathless pace around the old city, down one passageway then up another, short-cutting by dodging through arched courtyards and often doubling back on themselves in what Mels quickly recognized as an unsubtle—but successful—attempt to confuse him. At length they stopped by an entranceway barred by an old wooden door on which Mels' guide knocked three times, paused, then knocked again—twice this time. A small, iron-barred hatch at face height opened sufficiently for a few words in Armenian to pass. This was followed by protracted sounds of various bolts and locks being unlatched. The door then opened just enough for them to enter in single file. Mels had barely put his foot over the threshold when a coarse sack smelling of chemicals was pulled roughly over his head. He struggled to breathe for a few seconds before lapsing into unconsciousness. He imagined himself being shouted at from the end of a long, long corridor or pipeline. Amidst a backdrop of several echoing Armenian voices he heard the voice of his erstwhile guide speaking in Russian and felt a dull ache in his upper torso.

"That's for the grass stains and the long walk, asshole."

He woke with a splitting headache and a sharp pain in his ribs. His hands had been tied in front of him and he was in a sitting position with his back against a wall. The hood was still over his head but he could see just enough through the sacking to tell that he had been dragged into an interior room. There was a smell of cooking coming from somewhere nearby and the amplified voice of a television was blaring in Russian. Several male voices from within the room were apparently commenting on the program in Armenian. When one spoke, the others responded with a purling chorus of "Che, Che!" as though in agreement, even though Mels knew that this actually meant "no" in Armenian. His mouth felt dry from breathing through the dusty sacking. He decided to risk speaking up.

"Hello?"

Through the burlap he saw one of the figures approach and squat beside him.

"Are you awake, now, Professor?"

"Can you take the mask off me? I get claustrophobia and I can't breathe."

"Not now. But soon. We know you're not a cop, Professor Ignatiev. And we know that Hamlet escaped from Mashtagah. We got word from some kid an hour or so ago, while you were still out. We're also prepared to accept that—despite your passport—you're also really this 'Ivanov' character young Kasoum told us about. Now, I have to tell you that Leningrad telephone number in your pocket has been disconnected and you might want to get that jacket of yours aired before you take your luxury class airplane back home. But, in general, we've checked you out and, well, we 'like' you. What you did for Hamlet was a good thing. Unfortunately, if we let you see our faces . . . well, let's just say none of us would feel comfortable with you running around wherever you live, knowing what we look like. It's only three years since some idiots in Moscow let off a couple of bombs. Before any of us even knew what had happened we were being dragged into KGB cells and accused of being nationalists."

"And you're not?"

"All Armenians are nationalists! But we have a business to run here. You don't get rich by letting off bombs."

Mels decided this was not the time to inquire about what kind of business they were running.

"How long have I been here? Can I at least get a drink?"

"You've been here for about six hours. We were worried about you for a while there. The chloroform doesn't usually put people out like that. If you want a drink, we have the best Armenian brandy."

"No brandy. I haven't eaten yet today. Do you have water? I guess I was tired. It's been a busy few days."

Curious, the man waited for Mels to elaborate.

"No offence, but I don't think *I* would feel comfortable with you knowing all my secrets, either."

Through the fabric, Mels saw the man shrug. He called out something in Armenian and was soon joined by a second shadowy figure. A slit was cut in the material then a glass of water was held to Mels' lips.

"We'll get you some food soon. There's *plaki*—that's Armenian bean stew—cooking."

Mels leant back against the wall. The sounds in the room returned to the loud baritone of a Russian news announcer—currently deriding the Chinese for breaking off border talks—and the crackle of Armenian commentary that drifted, randomly, into Russian in senseless snippets in response to what was on the screen.

". . . now that's a beautiful woman."

". . . that's an *Armenian* woman!"

". . . that car is a two-liter."

". . . six thousand rubles! They robbed you, my friend."

Eventually, food arrived. Even then, they refused to untie his hands and one of them had to feed him, describing each mouthful he was preparing for him as though he was talking to a baby.

"This is *lavash*. Here, I will tear off a strip. Now I put scallions, herbs, and cheese in it. Now I roll it up tight and you eat. *Lavash* is bread but *lavash* is also a plate and *lavash* is a napkin. This is *kufta*. It's made of meat, nuts, herbs, spices and brandy. Good, eh? Now here is *plaki*. Let me try this first. Hey, who cooked this?!"

An answering voice came from another room. Mels recognized it as Rapik's.

"Who do you think you are—Mikhail Talebov?! This is the worst *plaki* I've eaten."

There was laughter from the others in the room.

"Who's Mikhail Talebov?"

"That's *Lieutenant Colonel* Talebov to you, my friend. He's a local boy—an ethnic Uzbek but born here in Azerbaijan. He's one of Aliyev's proteges. Like his master he went south of here to spy on his moslem brothers. He lived in Kabul with forged papers and got a job as a chef in the presidential palace. Even in Afghanistan they like Uzbek food! But then—get this—he couldn't poison the president, Amin. He put poison in the guy's orange juice but Amin never trusted anyone so he mixed his orange juice with everyone else's and they all got mildly sick but no one died. Aliyev was furious. Finally they sent down an assassination team to finish the job."

"How do you know all this?"

"Let's just say we make it our business to know things."

One of the others spoke up.

"They also killed Amin's five-year old son. Russians are Christian people. One of the team that killed Amin had a conscience about his son."

Christian people? thought Mels. He was about to make a remark about pogroms when he remembered that he was supposed to *be* a Russian. Besides which, knowing that he was completely in their power, he didn't want to antagonize his captors. He changed the subject.

"When can I see Hamlet?"

"Tonight. When it's dark. Don't worry. We're *Armenians*. We are men of our word."

"Well could you at least put me in a room where I could remove this mask. I'll put it on again before we go but I feel like a blind man."

"A blind man! You should be honored to be in our protection! You know the difference between a Russian, a Turk, and an Armenian? If a man were dying in a ditch a Russian would leave him to die. A Turk would kill him out of cruelty but an Armenian *would lift him up!*"

So much for Russians being conscience-stricken Christians thought Mels. It was a tale he had heard before. He remembered Elmar Shahtahtinsky's alternative ending from the Azerbaijani perspective ("Oh, sure. An Armenian would lift him up, all right. *And* take his wallet.").

One of the other men joined in.

"You know, one of Armenia's greatest historians was blind. His name was Leo. When he got old he told his daughter that he had one last book he wanted to write before he died. He wrote for months and never saw a word he'd written."

"What did he write?"

"Nobody knows. His daughter didn't want him to make a mess so she never put ink in the inkwell."

Everyone laughed. The conversation turned to women and—as the men's boasts of their womanizing prowess became more outlandish—the language reverted to Armenian. Mels was ignored for the rest of the afternoon until it was time to leave. A dispute broke out between the men about who was to drive the car, a borrowed military jeep that they were 'using' for the evening.

"I'll go with Ignatiev. I know the way to *Lokbatan* with my eyes closed."

"Were *you* in the army? You can't drive a jeep."

"If you drive then I go, too. You don't want to get lost around there, and not just because of the Azerbaijanis and the military patrols. The place is haunted."

"Haunted?! Do I look like I'm afraid of ghosts?"

"No, but you could get lost in three birches."

Mels was lead down some stairs and into the back of the jeep. A blanket was thrown over him and then he was told to keep perfectly still and quiet. The jeep's harsh suspension bounced erratically as the vehicle gradually left the traffic noises of the city behind and headed into the quiet of the countryside. They were stopped just once at some kind of checkpoint. Mels heard a thick Azeri accent demand cigarettes and a brief exchange of words before the car continued on its way.

He lost track of time after that and probably would have fallen asleep but for the lurching and bouncing of the jeep. When the car eventually stopped, one of the men in the front pulled the blanket off him. He recognized the voice of the man who had insisted on accompanying the driver.

"We're past the brine lakes now, so we're going to let you out here. This is a strange place where the earth shakes and fires come out of the ground, but you cannot get lost if you keep going *up* the hill. It's a clear night and the moon will guide you. Be careful at the top. There are pools of bubbling mud up there. *Lokbatan* means 'the camel got stuck.' Mind your step or you will, too."

"You're not coming with me?"

"You're on your own. We're Armenian and we have no guarantee of our safety. Just remember—you are not in Baku now."

Chapter 11

I may as well have left the damn mask on . . . that driver should try finding his way up a mud volcano by moonlight! Mels picked himself up for the second time after tripping on the uneven surface. He paused to catch his breath and stared up at the summit, noticing that the red glow he had seen from the base of the hill actually comprised several separate fires, which would flare dramatically for minutes at a time—roaring like mythical dragons—then suddenly disappear. He knew enough about mud volcanoes to know that these were natural gas seeps from deep within the earth but he was amazed by their scale. He continued up the hill until he found himself at the lip of the caldera. Dimly visible ahead of him, five or six clay stalagmites stuck up from the depression like low chimneys from which flames sporadically burst. Approaching one of these, he saw that a steady stream of viscous mud accompanied the eruptions. Bubbles burst with blue flames from the shiny wet surface. Fascinated, he reached out to touch the mud and had just time to register surprise that it was cool to the touch before loud canine baying broke the silence. A distant voice in Azeri was followed by one in Russian.

"Ivanov? Is that you?!"

"I'm over here. The dog will guide you. Don't be frightened of it—but don't try to touch it, either!"

Even in the semi-darkness, the dog was hard to miss. It was white in color and huge. It did not so much guide as herd Mels to where Hamlet sat with a group of Azerbaijani men around a campfire on which a small lamb was being spit-roasted.

"Have you eaten, Comrade 'Ivanov,' or should I call you 'Ignatiev,' now?"

"You can call me what you like. But, thanks; your, er, 'business associates' fed me."

"Not Rapik's *plaki*, was it? It's bad enough to be held captive without being tortured!"

Mels laughed.

"Well if you're still hungry, I'm sure these gentlemen will share their lamb with you."

The Azerbaijani men were staring at Hamlet with barely disguised hatred. One spoke up in a thick Azeri accent.

"That's not part of our deal, Armenian."

Hamlet's reply, though *sotto voce*, was unmistakably in American-accented English.

"Faithful to your little girlfriend even in death. How touching!"

Mels was astonished. He answered in English.

"So you speak *English*, too?! I don't believe you learned that in Baku."

"As a matter of fact, I learned that from my parents. They were American. And, literally speaking, so am I, though I left there when I was five years old."

"No crap?"

"That's 'no *shit*?' And your accent is terrible. You sound like an Englishman. Did you get that from the BBC?"

Mels laughed.

"I didn't know I *had* a British accent! I don't get that much chance to practice with native English speakers. I suppose the tapes we listened to at school were British. So do I sound like Prince Charles?"

"Well, no one's going to mistake you for Jimmy Carter."

Mels thoughtlessly switched back to Russian.

"So tell me, Hamlet, how did a Yankee boy like you end up on top of a mud volcano in Azerbaijan?"

Hamlet's eyes flashed.

"Don't speak Russian! These country hicks may look like they just stepped out of the wild forest but they speak Russian every time they take their flocks into town. I'll tell you my story—after all the KGB already knows it—if you tell me yours. 'Ignatiev' doesn't suit you, either. You're Jewish aren't you?"

"You're not as easily fooled as your associates."

"That's right. Did they tell you the story about the Armenian, the Turk and the Russian?"

"I'd heard it before."

"Well what you should realize is that to an Armenian, the world is made up of 'us' and 'them.' 'Them' consists of 'Russians'—who are usually neutral but sometimes helpful—and 'Turks' whom you can never, *ever* trust. Azerbaijanis are 'Turks.' Russians are 'Russians,' of course, as are Jews, Georgians, and even Frenchmen and Americans. Greeks are a special class of 'Russian'. After all, who else hates the Turks more than the Greeks? But when it comes down to it you can only trust an Armenian."

"It sounds like a very insular world. If you ask an Azerbaijani, the words 'trust' and 'Armenian' don't often appear in the same sentence."

"They have their own way of looking at things. But let me tell you a little bit about the history of the Armenian people before you make these moral judgements, Comrade 'Ivanov.'"

"It's 'Katz.' Mels Katz."

Hamlet laughed.

"Well, Mels Katz, a Jew with a first name like that should certainly appreciate *this* story. Your dad was a Communist, eh?"

"Obviously. Like everything else, irony was in short supply in Leningrad in 1945."

"Yeah, well my dad was, too. He used to have a map on the wall of his shop in California that showed the progress of the Red Army against the Fascists. Just after the war in Europe ended, a sharply dressed guy appeared in the shop. He spoke Armenian but with a different accent—my father's family came from Lebanon and before that, Turkey—but this guy spoke with a Yerevan accent. He knew my father's name and mentioned the names of several mutual acquaintances in the community. He'd been well briefed. To cut a long story short, he wanted my dad to go 'back' to Armenia and help rebuild the country. And of course my dad fell for it, hook, line, and sinker. . . ."

"What . . . ?"

"You should practice your idioms. I mean he fell for it *completely*. The problem with Armenia is that it's like Israel. It's a small, rocky country with no natural resources surrounded by a sea of Islamic neighbors who hate it. And just like Israel, it couldn't survive if it didn't have a 'big brother.' In Israel's case, it's America but all we have is Russia. And the Russians know that, and they use us as their proxy in the region and so the Turks and *their* little brothers—the Azerbaijanis—hate us all the more. Some general in Czarist times said 'Russia has need of Armenia, but it has no need of Armenians.' And Armenians feel the same way about Russians. Except my dad, of course. Well, I take that back—it wasn't a Russian he trusted—it was a Georgian."

"Stalin."

"That's right. The old murderous bastard managed to convince about three hundred Armenians to throw over the good life in the U. S. of A and come 'back' to Armenia to build the Socialist future. This is the same man who sold us out over Nagorno-Karabakh and gave it to Azerbaijan."

"The Azerbaijanis say he sold *them* out by making it an Autonomous Region, run by Armenians."

"Yeah, I know. I'll say one thing for the Azerbaijanis, they were never fooled by Stalin. He fucked Armenia and what did we do? We built the biggest statue in the world, right in the middle of Yerevan. You know that was the last statue of Stalin that was erected in the whole Union? Six men died putting it up and another six tearing it down in Kruschev's time. And as for all the Armenians that came with my dad, well, within months all of them had asked for their passports back. But they were stuck.

The Americans didn't do anything to help—at least not at first—after all, most of them were Communists and they didn't *want* them back! After a year, my family moved to Baku, to the *Armenikand*."

"That's a little ironic, isn't it, given what you feel about 'Turks'?"

"Baku isn't typical of Azerbaijan. It's always been a multicultural city. At least until recent years. Now Aliyev is moving his clansmen into the city. Still, there's more opportunity here than in Armenia."

"So how did you fall out with the authorities?"

"Well, you can imagine how much surveillance we were under—being 'Americans' and *refuseniks*. I started doing a little private enterprise—just amber jewelry that I'd get from a man from Vilnius and sell on the streets. The militia picked me up a few times but I usually got off with a warning. I could have ended up as some petty criminal if fate hadn't intervened. Then, one time, this judge thought she'd really scare me so she sent me off to the military. It was the best training I could get."

"You mean self-defense?"

"No! I mean it let me travel all over the Union. I was in an engineering battalion that built bridges, so I could meet people in the construction trade, make contacts, learn how the heavy industrial plants get their money. And when you're in the army there's always something to sell. By the time I'd spent my two years I had enough money to start up on my own with a chain of contacts from Leningrad to Vladivostock."

"I don't think I understand. By 'heavy industry' you mean you built trucks and cars?"

"Well, not at first. You have to start small. But you'd be amazed how quickly these things take off. You have to have patience, though. You need to wait until exactly the right opportunity comes along and then not kill the goose that lays the golden egg."

"Kill the goose . . . ?"

"It's just a saying. Like 'don't milk a cow 'till its udders bleed.'

The problem is that people get greedy. I'll give you a good example. We had a factory in Siverskiy that built tractor engines. The State Inspection Committee certified that the plant was ready to produce in December of seventy-eight. By February of last year the Ministry of Agricultural Machinery had assigned production quotas for it."

"You mean Siverskiy, just south of Leningrad? There's no tractor engine plant in Siverskiy."

"That's right. But, thanks to 'our' people in Moscow, the Central Statistical Office reported the work of the non-existent plant for more than a year. We were making a fortune! We looked so good on paper that people started sending their tractors to us to be repaired. So much money was coming in that we subcontracted the real plant—the one this 'factory' was supposed to replace—to repair the engines. Everyone was happy. The managers were paid off, the workers were getting overtime, the tractors were getting repaired in half the time it usually took. All it took was a little organization. And then someone got greedy."

"What happened?"

"Well the old factory could do the repairs because it had all the parts. I mean, it wasn't making any new tractors because *we* were supposed to be doing that. Then someone had the bright idea of liquidating its inventory."

"You mean selling off the parts?"

"That's right. But to do that, the old plant had to be shut down. That was a dumb idea. Broken tractors started to pile up with nowhere to go. People started to complain. There was a lot of ill-feeling."

"I can imagine! You must have had a huge workforce!"

"No, I meant the customers. Always keep the clients happy. That's the first rule of business. We moved some of the ancillary staff into our gasoline business and shifted the mechanics to Togliatti. They 'finish' Zhiguli cars, now."

"'Finish'?"

"People wait three years for a car and then discover that it's one that's made at the end of the month when the factory is trying to catch up with its quotas. They're so happy to get it that they sign a piece of paper saying it's been received in good shape. I mean, chances are that it's the first car they've ever owned so how are they going to know? Then afterwards they find out it's a piece of crap; the windows don't wind up, the indicator lights don't work, sometimes even the wheels fall off because some idiot on the assembly line fitted the wheels with one bolt! So what do they do?—they come to us! We get the parts through 'our' guys at the warehouse and then 'finish' the cars. Skilled work like that is best done by as few people as possible. You give me a couple of guys who know what they're doing and I'll make sure we give you a quality product—and then you'll come back, right?

No—to get back to your question—as far as labor is concerned, our biggest problem is in the construction business. That's where the big money is but you need a lot of people on the payroll and it restricts mobility. Plus the more hands, the more mouths; you have to feed them or they start talking.

Tell me, do you live in a co operative, Mels?"

"No. I've never had the money to buy my own place."

"Well, we *build* co operatives. People like them. You ask the average 'intellectual' and he'll tell you that Krushchev was too much of a peasant to be Premier. But let me tell you, he knew what every peasant knows—people want to own their own home whether it's a hectare of land or a co-operative apartment. So they can leave it to their kids or sell it if they want to.

But even though Krushchev legalized them, there's always been a shortage because builders don't like building them. Private owners aren't like Housing Ministry officials. They *won't* sign papers saying they're in good order unless they really are. Your average Russian may not know a carburetor from an alternator but he knows when his kitchen closets don't shut properly! So builders lose their production bonuses. That's where I come in. I can get *shabashniki*—private teams of workers—to build them for a lump sum. I pay them well so I can keep a group of guys that I can trust. You have to have good ones that can do a bunch of different things. You don't want to be waiting all day for some electrician or plumber who got drunk the previous night to show up. And I need guys that can build a house one day, then maybe a barn or even a road the next.

The big problem now in Moscow is the Olympics—"

"But I thought there was a lot of building going on there?"

"Oh, there is. But the problem is that they got so far behind that they started releasing prisoners from jail to work on them. They're unskilled thugs but they're being paid so much that they're spoiling the market. Plus there's a crime wave going on. They can't keep an eye on the ex-convicts all the time and these apartments and hotels that are being built for foreign visitors have to have bugs installed by the KGB. When they do that, they clear the site and these guys go off and get drunk and start terrorizing the neighborhoods. There are some suburbs near the Olympic stadium where rapes are so common the locals have formed vigilante groups!"

"So what does a 'businessman' like yourself do in a situation like that?"

"Oh, that's easy. Forget Moscow. Siberia's always been the place where you can make most money. There's *always* a shortage of workers out there so I put my people in as stevedores on river ports or temporary firemen, wherever people need them."

"Where do you get them from?"

"Moscow, usually. Even before the Olympics, people would go there from all over but they don't have residency papers so they end up living like bums."

"The *limitchiks*, you mean?"

"You know the term?"

"Sure. We have them in Leningrad, too; people who can't live in the city because the authorities put a limit on the number of people who can there."

"In Moscow, they say 'Moscow is not made of rubber,' but it is if you know the right people. And that's where we come in. The *limitchiks* will pay fifteen hundred rubles—which for these guys is a year's salary in the jobs they had before they got to Moscow. For that we'll arrange for them to marry a Muscovite and qualify for city housing. Then, if they want, they can get a job in Moscow. You need six months of marriage to qualify for a resident's permit. A lot of these guys don't have fifteen hundred rubles though, so we'll lend them the money but they have to work off the debt."

"Like serfs?"

"Moralizing again? Look, nobody's forcing them! You should see them. There are whole camps of them in the forests in summertime, living on squirrels and mushrooms! Others live on garbage dumps outside Moscow. They're good workers—if you can get to them before they hit the bottle. You ever go to 'Electric Corner'?"

"No offense, Hamlet, but when I'm in Moscow I don't visit garbage dumps. OK, so you have these workers in Moscow. But the money, you say, is in Siberia. I've been there. It's a long way. Don't tell me you have your own airline, too?"

"Airline? Don't be stupid! They can go by train or riverboat. You don't need an Internal Passport for those. Where did you go in Siberia?"

"We were based in Akademgorodok but I spent most of the winter in a camp up around the Ob River."

"What's that like?"

"Akademgorodok is pretty boring. It's built in the forest south of Novosibirsk and there are three thousand bored, under-worked doctors of science plotting petty intrigues against each other to try to stop their brains from turning to mush. But you're right about the money. Even machine operators get paid two hundred and seventy rubles a month, plus a New Year's bonus. The food is surprisingly good, too; salmon caviar, reindeer tongue, meat pies, tomato-and-cucumber salad. Better than we get in Leningrad. And there's always fish from the river—though that's frozen from October to April so you have to cut holes in the ice.

But you haven't finished your story. If you're such a successful entrepreneur, what went wrong?"

"Ah! Well, I told you about that Siverskiy plant, right? Anyway, some of our disgruntled clientele had friends in high places. I was walking along Nevsky Prospekt one day when a Volga car pulled up alongside and the next thing I knew I was picking myself up off the floor in the Big House. They knew everything! The suppliers, the officials in the Ministry, even the drivers' names. I thought I'd be looking at a firing squad. Then some tall, soft-spoken guy came in. High ranking, I guess, though he wasn't in uniform. I never heard his name but the others called him—"

"'Asparagus'?"

"That's right! Well, my friend, I see we are both part of the 'Asparagus' fan club. Anyway, this Asparagus guy told me he admired my business acumen! He said he was impressed by the way I'd marshaled all the forces under my command. Told me they still hadn't rounded up all the parties involved—I guess he meant my cohorts here—but that he'd never come across such a well-organized scam in his career."

"What did you say?"

"I told him Article thirty-eight of the constitution states that citizens have the right to work and choose their profession."

"I'll bet that went down well?!"

"Well, you should understand that I thought they were going to kill me anyway at that stage. But he just laughed and told me that Article fifty-eight says that avoiding socially useful work is incompatible with the principles of a socialist society. And as I hadn't had a job for six months I could get charged with parasitism under Article 209. Parasitism! He called me a *sharomyzhnik*—whatever that is."

"Sounds like Asparagus has an ear for history. That expression dates back to the Napoleonic wars. From French soldiers going round saying *'cher ami'* and begging for food after Napoleon abandoned them to freeze in the retreat from Moscow. It means 'beggar.'"

"*Beggar?!* I *work* for my living. I don't beg."

"But parasitism is—how do you say?—'small vegetables.' What about corruption, theft of state property?"

"That's small *potatoes*! He said the other charges would stay on the file. But he told me that in return they had a 'little job' they wanted me to do. He said there was an American official they were trying to 'turn' but none of their usual methods were working. It seems that 'we' Americans are smarter than you might think. They sent over this guy who's openly homosexual so he can't be blackmailed."

"Brantley Logan."

"That's right, too! Looks like we were working on the same case, partner!"

"Not quite. But go on with your story."

"Well, there's not much more to tell. I was supposed to exploit my 'American' connections to get close to Logan and then involve him in some corruption scandal involving stolen Zhiguli cars. Can you believe it?! They figured that if they couldn't use sex to blackmail him then they could use money. It was pathetic, really! Logan was sympathetic about the nationality thing but when Asparagus pushed me to get him involved with the car deal he just laughed in my face. He said he wouldn't be seen dead in a Russian car. And it turns out his family owns a winery back in California so he didn't need the money. Well, I knew it wouldn't work but I didn't want to piss off this Asparagus guy, so I tried a different approach. I got Timor, his little boyfriend, interested in the car deal, figuring he could persuade Logan to buy one for *him*."

"And that was where the accident with the tram came in?"

"Not quite. You see, the KGB gave me a new Zhiguli for bait. But I figured that was a hell of a waste of a brand new car, so I got hold of one that had been in a wreck and took it down to Petrodvorets."

"Petrodvorets? You mean Peter the Great's palace?"

"Yeah. You should go there. The Fascists reduced it to rubble during the *blokada* but they've nearly finished restoring it. The inside is all lacquer work. It's beautiful—really! Anyway, one of the guys working there was one of 'ours' so I got him to patch up the wreck with lacquer. He did a fantastic job. It was all I could do to stop him painting cherubs on it! The problem was that the car had an alarming tendency to pitch to the left when you applied the brakes. Anyway, I arranged with Timor to meet him on the day of the accident. I had a little side deal to pick up some vegetables from the private gardens people keep down there and sell them to a hotel. I normally wouldn't waste my time with small deals like that but this was asparagus—strangely enough—that was needed for a big reception so they were going to pay top dollar for it. Problem was I'd piled it all on the seat next to me and when the car lurched to the left, some rolled under the pedals. The next time I tried to brake I couldn't, and the car got its fender wrapped around the running board of that tram."

"So how did you get back to Baku?"

"Courtesy of the KGB. Luckily I hadn't actually sold the car they'd given me so I bluffed my way out of *that* problem. But I think they figured I was better off out of the way for a while. They drove me to Mashtagah from Leningrad."

"That's an amazing story. What are you going to do next?"

"First you tell me your story."

"There's very little to tell. Three days ago I got called into Ignatiev's office. I should explain; I'm a geophysicist and he's my boss. He told me he wanted me to present a pseudo-scientific paper at some conference. When I refused—the paper was crap—he called in the KGB to threaten me. Then I accidentally picked up the bag with the money Timor was going to give you for that car. Stupidly, I left it at my ex-wife's place. I came to Baku to try to find out why the KGB is even interested in such a trivial matter as this technical paper. Now they've put an obituary in the paper saying I'm dead."

"*That's* not a good sign! What are you going to do next?"

"I don't know. How about trying to get over the border into Iran?"

"Good luck! They've doubled the border guards on this side of the border to stop people fleeing in *this* direction from the fighting with the Kurds and the Arabs. And the Iranians are paranoid about foreigners since the Americans tried to rescue their hostages. Oh, and don't even *think* about getting through the Turkish border. They have checkpoints a hundred kilometers away."

"Well, what about you? Where are you going?"

"Siberia, I suppose, though the chances are that they'll be looking for me in my usual haunts. I don't know this Ob River region, though. Akademgorodok sounds too small to hide in. Tell me more about Novosibirsk."

"I don't know much about it. I mean, it's a big town and they make fighter jets and military vehicles there, but we'd just change planes at the airport. I was working up in the marshlands, near the Samotlar oilfield. That's 'dead lake' in the Khanty language. You can only shoot seismic data up there when the swamps freeze in wintertime. It's dark for twenty-three hours a day and the temperature gets down to minus forty degrees. And when the winds blow, the snow feels like sandpaper on your face. The first time I went there, I took my dog, Laika. It was too cold to take her out in the field so I left her back at the camp. When I got back the cook had made a stew out of her."

"Bastard! You should have killed him!"

"Easier said than done. The cooks and most of the laborers were convicts. Only the tough survive in the *Gulag*. I half expected to be the next night's meal myself."

"It sounds a rough place but that's fine. They wouldn't look for us there. We'd have to go separately, of course. I have contacts that can take us there from Togliatti, but the hardest part will be getting to there."

"Togliatti's on the Volga. Didn't you say you can go by riverboat without an internal passport?"

"Oh sure, but don't you think they'll be looking for you here by now? How are you going to get *on* the boat?"

"How about catching it in Sukhumi? They won't be looking for us there. We could take the train to Sukhumi from some rural station where they won't check."

"It's a nice idea but the Sukhumi train is non-stop from Baku to Kirovabad, then it stops at Tbilisi and all the small stops from there to Sukhumi. We'd have to find a way to get you on the train in Baku. If it works you could be in Novosibirsk inside a month. What's it like in August?"

"It's a different world. The weather is hot and humid. I only spent one summer there. It was years ago. I was leading a field trip but we couldn't get anyone to come with us into the swamps. The convicts were more trouble than they were worth and the Khants refused to go because they were frightened of the bears in the forest. They were right, too. See this?"

He rolled his trouser leg up in the firelight to show Hamlet a twisted white scar on his calf.

"I'd been fishing and I was walking back across a pipeline over the swamp with my rod and a couple of fish. I looked round and there was this big brown bear, ambling after me. I tried running but you'd be surprised how fast those things can move! Finally he caught up with me and swiped the back of my leg with his claw. He lost his balance and fell into the swamp where he got bogged down in the mud or I wouldn't be around today! I limped back into camp and got my leg sewn up by some convict medic.

The worse things, though, weren't the bears. I lost a lot more blood to the mosquitoes. They were as large as swallows. We had to wear beekeepers' outfits for fieldwork. You could never tell who was who—"

"That's it! That's how we'll get you on the train. All we need are bees! Who's going to get close enough to check your documents?"

"Actually, that's not a bad idea. But what about when I get to Georgia?"

"Ditch the bees! Who cares?! And take my advice, when you get to Sukhumi don't refer to it as 'Georgia.' It's 'Abhazia.'"

"Surely that's the same thing?"

"There are many things you don't understand about the Caucasus, my friend."

"You're right about that. Here's one that's been troubling me since we met in Mashtagah. How *did* you get out of the mental hospital?"

Hamlet laughed.

"That's easy; *basturma*."

"Spiced meat? What do you mean?"

"You ever eat it?"

"A couple of times. It's too hot for me, to be honest. Why?"

"Well if you think that spice is hot on the tongue you should try it in the eyes. It's an old trick. The only novelty is the 'delivery vehicle.' You can use a drinking straw with one end blocked with cotton. Or a cigarette—double-thickness of paper for stiffness with a small plug of tobacco at one end. Or a ballpoint pen—though not a transparent one, obviously. Just point and blow. Simple. Other than that, like I told you, it's just a question of taking advantage of opportunities when they come your way."

"Just like in business?"

"Just like in life, Mels. Just like in life."

They sat and watched the embers glow in the darkness. Unable to follow their conversation, most of the Azerbaijani men had fallen asleep while they were talking. Only the one who had spoken earlier stayed awake, his eyes glowing with a hatred as hot as the embers.

"Who's your friend over there?"

"Oh that's Kasoum's father."

"Kasoum! I'd forgotten about him. Where is he? I'm surprised not to have seen him here."

"Kasoum is in Baku. He's my guarantee. If anything happens

to me they don't see him again. Don't look so shocked, Mels! What you did for him *and* for me was very noble but we're talking about survival here. They know you saved him from dishonor. I told them that. So you're safe tonight, even if they won't feed you. But you'd better not outstay your welcome. My colleagues will return tomorrow before dawn. They'll take you back to *Icheri Shekher* until we can arrange to get you out of Baku. For now, here's a blanket. You sleep with your back to me, OK? Good night, Mels"

"Good night."

Chapter 12

By the dawn light, the caldera looked like a lunar landscape. No grass grew in the gray, sterile mud that had been ejected by the mud volcano and the ground had a scaly, dried-up appearance like chapped skin. All the shepherds were already up and about, driving their flock to more fertile grazing areas. Hamlet handed Mels a piece of cold barbecued lamb wrapped in *lavash*.

"Here—eat this. I don't want it. You can feed an Azerbaijani nothing but *shashlik* three times a day and he's happy. If these guys spend a day without meat they feel hungry!"

"What about you?"

"The guys in the jeep will bring me something. You'd better hurry. I think that's their headlights coming now."

At the base of the hill, a long conversation in Armenian ensued between Hamlet and the two men inside the jeep. Mels sat feeling self-conscious by the side of the track with the sacking mask over his head. At length the talk trickled to a halt and they opened the door and helped him climb in the back.

"OK, Mels, all is arranged. I'll see you in the swamps!"

Bees, however, were not all that easy to arrange. The next two days were excruciatingly boring to Mels, deprived—as he was—of the sense of sight. Other than eating and sleeping, he spent his time being lectured about Armenian culture. While some of the statistics seemed rather bogus (*how can Armenian be the oldest unchanged alphabet in the world? What about Chinese? Or He-*

brew?) and others rather dull (Armenia, apparently, had the lowest divorce rate in the Union), he was frankly glad to have someone to talk to.

Their relationship had subtly changed. They no longer regarded him as their captive and, indeed, he often found himself giving *them* instructions when he was hungry, hot or cold. But the atmosphere was never entirely relaxed and could become tense in a heartbeat if he made a thoughtless remark—for example on the one occasion when he inquired about Kasoum's welfare and was told that the boy's safety depended on his silence. The alternative source of news—the ever-present and never-silent television—produced a steady diet of even more dubious propaganda, much of it about the activities of Geidar Aliyev. From his guardians he learned a different story about the man. It seemed the dynamic, fifty-seven year-old leader of Azerbaijan—nowadays always immaculately tailored in English suits—was actually from a poor village in Nakhichevan on the Iranian border and had risen up through the ranks of the KGB. Fluent in Farsi, Turkish, and Arabic as well as Russian, in his youth he had spent much of his time south of the Araks river, fomenting unrest in the Iranian oilfields and organizing the Tudeh, the Iranian Communist Party. A favorite of Andropov, after gaining the leadership of the local KGB, it had taken him a mere couple of years to overthrow his predecessor on a corruption charge and become *de facto* President of Azerbaijan (it was a source of amusement to the men relating this story that anyone could be overthrown in Azerbaijan for corruption. It is as ingrained in the soil as crude oil, they said).

Mels tried to explain his idea of upward mobility to them—illustrating his theory with the example of Romanov's rise and fall in Leningrad—and was surprised by their response. To them, the comings and goings in the higher echelons of the Communist party represented not so much a physical law as a sinister puppet play. Self-centered as they were, they insisted that what had happened in their tiny republic had been orchestrated in Moscow at the highest levels. In the emotionally-charged environment of the room in *Icheri Shekher* this almost made sense and he began to feel that maybe there *was* some larger drama unfolding beneath the surface—something inexorable, like the movement of tectonic plates beneath the continents. On later reflection, he decided prolonged sensory deprivation and claustrophobia had made him temporarily lose his grip on reality.

On the third day he heard a car being reversed through the small archway that lead into the courtyard from the world outside. As it was unloaded he heard the unmistakable buzzing of bees. That meant freedom!

A couple of hours later he was loading the trays of bees into the baggage car of the Baku-Sukhumi train. The conductor gave him a wide berth, as had the unusually strong police presence at the station entrance. He sat on a small suitcase containing his few portable possessions—a parting gift from his erstwhile captors—as the train pulled out of the station and threaded its way through Baku's steep suburban hills.

The connecting door that lead from the baggage car to the rest of the train opened several times as passengers looked for additional space on the crowded train but was quickly closed as soon as the presence of the bees was noted. Each time it opened the smell of coal smoke permeated the car, triggering in Mels long lost memories of train travel with his mother and father. The acrid smell came not from the locomotives—mostly diesel or electric for many years now—but from the old-fashioned boilers used to heat water for tea making.

When Mels was a small boy, his father used to take Mels' mother for train journeys out of Leningrad most weekends during summertime. In later years, Mels realized this was his attempt at therapy for her; an attempt to convince her that the *blokada* was truly over. He remembered her sitting silently, stiff-backed and white-knuckled in her seat, while other families around them would noisily plan picnics, swimming trips and visits to relatives.

The view from the window had become monotonous now; bare brown hills and dusty valleys with occasional vivid patches of green where canals from some distant river brought irrigation to small villages.

Mels lay back on the sacks and suitcases in the car. The buzzing of the bees and the rhythmic motion of the train lulled him into a sleep from which he was awakened a few hours later as the train came to a halt in Kirovabad.

Accustomed as he had become to regular meals in his sojourn in *Icheri Shekher*, he found to his surprise that he was hungry. A voice over the train intercom announced that they would be stationary for twenty minutes. Although he had been given strict instructions not to leave the train under any circumstances, he was bored and the car had become unpleasantly hot now that there was no breeze coming through the windows. He scrutinized the comings and goings on the platform, gauging the risk of stretching his legs.

It was a small station for the second biggest town in the republic. At one end of the platform there was a small cabin and a vendor selling cooked cobs of corn and *ayran*, the local yogurt drink, from a cart. At the other, there was one militiaman standing next to the ticket collector at the exit. Otherwise, the station seemed to have *no* security measures in place. It was too great a temptation for Mels. Disembarking, he walked to the vendor and asked for two cobs of corn and a glass of *ayran*.

"You can have it for free, Comrade, if you watch my stall for a moment."

"Where are you going? I have to get back on the train."

"I'll only be a moment. I have a phone call to make. You see this cabin? That's the axle-inspector's. I can make a phone call from there to anywhere in the Union. Why pay to do it from home when I can do it here for free?"

As a frequent rail traveler, Mels knew that much of the axle-inspectors' job had been made irrelevant in recent years.

Originally their function was to go from wheel to wheel when the train was in the station, tapping the metal to listen for telltale sounds of metal fatigue. They also served a security function in that they could look for stowaways clinging to the axles of the cars. For non-stop trains, they were supposed to stand at attention, flag in hand, while the train went by, checking for open doors or any other irregularities, In practice, most of them nowadays did their inspections from the comfort of their cabins. In place of flags to wave they now had long-distance phone lines to call the stations down the line in case anything was amiss.

"Where *is* the axle inspector?"

"Right now, I'd guess she'll be on her second cigarette with her colleagues in the restaurant car of your train. Don't worry, she won't come out until the train's ready to go."

"I'll pay you double if you let me go first!"

He dialed Tanya's number. Without the usual long distance operator making a manual connection, the line was almost free of static. A female voice at the other end refused to fetch Tanya to the phone until he identified himself.

"It's Sasha, from Petrozavodsk."

Tanya's voice came on the line, sending an electric thrill through Mels.

"'Sasha?' Can you talk?"

"Not really. I just wanted to tell you I talked to my Uncle James, in America. He's going to Malibu for a few days, then he'll be going to Detroit. He'll get a message to you when he gets there."

"'Detroit.' OK. Anything else?"

"He was anxious about his daughter. She worries when he travels. He doesn't want her to know *where* he goes as it could be dangerous. But he likes her to know he's OK. Oh, and Tanya?"

"Yes?"

"He told me he especially misses his girlfriend."

"I'm sure she misses him, 'Sasha.'"

"See you. . . ."

Nervously he put the receiver down. As he left the cabin, he checked the new imitation Rolex watch he had bought from his former captors. He had been on the phone less than a minute. *Surely even the KGB can't trace me that amount of time?*

"That was quick, Comrade. Look, I won't charge you for the corn and the *ayran*. Just watch for me, will you?"

He stood guard, munching on the cobs and sipping the cold yogurt drink, until the train whistle announced it was time to leave. The vendor stepped nonchalantly out of the cabin just a few seconds before the grayish-blue uniform of the axle-inspector descended the steps of the restaurant car. As Mels resumed his position in the baggage car, she walked back to her cabin where she had a loud conversation with the corn-seller that ended with him pointing at Mels' face in the window. Just as the train was pulling out, she ran up to him and rapped on the pane. Mels stood aghast, heart pounding, as he watched her panting face through the glass.

"Comrade!" she yelled, "Do you have any honey to sell?!"

After Kirovabad the countryside started to become less boring. Distant mountains came closer and finally surrounded the track on both sides. The villages now had buildings closer to the rails, pressed in by the steep slopes on which they were built. As the train worked its way westwards, the red-tiled roofs, treetops, and small courtyards of the towns were almost close enough to touch from the car's windows. Then, abruptly, signs of human habitation disappeared and were replaced by rugged mountains and narrow gorges. Looking down, Mels could see the turbid water of the Kura River. It was his first glimpse of the Caucasus but it seemed to him deeply familiar from a childhood spent reading Pushkin, Lermontov, and Tolstoy.

The poetic mood dissipated as the train reached the outskirts of Tbilisi. Though the center of town was as picturesque as any that Mels had seen, the effect was spoiled by the train's approach through the ubiquitous suburban concretopolis.

The train stopped in Tbilisi for an hour and a half, which gave Mels ample time to disobey his instructions to stay on the train. He disembarked with the other passengers still wearing his beekeeper's garb, which he stored in a locker on the station concourse. The town had a distinctly Mediterranean flavor after Baku. The old city consisted of a series of narrow winding streets where the houses seem to hang from the hills on which Tbilisi was built. As he walked past an old bathhouse, he smelled the characteristic sulfur smell of natural spa water. He noted, at first with amusement, that Georgians seemed to regard their cars as latter-day donkeys. Each house had a low metal pipe cemented into its façade to which chains were attached that were used to padlock the owners' cars. When he remembered Hamlet's story about how few keys were needed to steal cars, his condescension turned to admiration at this commonsense precaution.

Mels would have liked longer to look around Tbilisi but his train awaited him. He bought a local cheese pie called a *khachapuri* and some smoked mountain trout and *Sameba* wine and walked back to the train station along a road lined with plane trees in a better frame of mind than he had experienced for days. The claustrophobic atmosphere of the room in *Icheri Shekher*, complete with its high-level conspiracy theories, had stretched his nerves to their limit.

Unfortunately, he was in for a sharp reminder of his fugitive status on his return to the station. A team of militiamen with a dog was waiting on the platform, letting passengers through in groups of ten or twelve at a time. To his horror he saw that one of them was carrying half a facecloth on which he could clearly make out the word "Hilton." As each group went through, the dog was allowed to smell the facecloth then was set free to sniff excitedly at the embarking passengers.

He changed into his beekeeper's costume in the station restroom then returned to the street. A block away he remembered seeing an old-style ironmonger's and general store. Reflecting the eclectic taste of its manager, it had a small photograph of Stalin next to a handwritten notice advertising Aquarium's Tbilisi concert in the window. He entered the shop and was greeted in Georgian by a jovial heavyset man in an old-fashioned shop apron. On seeing Mels, he immediately held up a device shaped like a cross between a blowtorch and an 'Arabian Nights' style oil lamp.

"How much is that, er, thing?"

The shopkeeper switched into Russian.

"The smoker? Twenty rubles."

It was an outrageous price as they both knew but Mels had little time to haggle.

"Throw in the fuel and I'll give you fifteen,"

The shopkeeper shrugged and tried to look hard done by but he handed over the smoker with only too evident satisfaction.

Mels lit the fuel outside the store and ran the pungent incense-like smoke over his outfit. He rushed up to the departure gate. Most of the passengers had already boarded the train.

"Comrades, let me through, please. Here is my ticket. I have a cargo of bees on the train who are getting ready to swarm."

"Not so fast, beekeeper!"

Despite its repeated exposure to Mehri's face towel, the police dog seemed to have retained its interest in its odor (*hardly surprising*, thought Mels as he watched, *considering their shared interest in scatology*). As Mels had anticipated, the dog was far less inclined to approach *him* after his saturation in smoke. Fortunately the conductor was down at the other end of the train as Mels boarded. He discovered that it was considerably easier to ignite the smoker than it was to extinguish it. Almost overcome by the fumes (though it *did* lull the bees into somnolence) he threw it from the moving train as they passed Mount David on their way out of Tbilisi.

Having slept earlier, Mels did not expect to sleep at all but, as the afternoon light turned to night and the train stopped briefly at Gori, the combined effects of the dark amber Sameba, the food and the train's rhythm worked their magic. He lapsed into a deep sleep from which he barely stirred until they reached Sukhumi early the next morning.

If I were an Azerbaijani bee, thought Mels, *I'd think I'd died and gone to bee heaven*. Compared with the dry dusty moonscapes of Azerbaijan, the lush greenery of Abhazia was like waking up in a tropical paradise. The city of Sukhumi seemed to be one big park. The avenues were lined with laurels, palms, and Himalayan cedars and the plentiful public gardens were full of eucalyptus, citrus, and banana trees. He released the bees in a thirty-hectare forest park on the slopes of Mount Sukhumi where a sign boasted that the plants within had been selected so that there would always be some species in bloom. As he stripped off his smoky beekeeper's outfit in a sheltered part of the park and changed back into his "civilian" attire, he was aware he was being watched. A small man, about thirty years old, with dark hair and moustache and carefully trimmed sideburns stepped forward. He was wearing a light blue suit with wide lapels and flared pants and white shoes.

"Professor Ignatiev?"

"Who wants to know?"

"I'm Nestor. Nestor Ardzinba. Hamlet sent me. I followed you from the station. I'm your contact here in Aqw'a."

"'Aqw'a'?"

"Sukhum. Sukhum*i*, as you call it."

"All right, Nestor. Nice to meet you, I'm sure. Where do I get the boat?"

"Not so fast, my friend. You can't just get on *any* boat. Togliatti is a closed city. The boat you will go on leaves tomorrow night. We've booked you into a hotel tonight in the southeastern part of the city near King Bagrat's castle. Don't look alarmed. You won't have to pay anything; Hamlet has arranged this. But it's an Intourist hotel, which means that your room will be bugged and your guests will be watched. Those hotels are sixty percent glass, thirty percent ferro-concrete and ten percent microphones. So once you are in there we cannot contact you directly. I will give you all the instructions you need today and I will see you tomorrow at a designated place."

"That's just asking for trouble! Why must I stay in an Intourist hotel? Why not stay in a safe house somewhere?"

"Because you will be going on a tour for foreign tourists only. They will pick you all up from the same hotel. There is a party of 'fraternal delegates'—foreign Communists—who are being taken to Moscow for the Olympics. Naturally they will stop at all the 'Potemkin villages' en route. You will disembark at Togliatti.

Hamlet informs us that you speak English with a British accent so we have arranged a British passport for you. Of course, we will need a photograph of you so we will go to a photographer friend of ours today. I am not good at foreign names but I think your name is 'Jan Morgan.'"

"That doesn't sound very British. But how did you get the passport? Isn't this 'Jan' looking for it?"

"Odessa. You can find anything in Odessa. Maybe even Jan Morgan if you know where to dig."

Mels was silent for a moment as he mulled this over. Whether the story about this Morgan character was true or not, Ardzinba was obviously sending a message that there were some questions that he did not want to answer. Nevertheless, there were some practical considerations that needed to be addressed.

"Look, Nestor, I'm very grateful to you for your efforts but do you think this is going to work? *I* think I speak pretty good English and Hamlet tells me I speak with a British accent but do you think I'm going to be able to fool real British people? I mean, I'm going to have to be 'British' all the way to Togliatti. That's a week in these people's company, eh? Don't you think this is just drawing attention to me?"

"We've thought of that. That's why you're going on this particular vessel with a boatload of Communists. First, you'll be the only Englishman on board. They're all Europeans—Italians, mostly. Actually, that's why they're going to Togliatti. Trust me— I have been a waiter on one of these boats—the Italians will expect you to sit on your own with your nose stuck in the air. And, second, you're a *Communist*—some loser with a chip on his shoulder who thinks he's come to the workers' paradise—so the KGB won't waste their time trying to 'turn' you. I mean what kind of spy would *you* make?

The boat will be pretty empty. All the Americans cancelled their trips because of the Olympic boycott. Just beware of the girls who work on the boat. They'll try to sleep with you because you're foreign."

"And they might inform on me?"

"No! But you might catch a dose of something."

They took a bus to a street lined with oleander in the town center, where Mels was shown into the back room of a photographer's studio. Afterwards, they drank coffee in a deserted corner of the terrace of a nearby café while they waited for Mels' new identity to be completed.

"It should take less than an hour, he said."

"That's good. It's 'Ian,' by the way."

"What is?"

"My name. I saw it in the passport. It's pronounced 'Ian.'"

"Whatever. I'm not good at foreign languages."

"Yet you speak Abhazian and Russian?"

"And Georgian, too, though not by choice."

"So that's three languages. I can only speak two."

"I'd like to say Georgian is a foreign language but unfortunately, it's not. And everyone here speaks at least two languages. We Abhazians are always expected to speak Russian and Georgian but no one forces the Mingrelians to speak Georgian. Sadly, we were fucked by both Stalin *and* Beria—a Georgian and a Mingrelian—who moved their people into our country and took away our independence."

"It's a familiar enough story in this part of the Union."

"Oh, I know what you're thinking. You've been listening to Hamlet's friends tell you 'the Armenian history of the world' and now you're thinking I'm going to give you a sob story about the Abhazians."

"And you won't?"

"No! I'll tell you a *joke* about the Abhazians. A Georgian is driving his Chaika limousine on a mountain road in Abhazia when he hits a big pothole. The car is ruined. He sees an Abhazian peasant walking by and curses him 'Why don't you fix your roads in Abhazia? I worked all summer to save for that car!' The peasant shrugs. Then a Latvian comes along and drives his Zhiguli into the same pothole. Same result. He says to the peasant 'I worked all year to save for that car!' But the peasant just shrugs again. Lastly, an elderly Russian then drives his little Zaporozhets into same pothole and it disappears entirely. He climbs out. He's completely inconsolable. He says to the peasant 'I worked my entire life to save for that car. . . .'" The peasant replies 'I'm sorry for your loss but you know you really shouldn't be driving such an expensive car on these mountain roads. . . .'"

Mels laughed.

"You see there's a difference between us and those guys in *Icheri Shekher*. They see everything as a conspiracy aimed specifically at them. They don't see what's happening in the wider world."

"I have to admit I didn't hear very many jokes at their expense but what do you mean exactly?"

"Well, Hamlet is the smartest guy I know. He sees moneymaking schemes where the rest of us see nothing. But he's losing touch with what's going on. It's not his fault. He was outvoted on a deal we had going up north—"

"Siverskiy?"

"Right. He told you about that, then? Well, then you know it went wrong and now important people are after his hide. Ever since he's been out of the picture we've had troubles. *Big* troubles. There's something going on. I don't know what it is. . . ."

His voice trailed off and he stared down into his coffee.

"Look, Nestor, I don't pretend to understand what Hamlet does but he seems to keep on top of things—"

Ardzinba's voice became heated.

"Listen, Ignatiev, we've lost a number of good men lately. This region used to be wide open. You could drive over the border into Krasnodar Territory and get anything you wanted—drugs, jewels, cars—and the militia would recognize your face and turn a blind eye. *The Party secretary of the Territory was one of 'ours'!* Now things have changed. Our guy, Sergei Medunov, got into some fight with the little shit that runs Stavropol Territory-"

"You mean Gorbachev?"

"Yeah, the country hick with the birthmark. Andropov is from Stavropol originally. Rumor has it he's big buddies with Gorbachev. He even comes down to Stavropol for his vacations."

"Krasnye Kamni?"

"Krasnye Kamni! So when Andropov tells Gorbachev to stick the knife in his neighbor next door in Krasnodar, Gorbachev is only too pleased to do so. It was the same in Azerbaijan with Aliyev. Now Andropov's other protégé—that's Shevardnadze—has to show his boss that *he* can be just as tough. We used to have a string of businesses here—jewelry manufacture, fruit juice, restaurants—that Shevardnadze has closed down. We've had to move our operations to Stavropol Territory."

"But that's Gorbachev's home turf!"

"That's right! You don't get the idea, do you? These guys don't really care about us—we're too small to bother with. They're just trying to look good in front of Andropov. And that means making each other look bad! So, if Shevardnadze wants to close us down, that means Gorbachev will keep us open. Jesus, Ignatiev, you come from Leningrad. Surely you know what happened to Romanov?"

Mels started again to explain his mathematical theory but was quickly interrupted.

"That's just bullshit! Andropov hated his guts and got him expelled from the Kremlin."

"You seem to know a lot about the KGB. Do you know anything about 'the ballerina'?"

"In what context?"

"'Tripping the ballerina'?"

"'Tripping the ballerina,' eh? Maybe that's what I was just talking about."

Chapter 13

But before Ardzinba could say more on the subject, a honeymooning couple came to sit at a table nearby and the two of them were forced to switch to less controversial topics of conversation until the hour was up.

Mels was puzzled as to what this massive Machiavellian plot could possibly have to do with his ex-wife but—now that he had broached the subject—he was unsure how to reveal what he knew about her activities without tipping off Ardzinba as to his true identity. Although he trusted Hamlet, he felt uneasy about revealing his real name to anyone else.

The photographer-cum-forger had done a good job of substituting Mels' photo into Ian Morgan's passport. Mr. Morgan's visa was valid for a month; enough time, hopefully, for Mels to find his way to the relative safety of the Siberian swamps.

"Now you can check in as 'Ian Morgan.' Let's look at you. Hmm, your jacket looks a little dated but you're an English Communist, so no one will expect you to dress well. I will take you to your hotel, now. Tomorrow we will meet in the Amza restaurant at lunchtime—it's near the park where you released the bees—and I will hand you your tickets and other documents you will need to get to Togliatti. Enjoy yourself. There is always plenty to do in Sukhumi!"

Ardzinba was right. There *were* a lot of things to do in Sukhumi. Mels strolled along the elephant palm-lined seashore in front of pastel-colored tourist hotels, feeling more like he was on vacation than on the run. Girls in bikinis played in the velvety, aquamarine waters, watched by lobster-red fat men dressed in tiny briefs. The heart-rending shrieks of tame peacocks filled the air. Children built sandcastles in the sugary sand or ate improbably colored ice creams while their mothers sat in deckchairs or lay on towels. Everyone seemed focused on one goal—to be as naked as the law allowed to maximize exposure to the sun.

At lunchtime it was difficult to find a restaurant that was not full. When he finally found one that had seating, he was told that it had been reserved for a wedding. However as he turned to leave, the party itself arrived and insisted—against his protests—that he stay as their guest ('Any guest is God's messenger,' they contended). The bride's name was Gunda. She was Abhazian and the groom Georgian. Perhaps because of this, the conversation and toasts at the wedding were all in Russian. However, it was soon evident to Mels that there was some rivalry between the groups—at least among the younger relatives.

The *Tamada*, or toastmaster, called the people to order then held up a silver-embossed bull's horn filled with wine to propose a toast to the young couple.

"Let the steps that lead to your home be made of the hardest stone and let it be worn away in a year by the footsteps of guests who visit your home...."

However this provoked a comment from one of the more distant tables that good Georgian stone was too hard to be worn away, to which came a rejoinder that Georgian hearts were made of the same material. The *Tamada* squelched this with another toast about Abhazia being the country of long life—as was evident by the number of centenarians who lived there—and his wish that the couple would spend many years in each other's company. The meal proceeded in relative harmony for several courses, each proceeded by a toast, until wine and proximity unleashed a renewed round of insults and counter-insults.

"A year in the company of a Georgian is like a century!"

"For an Abhazian to last a year with a Georgian is a miracle."

"He would leave first!"

"He would die first!"

Inevitably, the verbal jousting became a little too personal and the two principal protagonists left the restaurant to settle their differences outside. To Mels' surprise, the other guests did not appear in the least discomfited by this and dismissed it as quite normal. Although some older relatives were finally sent outside to separate the two youths—who, as it transpired, had merely been cursing each other out rather than hitting each other—the respective family groups seemed to take some perverse pride in their mutual antagonism. Extravagant boasts and insults were still being traded back and forth when Mels left, an hour later.

At his hotel he had been handed a suggested itinerary in English that listed such attractions as the oldest choir in the world, the botanical gardens he had already visited, a guided tour of the ruins of King Bagrat's castle, and bus trips to nearby spas, forests, and beaches. Knowing that he was doomed to spend a week in their company, he decided to forego these delights in the interests of reducing his exposure to his fellow guests. One item, though, seized his imagination, not least because it had been used as an in-joke amongst his colleagues at the Institute.

The Soviet Academy of Sciences maintained a monkey-breeding farm in Sukhumi that was actually listed as a tourist attraction. Back in Leningrad his fellow scientists had often compared their own fate at the hands of the Academy of Sciences with that of the baboons and macaques ("they get all the food and pussy they want and don't have to attend political meetings!"). Of course, the Academy of Sciences did not send the scientists from Mels' Institute to secret laboratories to be injected with biological weapons viruses or exposed to nerve gas, but the scientists liked to maintain the myth that the monkeys were better treated. In any case, Mels wanted to see the Institute for himself.

The monkeys lived on a series of bare terraces linked by

metal stairways. They had been provided with some concrete pipes and a few boulders to play with but there was no shade except for a small hutch that also served as their sleeping quarters.

"It's rather depressing, isn't it?"

The middle-aged woman in a white coat to whom Mels addressed his question nodded in agreement.

"Apart from the macaques, we have mostly baboons here. Plus some minor species. About two thousand altogether. Usually they just sit there. They seem unusually active today. Sometimes I think they know what's going to happen to them."

The monkeys behind them were idly scratching themselves or picking at each other's fleas. A large male slowly walked on his knuckles over to a subordinate group and started bullying an adolescent who then ran screaming to the protection of his mother. With the exception of one solitary individual who was vigorously masturbating in a corner of the cage, the word 'active' seemed inappropriate.

"What *does* happen to them?"

Sensing disapproval, the woman became defensive.

"Scientific research. *Essential* scientific research."

"Of course. I was wondering what kind."

"Well—for example—the incidence of skin cancer is rapidly increasing at the moment. We expose the monkeys to radiation to research this."

Mels thought of the scarlet-colored vacationers on the beach.

"Don't you think it might have something to do with the sun?"

She laughed.

"Of course it has, Comrade! Look, you seem like an educated man. Think about it; this is Sukhumi. We have people from all over the Union come here—most of them trade unionists from the higher latitudes—who are determined to return home with a suntan to impress their less fortunate neighbors. The whole economy here depends on tourism. What would happen if we told people *not* to come here and sunbathe?"

They watched the monkeys feuding in the bare cage.

"There's always have a dominant male. He eats first, then the other males, then the females."

Mels was reminded of the meal at Kasumov's dacha.

"Sounds like a good life."

"Not really. The dominant male has to spend his whole life guarding his position against rivals. There are always factions trying to take control of the troupe. Ironically, even his females are routinely unfaithful to him. It happens in the wild, too, but in captivity the jockeying for power becomes more intense. One day he just gets too old to keep them all in line and the next day we find a usurper as dominant male. We have to act quickly then to move out the old male's progeny before the new male kills them."

"And then the cycle continues?"

"Of course."

On the far side, a group of smaller monkeys were grooming each other. The big male strutted around the enclosure until he reached them but they all eschewed his company, fearing another outburst of bullying. He climbed up on the highest boulder in the cage and sat. He looked bored.

"Couldn't you plant a few trees in there?"

"We tried that but they chewed up all the vegetation."

"Maybe they were sending a message?"

"That they want their freedom? It's easy to romanticize, Comrade, but it's a tough world out there, beyond the fence."

But Sukhumi doesn't seem like a tough world, thought Mels. He walked along streets of picturesque buildings in fanciful styles; some turreted, others with semi-circular balconies, many in multi-colored brick. It was easy to see why the area had been a vacation and retirement spot for Russians since Czarist times. At dusk, the local teenagers came to the main thoroughfares dressed to kill, walking arm-in-arm, eyeing each other and making suggestive comments. The outdoor cafes were full and musicians played to entertain the crowds.

He returned, late, to his hotel. In sharp contrast to the surly *babushka* that had been on duty that morning, the floor concierge was an attractive young woman wearing lipstick and eye shadow. She stood up as he exited the elevator, as if expecting him.

"Can I get you anything?"

Just in time, Mels remembered that he was supposed to be Ian Morgan. He give her a theatrically puzzled look. She repeated the question in English.

"I'm not sure. Do you have tea?'

"Oh. You're with the Togliatti group?"

"Yes."

"We don't serve tea."

It was all he could do not to laugh out loud. Ardzinba had been right. Whatever she had on offer, it was not available for Communists. The light switch in his room did not work so he undressed in the dark and fell asleep immediately.

He got up early the next morning. The light was already coming through the thin curtains. A notice in the front lobby had a list of names—Morgan's included—of those who were to be picked up that afternoon and taken to the harbor to embark on their cruise ship. He skipped his Intourist-provided breakfast at the hotel and spent the morning visiting the nearby ruins and a cave full of stalactites before his lunch appointment with Ardzinba.

Mels was hungry when he got to the Amza restaurant, outside which a crowd of tourists stood waiting to be admitted. According to the rather garish brochure he had picked up at his hotel, it supposedly served authentic Abhazian food. But, once seated, Mels saw little difference between the lamb kebabs being placed in front of the patrons around him and the Georgian, Armenian and Azerbaijani cuisine he had eaten in the previous few days.

He ordered a Borzhomi mineral water and waited for Ardzinba to show up. He delayed ordering for as long as he could but a persistent waitress passed by his table every few minutes with comments about the line of people outside. He mused on his options as he ate. Ardzinba's absence was troubling. Mels did not have the tickets for the boat nor instructions about where he was expected to meet his contact in Togliatti. Although he still had a wallet full of rubles, these would not last him a week if he had to maintain his cover as 'Ian Morgan' and live like a foreign tourist in Sukhumi. He was wondering whether he could risk using Ignatiev's documents again when the bill arrived.

A small envelope was on the saucer under the bill. Inside were a thousand rubles and a typewritten note in English:

"Order the Freshly Made Espresso."

He called the waitress over.

"Do you serve Espresso?"

"I don't know. What is it?"

"Coffee. No? Well, who gave you this envelope?"

"He did...."

She pointed to an empty chair several tables away.

"He just left. He asked me to give it to you."

"What did he look like?"

"Oh, I dunno. Kind of average."

"'Average'? How old was he? Was he Abhazian? Did he have an accent?"

"You mean like yours? No. He was about your age, though."

Sensing the futility of further inquiry, Mels paid and returned to his hotel. His fellow tourists—some two dozen generally elderly Italians with a handful of French people and one East German—were already gathering in the lobby. He gathered his suitcase from his room and returned to the lobby to check out. As promised by Ardzinba, his bill was paid. The receptionist called over a uniformed Intourist Guide who, to Mels' relief, handed him his boat tickets and hotel and meal vouchers.

"Mr. Morgan, we have been looking for you. You missed the bus tour yesterday."

"I'm sorry. Where did you go?"

"Well, we planned to go to Lake Ritsa and Gagra but the guests took a vote and decided they wanted to go to Gori instead—"

"*Stalin's* birthplace?!"

"Well, yes. There is a museum there."

"On second thoughts, I'm *not* sorry I missed your bus tour."

The Guide looked hurt.

"We had a picnic under his statue. It was very jolly, as you English say."

Mels boarded the bus feeling like there was a dead weight around his neck. The feeling did not dissipate as his fellow tourists started to sing the *Internationale* on their way to the harbor.

To Mels' surprise, he was given a two-bunk cabin to himself. He chose the top mattress as there was a stain on the lower bunk where water had come through the double-glazed porthole. The boat itself was big, about a hundred meters in length. It was almost new and smelt of recently applied paint. He was told that meals would be taken communally on board, unless the boat was stopped at one of the towns en route. A vast staff of surly waitstaff—resentful at the absence of over-tipping American tourists—attended their every meal.

They cruised through the narrow gateway of the Sea of Azov, then entered the Volga-Don canal system. Mels was in his cabin, reading a book he had borrowed from the boat's well-stocked library, when the intercom announced that they were approaching Rostov-on-Don.

Although the historical importance of the area had already been established by the time of the Ancient Greeks, the town itself only dated back to the establishment of a customs House on the river in the mid-eighteenth century. Still, as a native of a city only a few decades older, Mels was looking forward to seeing

Rostov-on-Don. He had not, however, anticipated the tastes of elderly Italian communists. Rather than visiting the few historic monuments that had survived the Nazis, they were more interested in seeing those buildings that had historic "significance." Loosely translated, this meant only those pre-1917 sites at which the causes of Communism had been furthered. This was especially galling to Mels, as he knew that the Cossacks of Rostov-on-Don had resisted every outside attempt to subdue them—whether by Tatars, Turks, or indeed by the Bolsheviks during the Civil War. That this rebelliousness against authority had now manifested itself in Rostov-on-Don's involvement in the criminal underworld was used as an excuse by the tour guides to forbid him going off on his own ("It's for your own safety, Comrade").

Instead of visiting early Don Cossack forts and any of a number of impressive churches in the surrounding region, Mels was treated to a (mercifully short) tour of the Museum of Local Studies and the Fine Arts Museum (*neither of which*, thought Mels, *compares with one room of the Hermitage in Leningrad*) and a bus tour of the post-war reconstruction in the western suburbs. The tour guides gave a running commentary in Italian first, then English. Since only one of the four French people on the bus understood English, this meant that there was always an echo effect in French following the guides' remarks. The lone German was left to figure things out for himself, though it seemed to Mels that he usually paid more attention when the guides were speaking among themselves in Russian.

"Here are the ornate facades of the Stalinist era. We compare those with the architecture of the Krushchev period. You will note many improvements. Finally, we see the Brezhnev era. These are the most beautiful of all."

Mels looked up from his book of Pushkin's poems. The hot sun was shining on a monolithic cliff of reinforced concrete and glass that housed several hundred families.

"Do those windows open?"

"There is no need, Comrade. All Soviet apartments are fully air-conditioned."

"Where are the air-conditioning units?"

The two guides on the bus conferred in whispered Russian.

"What the fuck is the Englishman talking about?"

"I have no idea. Make something up and keep an eye on him."

Smiling, the younger guide replied in English.

"My colleague informs me that the air-conditioning units are round the back of the building, As they are of a revolutionary design, we normally take tours to see them, but unfortunately we are pressed for time at our next stop."

The next stop was the Snake Ravine, where they were to see one of the region's most disturbing memorials: a museum of Nazi atrocities. Historically "significant" though this undoubtedly was, it had a naturally depressing effect on the company. Mels found a group of them standing in front of a Fascist propaganda poster of an Italian soldier chipping away at a statue of a Russian bear.

"What does it say?"

A tall gray-haired Italian man in his seventies answered in slow but understandable English.

"In Italian it says '... *se non ci fosse stata la Marcia su Roma non ci sarebbe oggi la marcia su Mosca*.' That means 'If there hadn't been the March on Rome, there wouldn't be the march on Moscow today.' Mussolini sent two hundred thousand Italians to fight on the Eastern Front. Few of them returned. I was in the mountains, fighting with the Partisans, or maybe they would have sent me. I had my share of fighting for Mussolini in Abyssinia. You know, Comrade, I understood your conversation with the Tour Guides today. You were right. You don't build Communism by lying to people."

Oh yes you do, thought Mels, but the old man meant well.

There was little talking on the bus that took them to the restaurant where they were to eat that night. Mels should have been forewarned by the absence of a line outside. They were not expected and the restaurant was closed. Embarrassed and intimidated by the presence of a large party of foreign guests, the manager did his best to oblige but the scant supply of basic foodstuffs that prevailed in the north seemed to have stretched as far south as Rostov. The "Chicken Kiev" they were served was almost hollow and the cabbage soup watery. That there should be a scarcity of meat in Leningrad did not particularly astonish Mels, but the shortage of cabbages in a fertile agricultural region was surprising, to say the least.

They had been plied with abundant alcohol on their arrival while the kitchen staff were located and set to work. It seemed to have a galvanizing effect on the formerly somber gathering. One by one they berated the hapless Intourist guides that they had not saved for years to visit the Soviet Union only to find that the darkest lies of capitalist propaganda were true.

Mels woke with a hangover the next day as the boat was negotiating the Volga-Don canal system on its way to Volgograd, the former Stalingrad. As they approached the city, he could see dozens of factory chimneys belching rust-colored smoke. Hundreds of bathers in the shallow waters of the Volga were swimming just a few meters downstream of the giant shipbuilding yards, tractor factories, sawmills, and the huge Red October steel mill that stretched for kilometers along the riverbank. They were taken to the "Pantheon of Names" at Mamal Mound where the fiercest fighting of the battle of Stalingrad occurred. A statue over seventy meters tall—called "Motherland is Calling"—shared guard over the Pantheon with two soldiers who periodically marched in formation around the inner perimeter.

Mels saw the East German from his tour party flinch at the sight of the goose-stepping guards.

"Do they still goose-step in Germany?"

"In the East, yes, but I believe in the West they have stopped this."

"You seem very moved by all this?"

"Ja. This is not my first visit. I was here in the war. In the German sixth army. I was seventeen; just a child, really. We'd hardly seen any Russians since we crossed the border—at least any live ones—just miles and miles of steppes and scattered corpses. Then we came to Stalingrad. We could *hear* the Russians. They were on the other side of the street, sometimes in the next house. We would take buildings one room at a time . . . sometimes it would take a week and then we would be pushed back. These crazy Russians, they would fight for every meter. At the end we were fighting amongst, how you say, rubble. Then we started to pull back but the Russians had cavalry—men on horses! They cut off our line of retreat and I was captured with a hundred thousand others."

"At least they didn't kill you. A million Russians died, you know."

"No they didn't kill me, Comrade. Though many men died—on both sides of the conflict. They sent me to a labor camp that produced coal. I was there for ten years. I was never a Nazi, but it was there I became a Communist."

Oh, Lord, thought Mels; *he's going to make me feel sorry for a member of the Wehrmacht.*

"I suppose it was the same with you?"

"Excuse me?"

"Coal-mining. The conditions are brutal enough, especially when the workers never get to reap the benefits of their labor. Don't look so surprised, Mr. Morgan. I learned Russian in captivity. I heard the guides discussing your background in Wales, ja?"

Ardzinba could have warned me!

"Well, let's not spoil the day by talking about work, shall we? We're on vacation, let's enjoy ourselves!"

After the incident at Volgograd, Mels did his best to keep to himself, fearful of being drawn into a conversation in which he would inadvertently say something which contradicted his cover story. This was easy enough on the boat where he could stay in his cabin, but silence was impossible on the trips ashore. He did his best to keep with the French party, who made no effort at all to talk to him.

Isolated by language, it was interesting to watch the varied body language of the people around him. The Italians seemed incapable of talking without looming close to each other's faces, filling even that small space with expansive hand movements. The French would preface every remark with a curl of the lower lip and an audible exhalation of breath. Their gestures were more controlled, usually consisting of outstretched fingers held rigid while the entire hand was rotated about thirty degrees back and forth.

Although the guides did their best to separate them from the local people in restaurants, it always seemed to be logistically beyond their abilities to arrive at the scheduled time. So, after enduring a wait outside at the behest of doormen with an overdeveloped sense of territorial imperative, they were forced to share large tables with Russians. This, too, was fascinating to Mels who was accustomed to his countrymen's shyness and distrust in the presence of strangers. He knew that, in contrast to the tourists, the locals rarely dined out. Invariably, whenever a family found themselves the only Russians at the table with foreigners, they would ply the tourists with questions and candidly discuss what would normally be taboo subjects.

Of course, there were limits. People would talk critically of unnamed leaders but never say "Brezhnev" in case there was a snitch listening. But they would go through an elaborate mime, putting two hands on forehead, palms outwards like giant eyebrows. The visual code for Stalin, on the other hand, was usually a military posture and a stern expression. Two sharp raps on table were given—and the subject swiftly changed—whenever one of the two Intourist guides or other Russians came near. Whether they were speaking Russian or practicing their English, whenever they offered an alcoholic drink it was always accompanied by the same gesture he had seen in Mashtagah. The right index finger was first placed against the thumb as if the person was about to flick something away, then—with the head tilted to the left—it was snapped against the back of the right jaw, making a hollow, popping sound.

One day, the boat stopped at an island in the river for a day of hiking and picnicking. A barbecue was set up on a wide sandbar and most of the tourists sunbathed and swam in the Volga while they waited for the food to be prepared. Mels welcomed the opportunity to spend the time on his own and took off down a path between thick conifer trees, leaving the rest of the party behind. After twenty minutes or so, he found an abandoned church in what had once been a clearing in the forest. A trio of noisy crows left their perch on the rusted gutter, yah-yahing indignantly at his approach.

The old church was in a terrible state of disrepair, with shrubs growing from an onion-domed roof that had been gilded but now showed only patches of a faded canary yellow. Inside, he found that the interior had been vandalized many years ago, in some long forgotten campaign against religion. Obscene graffiti despoiled pillars that once had been painted gold. Someone, local villagers presumably, had stockpiled peat moss for winter fuel in what had been the aisle. Mels made his way up to the altar. There, amidst pigeon droppings and debris, were two bouquets of fresh wildflowers. From a faded icon, a sad-eyed Virgin Mary regarded the modest offerings with her usual all-forgiving kindness.

He heard a noise behind him. One of the tour guides stood with the caretaker, who—disturbed from his midday siesta—was in voluble mood.

"Who the fuck are you? What are you doing here?"

Mels pretended not to understand. The guide pretended to repeat the remark in English.

"The caretaker welcomes you to his church which unfortunately is closed for renovation."

"I thought God's house never closes?"

The guide repeated the process in reverse.

"He's making some smart-ass comment that 'god's house never closes.'"

"Maybe so but I'm in charge of this one."

"The caretaker says God should take better care of his house."

"Where is the priest?"

"Now he wants to know whether there's a priest?"

"Tell him the last one was thrown down a well in 1938."

"The priest is away on vacation at the moment."

"Do the villagers still come here to worship?"

"He asks if people come and pray here?"

"Not if I catch them."

"The caretaker says all are welcome but most of the villagers are scientific atheists."

"All are welcome in god's house, eh?"

"Well Mr. Morgan, I think it's time to return to the beach now. We have a French-style lunch today in honor of Bastille Day. If your German friend had not told us you were here you would have missed it. Come—don't frown—you will enjoy it. And afterwards we will discuss our itinerary for Togliatti tomorrow."

Chapter 14

The last thing Mels expected to see in Togliatti, Russia's self-proclaimed "industrial city of the future," was a group of gypsies by the railway station. Olive-skinned and anarchic, they seemed to have strayed into the wrong century as they flitted amongst the stolid Russians on their way to work, offering to read palms and begging for kopecks. One of the Italians raised his camera to photograph the picturesque group in their pavement-sweeping floral skirts, but an unsmiling militiaman appeared from the rush hour crowd and clamped a gloved hand over the lens while a colleague harried the gypsies from the plaza. A life-long Communist from Genoa was then given a ten-minute lecture on the evils of capitalist propaganda by the officious policeman. As the weight of public opinion was firmly on the side of the would-be photographer, the guides had no choice but to intervene and translate the exchange.

"Gypsies are fully integrated into the economic and social life of the Republic and to show them begging is to present a false picture. Second, they were not begging. Nobody needs to beg in the Soviet Union."

"I have come all the way from Genoa, the birthplace of Palmiro Togliatti, to this city. Tell me, Mr. Policeman, if they weren't begging then *why shouldn't I take a photograph?!*"

Unused to having his authority questioned so vehemently by someone who was sober, the policeman was lost for words. He summoned the other militiaman over.

"You misunderstood. My colleague did not stop you from photographing 'gypsies.' Look, here are no gypsies here. It is against the law to photograph railway stations and other buildings of strategic importance."

The photo opportunity having long-since past by, there was little point in arguing. The tour group boarded their Intourist bus and was driven to the Zhiguli car factory while one of the guides gave them information they had known for years.

"Palmiro Togliatti founded the Socialist newspaper *L'Ordina Nuova* in 1919—"

A chorus came from the bus.

"*L'Ordino Nouvo!*"

"Yes, *L'Ordino Nouvo*. And he was one of those who formed the Italian Communist party in er,—"

"Nineteen twenty-one!"

"Quite. Well, he was leader of the Italian Communist Party for thirty-eight years. When Mussolini was in power, he spent eighteen years in Moscow in exile where he founded the Comintern and was in charge of the resistance against the Fascists in Spain. He returned to Italy in 1944. Under his leadership, the Communist Party became the largest Communist Party in Western Europe, yes?"

The Italians nodded their agreement.

"So, when Fiat of Italy won the tender for building the automobile factory here, his name was an obvious choice. You are privileged to visit. Only foreign engineers working in the factory itself are usually allowed here. When we get to the Zhiguli factory—which is officially called the *Volga Automobil Zavod*—you will be given a guided tour by specialists from the shop floor. In the meantime I invite you to look at this beautiful city to see what the future looks like."

If she is right, thought Mels, *that would resemble some of the old science-fiction movies we were shown as children.* He looked out the window at a movie theater called "Saturn" constructed to look like a flying saucer. Even the apartment blocks had been covered with white ceramic tiles that gleamed in the sun. Visiting a car factory was not high on Mels' list of priorities but he knew his chances of being contacted by Hamlet's associates were higher if he stayed with his tour group.

As they turned into the VAZ gates, they stopped to allow the factory-appointed guide on the bus. Unusually, security guards from the VAZ plant also boarded the bus and checked their passports before allowing them to enter. While they waited, Mels saw shreds of banners, and the broken poles used to carry them, lying in the road outside the main entrance. It often took weeks in Leningrad for the streets to be cleaned up after May Day, but the lettering on the litter seemed curiously amateurish and home made. It was a minor point but he was curious enough about it to mention it to their new guide once he had taken over the bus microphone.

"That was high spirits on the part of the factory workers."

"High spirits?"

"Indeed. A spontaneous demonstration on the eighth of May to celebrate Victory over Fascism Day."

"Victory Day is May ninth."

"The workers were given both days off because of their high productivity."

The VAZ guide refused to discuss it further, turning instead to a dizzying array of statistics about production and export figures. Inured by lifelong exposure to Soviet statistics, Mels found little of interest in what was said until one of the tourists asked why the guide kept referring to "Zhiguli" cars when everyone knew these were "Ladas." The guide's clumsy attempts to prevaricate piqued the group's interest and they kept returning to the question until he was forced to answer.

"Look, 'Lada' is just for export. 'Zhiguli' sounds good in Russian but in English it means 'wobbly' and in Chinese it's apparently a brand of chocolates. However, at least we did not try to market a car called the 'No Va' in Latin America as the American Chevrolet did."

Everywhere they were taken, the factory seemed new and clean and the workers young and attractive. They were taken for lunch in the VAZ cafeteria and were served a three-course meal of steaks and fried Volga sturgeon, while the cafeteria workers' eyes followed their every mouthful. After the meal they were taken to the test track. As he stood and watched the cars being noisily test-driven around the eight-kilometer loop, Mels heard two of his fellow tourists having a shouted conversation in Italian. Only one word caught his attention.

"Excuse me, did you say 'espresso'?"

"Si! This meal, it's the best we have all trip, no? And the guide, he tell me that they have espresso in the hotel where we stay tonight."

The "Hotel Zhiguli" did, indeed have a coffee bar where they served espresso. Mels stayed in there long after his fellow guests had departed for bed. The next day was the highlight of the trip for the tour group and they wanted to get an early start so they would miss nothing of Ulyanovsk, the birthplace of Lenin. They had been informed that from this point on, they would be sharing their accommodations with domestic tourists; factory workers for the most part who had drawn the short straw for their vacation entitlement. Instead of heading south to the Black Sea resorts, this lucky crowd had been issued with coupons for two-bedroom chalets on the shores of the Valdai Hills lakes, south of Leningrad. In order to minimize contact between the two groups, the foreigners would now spend their nights in Intourist hotels ashore while the Russians slept on the boat.

At midnight, Mels was told the bar was closing. He had an uneasy feeling that he was being observed, which he rationalized as paranoia. However, fueled by caffeine and adrenaline, he knew he would be unable to sleep. He left the hotel to take a walk in the nearly deserted streets of Togliatti.

No sooner had he left the hotel than a woman's voice called out to him in English.

"Ian. Wait for me, will you?"

A pretty, snub-nosed woman in her early twenties hurried after him, one hand supporting her auburn hair, which was piled up on top of her head in a beehive hairdo that could have been copied from a nineteen-fifties Hollywood movie. Despite her slit-skirted sheer evening dress, her freckled face and overripe body were those of a young peasant woman. She put her arm through his in a possessive way then whispered under her breath in Russian.

"Keep walking. These people are snitches. Talk to me—in English—as if I am a prostitute you just picked up."

"Er, so there'll be a big tip for you if you know what to do."

As they turned the corner, she took a small package out of her purse.

"You're a strange one. You didn't have to take that note they gave you too literally, you know. You must have had six espressos! I'm supposed to be a prostitute. I was sitting in the bar trying to catch your attention but you looked straight through me. I've been waiting for you to go to your room so I could follow you and give you this in the elevator. (No. Don't open it!)"

"What is it?"

"It's some merchandise. They want you to take it to Moscow for them."

"I'm not going to Moscow. Ardzinba told me I would meet someone here who would arrange for me to go to Siberia."

She wrinkled her freckled nose and smiled mischievously.

"Now come on, 'Ian.' One hand washes the other, you know. You were given a lot of money down in Sukhumi, and they arranged your trip up here on a nice cruise ship. *Some people would be grateful.*"

"But what am I going to do in Moscow?"

"Whatever you like, dear. Go to Red Square if you want. But I *assume* you'll be wanting to use their contacts to get you to Siberia. Hamlet arranges that all the time."

"What if I say no?"

"Oh I wouldn't do that, dear. They don't like it when people do that. Personally, I don't think you have much choice, really. Caught between them and the KGB and all that."

"What's in this package?"

"I don't know. And I don't advise *you* to find out. If you break the seal on it they'll, well, they'll be really upset. *Really* upset. You just be a good boy and take that to Moscow, eh? Someone will contact you on the way. And don't go off on your own like you did on that island. People get worried."

"So you had someone on the boat, too? Why me? Surely you have other people who can transport it?"

"Well, maybe they're all on strike! Oh, you're not smiling? Hmm, you probably wouldn't have heard about that, would you, as you don't come from round here? The transport workers went on strike in May for a couple of days. They even managed to blockade the VAZ plant a short while before the strike was broken up."

"What were they striking for?"

"They were hungry, I believe. Plus some of them thought they were in Poland where you can get away with that sort of behavior. For those people without connections, there's been nothing but potatoes in the stores here all summer. Still, I expect *you've* been eating well, Mr. Morgan."

Mels ignored the comment.

"Why do I have to go all the way to Moscow on the Volga? There's a direct highway between here and there? Can't we just drive?"

"Do you think they have every single traffic cop between here and Moscow on the payroll?"

"Maybe not. But, well, suppose I agree to do this. What guarantee do I have that my daughter and I get to Siberia?"

"I don't know. They didn't tell me everything."

"What else *do* you know?"

"Not much, really. Let me think, I told you to get back on the boat until you're contacted. And I told you not to open the package, didn't I? That's about it, really. Oh yes, I *was* told that I was supposed to have sex with you if you fancied it."

"So you really *are* a prostitute?"

"They said you like to make moral judgements about people. Did I ask you for money?"

"Well, no."

"Then it's not prostitution, is it?"

Mels sighed. An offer of free sex was not exactly what he had planned on. Togliatti was supposed to have been the gateway to Siberia and the rest of his life. He looked at the unnamed woman in front of him and mulled over the proposal. Actually, she was not without her attractions, most of which were visible through the flimsy fabric of the dress. Despite his fealty to Tanya, if it was not for the thought of having sex in a bugged room at the hotel, he might have been quite tempted.

The package she had given him had a lead seal on it. He weighed it in his hand. *How much does heroin weigh? Or microfilm?* It was too light to be gold and too heavy to be cash. *Maybe it's some electronic device the CIA are interested in?*

"Look, I'll take a rain-check on the sex. Next time I'm in Togliatti, maybe?"

"Suit yourself."

"And—as you realize—I have no choice about rejoining the 'International Brigade' on the cruise ship. But I want you to go back and talk to whoever sent you here and tell them I expect to see someone with a little more authority at the next stop."

"Fine by me."

"So that's it?"

"That's it, 'Mr. Morgan.' Enjoy your trip."

But Mels did not enjoy his trip. For one thing, with the influx of Russian tourists on the boat, he found it hard to pretend he did not speak Russian. In his guise as a foreigner he found himself once again the target of ordinary people who wanted to talk about things they did not dare share with their fellow Russians. But the stories they told would just start to get interesting—tales of corruption, scandal, and intrigue—when the narrators' lack of fluency in English would get in the way and Mels would be left guessing at the details.

On top of which, the weather—which had of late been wet and windy—started to improve. The wide-open sky and the landscapes between the towns reminded him of Siberia. Judging from the scenes of pastoral life he observed from the boat, the pace of life along the riverbank seemed to have changed little since the days Volga boatman would haul cargo barges upstream by manpower alone. Old men with Tolstoyan beards herded gaggles of geese, women in headscarves washed baskets of clothes and children watered improbably large carthorses. Every now and then an inviting copse of trees would trigger some atavistic instinct in him and he was seized with the urge to go off on his own to explore.

By contrast, Ulyanovsk was torture. It was bad enough to have to stand in line at Lenin's tomb in Red Square. At least there was some scientific curiosity involved in seeing Lenin's corpse—was it real or had they really replaced it with a wax effigy? But to stand in line just to see the man's childhood home seemed to Mels a complete waste of a beautiful summer's day. He dutifully followed the instructions relayed by the redhead and followed his band of aging fanatics around what was, for them, a place of homage.

After the rather lackluster delights of Kazan (the tour guides refused to take the group to see any of the churches built in the wake of Ivan the Terrible's defeat of the Tatars, and took them instead to see the site of the technical institute where Lenin studied), the foreign tourists were not allowed to go ashore until after the boat had passed Gorkiy.

It was a muggy day. He lay on the bunk in his cabin, staring at Bunin's verses on the page in front of him, wondering what exactly had prompted the KGB to decide against sending him, like Sakharov, to exile in Gorkiy and instead to eliminate him.

Did they think he knew too much? About what—Zhanna's vice ring? Who would he tell? Leningrad had no investigative journalists who would take on the might of the KGB.

A wail from outside interrupted his reverie. He tried to look out through the open porthole but the angle was too steep to see what was going on. The wailing increased in tempo until finally a blast from the ship's horn alerted him to the fact that something really serious had happened. He left his room, ignoring an announcement over the intercom instructing people to return to their cabins. A scowling steward barred his way up the stairway.

"Please return to your room."

"What's happened?"

"Nothing has happened."

But others were also trying to make their way up the stairs and the steward could not hold them all back. They pushed him aside and went up on deck in time to see the lifeless body of one of the elderly Italians being winched out of the Volga while his widow screamed in shock and grief.

At dinner that night, one of their comrades explained that a group of them had become bored in the hot confines of their cabins and had decided to swim from the back of the boat. Unfortunately the cold water released from the Gorkiy reservoir, sourced from the north of Russia, was a lot colder than the warm, shallow river they had last swum in, way to the south. Presumably after suffering a sudden heart attack, the man had been unable to get a grip on the ship's ladder and drowned in front of his frantic wife.

Suddenly conscious, it seemed, of their own mortality, it was a subdued group that disembarked the next day at Yaroslavl, north of Moscow. Half the group—the die-hard sports enthusiasts—were leaving that day by bus to catch the opening heats of the Olympics. The remainder would stay with the boat for the remaining two days of the cruise.

But after the previous day's incident, many of the tourists

were too preoccupied to appreciate the splendors of the historic area, preferring to stay on the boat or doze on their Intourist bus rather than walk around the attractions of the so-called "Golden Ring" of towns.

Mels wandered round the Kremlin museum in the small town of Rostov with a much reduced tour party consisting of one of the French couples, the ever-present East German and the tall, gray-haired Italian and his wife. The church bells were ringing out at midday when he felt a tug on his sleeve. Without turning round, he saw a familiar face—with a finger over its lips—reflected from the glass of the display case in front of him. The finger moved away from the face, rotated through ninety degrees then hinged at the knuckle, beckoning him to follow. Mels watched his fellow tourists. No one seemed to have noticed. He backed away from the display case then turned a corner around which the figure was waiting.

"Hamlet! How the hell did you get here? Why aren't you in Siberia?"

"Shhh! You're in a museum! I had some business here before I disappear. Plus they told me you wanted to talk to someone with more 'authority'!"

"I did, but you're running a terrible risk. What's happening? Am I supposed to give the package to you? It's inside the U-tube under the washbasin in my cabin."

"Didn't want to get caught with it, eh? Smart."

"You're damn right I didn't! What's in it, anyway? Drugs?"

Hamlet shrugged.

"Don't worry about it. We'll get rid of it tonight. And after that we arrange your disappearance."

"To Siberia?"

"Unfortunately, not yet. You'll have to go to Moscow first. You'll go to the bar on the second floor of the National restaurant on Gorkovo Street. It's near the Kremlin. Ask the barman if Hamlet has been in. He'll give you instructions. It's an added complication but our network has completely broken down in this region. We had some problems with some of these halfwits from Electric Corner."

"I thought you said they were all 'trained artisans'?"

"Trained, yes. Artisans, perhaps. Halfwits, undoubtedly. I think I also told you we have a continuing problem with people getting greedy. Greedy and now forgetful, it seems. This area should be a gold mine. We're within a day's drive of Moscow and Leningrad for tourists visiting the 'Golden Ring' plus we have the river traffic coming from the port of Yaroslavl. And what do all those tourists need to get from town to town?"

"Transport?"

"Close. Bear in mind we're after the ones with money and *they* already have transport. No; what they need, my friend, is gasoline. And if you had a car you'd know how frustrating it is to try to get served from a State-owned gas station when the pumps are only open for a few hours a day. A typical tourist on a weekend break from his job in Moscow isn't going to begrudge paying a premium if he can be assured that he won't run out of gas. Even the Intourist tour bus drivers knew they could always get diesel at one on of our 'free market' gas stations. And of course, once you've established a niche, you can start selling sandwiches, tea, vodka and, say, little 'helpers' to keep Ivan the truck driver awake. Or maybe some 'company' if he wants to pull off the road for a while."

"Somewhat distasteful. But, you're right; it *does* sound like a gold mine. So what went wrong?"

"The halfwits were making so much money from out of hours trading that they forgot to draw their State salaries!"

"You're kidding?"

"I wish I was, Mels. The militia got a tip off from the Ministry's payroll department and staked out three of our unofficial gas stations/recreation areas. Ten of my boys—and I don't know how many of the girls—were pulled in for questioning this week. One of 'our' traffic cops showed me how to get here without being stopped but there are roadblocks on all the main highways."

"So how are we going to get out of here?"

"Leave that to me. For now, rejoin your group. The guides will notice your absence soon and get curious. When you get back to the boat, go to your cabin and retrieve the package then go to the ship's surgery."

"The surgery?"

"The medical clinic on the boat."

"What excuse will I give?"

"You won't need an excuse. You should find it deserted. Go in and wait for me."

Hamlet had been right about the heavy police presence in the area. The Intourist bus was stopped several times on the way back to the Volga embankment at Yaroslavl. Often Mels saw unmarked cars parked in the trees beyond the roadblocks themselves, waiting to tail any suspicious vehicle. Always, the driver or passenger was talking on a two-way radio as they passed, though none seemed to pull out to follow them.

The driver of their bus seemed less concerned about the frequent stops by the police than he was about where he was going to find diesel and slowed the bus to a crawl to preserve fuel. The only State-run service station that they passed had a sign outside which simply said "Closed for Cleaning."

At length an impatient Mels recognized the onion domes of the Church of the Nativity of Christ, which meant that they were approaching the embankment. Sleek hydrofoils skimmed along the Volga in front of the Nekrasov monument. They boarded the boat just as busloads of Russian tourists arrived back from their day of sightseeing. Mels lost himself in the throng and, as commanded by Hamlet, made his way to the ship's medical clinic with the sealed package hidden in the small suitcase from Baku.

Mels found the door unlocked and slipped inside the dark surgery. It was his first time there and he felt in vain for a light switch on the walls around the door. Groping in the blackness in front of him he found the cold metal of an examination table surmounted by what appeared to be a large wooden box. He ran his hand along the polished top surface. *What is this—an old steamer trunk?* The wood abruptly ended and his hand found itself touching something cool, like refrigerated meat.

Just then the light in the surgery came on and he realized that he had his hand on a dead human face.

Chapter 15

"What were you doing in here in the dark, Mels? The light switch is outside. And leave Signor di Ferranti alone. He's about to go into the meat freezer and any expression you put on his face is going to get frozen in place."

"So that's what we're here for—body snatching? What for? Surely you don't sell corpses to medical institutions?"

"Funny you mention that. I did look into it one time but it turns out they get more than they can handle from the *Gulag*. No, my friend, we are not 'stealing' Signor di Ferranti, we're just 'using' him. To be exact, we're using his coffin. You are going to get off this boat in it. Now don't go getting that horrified expression on your face again. It's a very comfortable coffin. Look, it's even got red silk cushioning in it. When my associates get here they'll help me carry the casket out after we screw you in."

"*Screw* me in! Are you out of your mind?! I'll suffocate!"

"No you won't. Look, it's huge. And we'll drill some air holes. Anyway, Signora di Ferranti will be accompanying you in the hearse. Italians are emotional people—she may throw herself on the casket and open it. We can't take a risk."

"Hamlet, no. I can't. I have claustrophobia. I'm not afraid of heights or the sight of blood or any of the usual things that people are scared of but small spaces freak me out."

"It's your choice, Mels. Now help me with di Ferranti. We need to wrap him up in a sheet. Luckily the kitchens are on this level."

But the "choice" Mels had unwittingly taken was one his acquaintanceship with Hamlet had forced him to suffer once before. After Hamlet's cohorts arrived, one distracted Mels while another put a gauze pad impregnated with chloroform over his nose and mouth. He was unconscious during the entire process of being manhandled off the boat and placed in the back of the converted Zil limousine.

He awoke an hour later inside the coffin and was immediately seized with a panic attack when he realized the lid was screwed shut. He took his penknife from his pocket and started blindly scratching away at the inside of the casket. After a few moments he heard a sharp knocking from the outside and an excited voice in Italian. A few moments after that, the coffin suddenly started to bounce around as if the car was being driven off road for several kilometers before being abruptly brought to a halt. Then the coffin lid was unscrewed and he saw a muted twilight through an overhead canopy of birch trees.

"You fucking idiot! Suppose there had been someone from Intourist in the hearse?"

Mels scrambled out of the coffin and tried to stand but felt dizzy so he squatted on the grass until the blood flowed back to his brain.

"I'm sorry, Hamlet. I just panic in enclosed spaces."

"I knew we should have used more chloroform. I just didn't want you to be unconscious for half a day like you were last time."

"Well what happened to Signora di Ferranti? Have you chloroformed her?"

"No. She fainted dead away when she saw your face. Now help me get her out of the hearse and tie her to a tree. We don't want her to wander off in these woods tonight."

"You're just going to leave her here?"

"Sure. It's July. It's not like she's going to die of exposure."

"I don't know, Hamlet, it's starting to cool down; it may rain later."

"Well, give me the hammer-and-sickle flag that was covering the casket. We'll wrap her in that. Don't give me one of your looks, Mels. Someone will be along here in the morning—it's a logging road. We can't leave her by the side of the main highway, can we?

You know, Mels, you are just damned fortunate that you didn't start throwing that fit closer to Yaroslavl. As it is, we only have another fifteen minutes drive to where we're going. But you're going to *have* to get back in that coffin, I'm afraid. You can wedge the lid open if you want but if we get stopped you'll have to close it."

Back in the coffin, Mels practiced deep breathing and tried meditation to still his anxiety. He made himself think of pleasurable things—of Tanya's smooth body next to his, of the quiet pride he felt when he taught Luba to drive a seismic truck when she was only fourteen, and of the satisfaction he felt when his students grasped what he was lecturing about. But even with the lid propped open by his penknife, it was the longest fifteen minutes of his life as a fugitive. When they finally stopped and he exited the hearse he was struck by how cold the night air was and realized that he was drenched in sweat.

They were parked in the driveway of a large dacha. Behind them, at the gateway, Mels made out a shadowy figure smoking a cigarette. Up ahead, the dacha loomed more like a miniature mansion than someone's summer cottage. Hamlet called out and someone turned on a series of security lights. Mels saw several other figures standing around the house. They seemed to be expecting someone.

"We'll go in the house and wait. Bring the package."

"Who are these people?"

"Security. Don't worry about it. All you have to do is hand the merchandise to the buyer. Just say it's the real stuff. Leave the rest of the talking to me."

"'The real stuff'? What's that supposed to mean? Suppose they ask me questions? What am I supposed to say?"

Hamlet gripped Mels arm.

"Listen, Mels Katz. I've told you all you need to know. All you have to do is give them the package and give them your word it's genuine. After that you leave the room. If you say anything else other than small talk you'll be very sorry. I personally guarantee it! No, don't say anything now either. Reflect upon this—you are in a bind. Your future and those of people dear to you depend on your behavior in the next hour or two. This is a small favor I ask. After this—"

"After this, the bar above the National restaurant, then Siberia."

"That's right. Tomorrow night you'll be on your way to freedom. Now just do as I say, OK? Your suitcase is in the hearse. Did you bring any clothes with you?"

"I brought everything your guys gave me in Baku. Why?"

"Well go and wash up and change your shirt. You look terrible. I'll give you a tie to put on. These are respectable people."

"Respect-?"

"Shut it, Mels! I'm serious. I don't want to hear any moralistic claptrap. Remember, do as I say!"

Hamlet directed Mels to a bathroom on the second floor. It was cold and Mels shivered as he dried himself and changed his shirt. The thought occurred to Mels that the house was probably always cold and damp, being surrounded by trees that shaded it from the sun during the day. No doubt the main rooms were heated by log fires. Unusually, the windows had no bars—indicating that whoever owned it could afford round-the-clock security. He heard a car engine outside and opened the frosted glass window opposite the mirror. Around the back of the dacha was a small car park with space for three or four cars. The hearse they had traveled in was being parked. Beyond it was darkness.

Standing in front of the mirror he tried to tie the necktie. He did not usually wear one and when he did he usually let Luba tie it for him. As he fumbled with the knot, he heard more cars approaching. In the mirror he saw headlight beams and heard cars being parked under the window. He waited a few minutes then went over to the window for a better view. Two large black

Mercedes cars had been parked next to the hearse. Whoever these gangsters were and whatever they did, they were evidently pretty successful at doing it. Even Hamlet seemed scared of them. *What, then, would happen if something went wrong with the deal? Supposing they did not want to pay whatever Hamlet asked? Suppose they did not feel like paying anything? What was the escape plan? Where the hell were they, anyway?* He could sneak out through the window—there was a drainpipe next to it which looked eminently climbable—but there was no way he could bear to travel all the way to Moscow in the trunk of a Mercedes. *They would have to steal a car.* And he was fairly certain even Hamlet would find a Mercedes a lot harder to steal—or "use," as he would say—than a Russian car. Just then, the interior light of one of the cars came on as the driver's door opened. Mels caught a quick glimpse of a fat neck under a chauffeur's cap before he ducked instinctively out of sight.

He exited the bathroom and walked towards the sound of voices, downstairs in the main reception room of the dacha. The stairway was decorated with posters from the Moscow circus and a large painting of an acrobat in mid-air. The new arrivals were warming themselves by the fireplace over which were the usual portraits of Lenin and Brezhnev. To his surprise, the main buyers were women. Not the archetypal gangsters' molls, either. From behind they appeared to be just two middle-aged overdressed (and overweight) women who were being unctuously served with drink by Hamlet. *Not that they seem to need it*, thought Mels, as the larger of the two women swayed from side to side and slurred her words. No one acknowledged his presence, so he sat on a chair by the door listening to their conversation.

"Where's 'Dog Shit'?"

"Don't call him that, Svetlana! That's a *family* nickname. He left with Yuri before me. They said they had to go to the Udarnik to pick up some shopping but personally I think he was going to visit his dancer friend before he came here."

"So we have to stand around waiting while your drunkard uncle tries to get it up with some young slut?!"

"No! We don't have to wait for *him*. You, Armenian, our credit's good, right?"

She turned to Hamlet with a regal expression. For the first time, Mels saw Hamlet actually look uncertain. He glanced over the fat woman's shoulder to the open doorway through which Mels had entered. From where he was sitting, Mels could not see who was standing there but whoever it was obviously made a gesture in the affirmative because Hamlet quickly agreed.

"Of course, Galina Leonidovna. You can pay us later."

"Well then, let's see what you've got!"

Hamlet gestured to Mels to approach. As he did so, the two women swung round, their eyes greedy with anticipation. Mels had the strangest feeling. The larger woman seemed oddly familiar, like a long-lost relative. The feeling was heightened when she immediately seemed to recognize him.

"You? You're the man whose picture was on television last night. With some god-awful Stalinist name—"

"'Mels.' 'Mels Katz.'"

"But I thought you were dead. Drowned, wasn't it?"

"'The report of my death was an exaggeration' as Mark Twain said. A case of mistaken identity."

"How strange. That young Academician, Ignatiev, was on the television last night. Said you were a genius. But I was sure he also said you died a couple of weeks ago."

Mindful of Hamlet's admonition, Mels said nothing. Was this "small talk"? Although he was curious to find out who the women were, nobody had introduced them so he assumed he was not supposed to ask.

"So, I understand you have a package for us?"

Mels reached out his hand with the package in it but this was intercepted by Hamlet who produced a small pair of wire-cutters with which he cut the lead seal before handing it on. The woman tore avariciously at the package. Hamlet looked at Mels and prompted him with a cough.

"Oh, yes. 'This is the real stuff.' That is, 'this is genuine.'"

"I believe you're needed in the other room now, Mels."

But after carrying it all the way from Togliatti, Mels wanted to see what was in the package. Obstinately, he stood his ground, watching while the woman opened the final wrapping to reveal the contents.

"Oh my god! Svetlana, look at these!"

In her hand she held at least a dozen large, sparkling diamonds.

"Let me see!"

While the women excitedly examined the stones, a rough hand gripped Mels' upper arm from under the armpit and pulled him away.

"Telephone call for you, Mels L'vovitch."

Mels was too startled to say another word as a burly security man half guided, half dragged him from the room and propelled him up the stairs of the dacha. The women's excited voices were still discussing the gems as he was lead to a small library on the second floor. For a moment he thought he heard the word "radioactive" before the guard's gruff voice drowned them out.

"Wait here."

The door was locked behind him and he was left alone. He was not immediately afraid. After all, Hamlet was still out there, able to plead his case even if he had overstayed his welcome. So he had been carrying diamonds, eh? It was quite a disappointment. He thought he had had military secrets or narcotics on him. And from the women's expressions, it looked as though Hamlet would get a good price for them. He was puzzled, though. He could not think *why* the woman's face looked familiar. And surely a buyer of gemstones would bring a jeweler along rather than relying on the word of a geophysicist, even one who'd recently been mentioned—and presumably had his photograph shown—on television?

What was it they were discussing just before I was locked in this library?—radioactivity. He laughed. That just showed how ignorant most Russians were about geology—only minerals containing elements of high atomic weight were naturally radioactive. He was quite sure that if he ran a Geiger counter over pure diamonds like the ones he had just seen there would be barely a squeak. *But, wait a minute!* The shock wave of consciousness hit him like a physical blow. "These are genuine" did not just mean they were real diamonds, it was supposed to imply that they had been produced by the very process using nuclear explosions that was described in Ignatiev and Kasumov's paper! *But why?* And how *did* Hamlet know about this? Mels had never told him.

He felt a sudden need to be a long way from the dacha, away from whatever dirty dealings were going on and away from Hamlet and his endless schemes. His eyes again instinctively scoped out his surroundings—as they had so often in the past few weeks—looking for an escape route. There was a skylight but no windows in the library and only one exit, now locked. He looked up at the ceiling. Maybe he could reach the skylight if he stood on a table?

He pulled a writing desk from its position against the wall and set it in the middle of the room under the skylight. Climbing up on it, he knocked over a framed photograph of a young-looking Leonid Brezhnev in uniform. He stretched up to the skylight but found that it could only be opened by a mechanical crank, which had been removed. He tried forcing it but it was no use. Disappointed, he jumped down from the desk and pushed it back against the wall. He bent down to pick up the framed photograph. On it had been written a message:

"To Galya with love, daddy."

"Galya?" Galina! *And what was that woman's name?*—Galina Leonidovna. *No wonder she looked familiar!* You could not go a hundred meters without seeing her father's face on a poster in the Soviet Union! So he, Mels Katz, had just told Leonid Brezhnev's

daughter that the diamonds he had given her were produced by a non-existent process!

Curses from outside the door indicated that someone was trying to get into the library and had found it locked. Mels heard the jingle of keys and then found himself in the company of two men. The elder one, by his eyebrows, was obviously a Brezhnev. The younger man was wearing the uniform of a general in the militia. Both of them had been drinking. The general scowled at Mels.

"Who the fuck are you? And what are you doing in here with the door closed?"

"I brought the package, Comrade. I was not aware the door had been locked from the outside. Your staff are obviously security conscious."

"Security conscious, my ass! Nobody steals books. I'll bet nobody's even read these books, eh Yacov? Certainly not my fat wife. So long as you weren't stealing my liquor."

He walked over to a bookcase and pressed the spine of one of the books, activating a hidden door. The bookcase turned out to be a false front to a large liquor cabinet. He grabbed two bottles of vodka, handed one to the older man, and closed the cabinet.

"Come on, Yacov. This dacha's dead. It's no wonder there's a fucking hearse outside. If we have to stay here tonight, let's find something to celebrate, for Christ's sake!"

They exited, leaving the door ajar.

Impulsively, Mels walked over to the bookcase and activated the liquor cabinet. He placed a small bottle of brandy in his pocket, slipped out of the door and tiptoed to the stairs. The security guard who had taken him to the library was standing on the landing under the painting of the acrobat, chatting to the fat-necked driver of the Mercedes. Mels recognized him immediately.

"Listen, Misha, or whatever your name is. I'm head of security here. I work for Galina Brezhneva Churbanova. Nobody's explained to me why the KGB decided to replace Galina Leonidovna's driver tonight, or why we locked that courier in the library. Unless I get an explanation—"

"'Unless you get an explanation'-what? I'm working on a top-secret project here. You think the KGB needs your fucking permission to lock up Jews?!"

"Would you mind your language? I would remind you my employer is Jewish."

"I think all Russia knows that. And if you have a problem with who is in charge here—"

"Who is in charge?! Yuri Churbanov is deputy head of the Interior Ministry. You think you outrank him?!"

Another familiar figure appeared from the reception room. It was Sergei, Misha's partner, whom Mels had last seen at the Sea Terminal.

"Would you two keep your voices down, please? What's the problem, here?"

"Your colleague decided to throw his weight around. I was reminding him, and will remind you, that I am in charge of security here."

"Of course, of course! Misha, I'm sure, was just allowing his natural enthusiasm to run away with him."

"Well what do you intend to do with the courier and that Armenian?"

"Oh, I imagine Galina Leonidovna has already offered for them to stay the night. Of course we wouldn't dream of allowing that to happen. As soon as the hostess and her friend are asleep we will be departing with your friend in the library."

"May I ask where?"

"You can always ask, my friend, but in this case I'm afraid I must decline to answer. Rest assured you will not be troubled with them again."

Mels tiptoed back along the corridor upstairs to the bathroom. Leaving the light off, he looked out the window at the cars in the parking lot but the glow of a security guard's cigarette showed that the line of retreat was cut.

His other shirt was draped over the bathtub where he had left it. Nervously, he wadded it up into a ball while he wracked his brains for inspiration. In the cool of the night, the shirt had not dried and was still sodden with perspiration. Watching the sweat drip slowly from his fingers into the tub a wild idea, born of desperation, came to him. He soaked the shirt in cold water from the faucet, then soaked all the towels he could find in the bathroom the same way. He baled them, using the necktie he had been given by Hamlet to connect the bundle to his belt. Then he waited until he was sure that the security guard outside was facing away from the dacha and swung himself out the window. He grabbed the drainpipe and climbed easily up to the steep roof. The tiles were slippery with wet moss but he was gradually able to ease himself up the slope to the chimneystacks. At full height, he was able to stretch and reach the pots, which he covered with the wet towels and shirt, then secured them with Hamlet's necktie.

Descending the roof in the dark was more hair-raising than climbing it had been. He couldn't see the guttering and had to gauge where the drainpipe joined it. He held on to an overhanging pine branch to get his balance then sat on the edge of the roof, his feet dangling, until he heard the sound of coughing from below.

"Yuri, are you completely incompetent? I asked you to make sure the chimneys were swept last Spring!"

An incoherent growl greeted this comment.

"Svetlana, we'll stay at your dacha tonight and go back to Moscow tomorrow. I'll come with you as we apparently are to be denied use of the back-up car. There's probably a dead squirrel or a ton of pine needles stuck in the chimney. Really, the countryside gives me the creeps!

Where's Uncle Yacov? Yuri, find 'Dog Shit' and take him in your car. Call ahead to the Schelokov dacha and warn them we are coming. Your driver knows the way."

In all the commotion, Mels' descent of the drainpipe passed unnoticed until he stood right in front of Galina Brezhneva.

"Galina Leonidovna, I wonder if I could request the favor of a ride?"

From under her plucked eyebrows, her eyes seemed to take a while to register who he was. She smiled almost flirtatiously as recognition set in.

"Why, Mels Katz; the man who brings me diamonds! It would be a pleasure."

He slid into the back seat between the substantial forms of Galina Brezhneva and Svetlana Schelokova. As the car pulled away from the dacha he saw the two KGB agents get into one of the other Mercedes and start to pursue them down the driveway until the lean figure of Hamlet Sirounian jumped in front of the second car and waved it to stop.

It was hard for him to follow the women's conversation in the back of the car as his attention was directed out the rear window, through which at any moment he expected the headlights of the Mercedes to reappear. To his initial surprise all was blackness. For a brief moment his faith in Hamlet was restored. Had he risked his own freedom to bargain with the KGB to let Mels go? Then the thought struck him that, as far as Hamlet and the KGB were concerned, Mels knew nothing about the KGB presence at the dacha. So Hamlet still thought that Mels trusted him. Smarter than the two KGB agents, he probably figured that it was not worth their while trailing him and arousing the suspicions of the two women in the process. After all, where else did he have to go except to Moscow, and Hamlet's trap?

As they approached a small town he noticed the driver eyeing him balefully in the rear mirror. *Is he a security guard, or KGB?* Actually, Mels reflected, it was pretty academic at this point; anything he said would be reported to the KGB. The ample forms of the two women pressed him from both sides as if they were trying to squeeze any remaining diamonds out of him.

"Galina Leonidovna, have you ever been to the National restaurant on Gorkovo Street?"

"Not for many years, but I know it of course. Why?"

"What's the nearest Metro station? How long a walk is it?"

Both women laughed.

"I'm afraid I don't usually use the Metro and I *never* walk. It is close to the Kremlin, though. I'll give you my Moscow telephone number—we live nearby—you must come when you have your next shipment!"

She batted her eyes. She was so close that Mels could notice that her artfully plucked eyebrows were starting to grow back. He smiled politely.

"Yes, yes. Well, ladies, I'm afraid I must bid farewell to you both here. I see the railway station in front of us. I *do* have an appointment to meet someone tomorrow night but perhaps I could call on you beforehand?"

"But you must come with us now! It's so boring up here . . . . "

Despite their protests, he insisted the two women drop him in the forecourt of the small rural station.

From the complicated schedule above the ticket office he discovered that there were trains going to both Leningrad and Moscow within the hour. He waited in line to buy tickets at the window reserved for ordinary passengers. At the next window a young Estonian conscript was trying to exchange a military docket for a third class ticket to Termez. The woman behind the glass was having trouble with his accent and was totally ignorant of any destinations that far south. A germ of an idea came to Mels. When his turn came he bought first class tickets to both Moscow and Leningrad.

Chapter 16

Despite the late hour, the station was still busy with dacha owners on weekend visits and sports fans Moscow-bound for the Olympics. The station restaurant and an adjacent pharmacy were doing brisk business. He followed the soldier into the restaurant where they stood in line for ten minutes to see the food menu, inhaling the scent of overcooked borscht before giving their orders to a bored sales clerk to add up the totals on an abacus.

"Let me buy you that, young man. I don't suppose you'll be eating well for the next week on the way to Termez."

"You know Termez? That Russian bitch—excuse my language—had no idea where I was talking about."

"Oh yes. Our main supply route to Kabul, then all the way to Qandahar."

"You've been there, Comrade? Or is it 'Comrade Major' or 'Colonel'?"

"I'm not in uniform. 'Comrade' is sufficient."

"So you *have* been there! Is it as bad as people say? Are we winning?"

The sales clerk handed Mels the register receipt and they walked over to a second line to pay.

"I shouldn't tell you this but, yes, it's as bad as people say. Worse, maybe. You've heard the *dushmans* make cartridge bags out of the scrota of captured soldiers?"

"Scrota?"

"Balls, my friend. Testicles."

The conscript reflexively crossed his legs.

"How long were you there?"

"Just a few months but long enough to see way too many 'Black Tulips' in the desert."

"Black Tulips?"

"Yes—the planes that take the bodies back to Termez. That's one of the sad things about war. So few mothers ever find out what happens to their sons. They're just buried in mass graves down in Uzbekistan."

The conscript said nothing but his eyes were as wide as saucers as Mels continued.

"I was with Lieutenant Colonel Talebov's unit in the palace. Special Forces, you know. You may think it strange but I actually miss the place. 'Course, that's because they give me all the easy tasks nowadays. Right now I'm supposed to be going undercover."

"Undercover?"

"That's right. I'm supposed to go and meet some petty criminal in a bar in Moscow. Apparently there's a ring where they smuggle draft dodgers to Siberia, Poland, Finland, wherever."

"Finland?"

"Yeah. Of course that's a real problem for the army because it's very easy for the Estonian recruits to pass as Finnish tourists because they look Finnish and they understand the language. Now Finland's a progressive country—we have friends in high places who will send back deserters if we put pressure on them—but there's that border with Sweden. Finns don't need a visa to cross it and then we can't touch them."

The conscript looked thoughtful as Mels paid the cashier and they went to the first food counter to get a bowl of mashed potatoes with a small amount of stew slopped over it. Neither of them spoke while they queued at a second counter to get borscht. There was a fuss at the third counter where they collected their black bread. As this was sold by the gram rather than by the slice, they had to wait while an officious sales girl in pigtails carefully sliced off a few grams over the limit. Mels sat at a table by the window, which had been partly obscured by a large cut-out poster of Misha, the smiling cartoon bear chosen by the Soviet Olympic committee to represent the spirit of the Moscow Games. The table had a large borscht stain on its oilcloth covering on which were set relatively clean glasses and some light aluminum forks and spoons. Mels produced Churbanov's brandy from his pocket and poured two large measures.

"Cheers."

"Cheers. So, is it dangerous?"

"What, Comrade?"

"This mission in Moscow?"

"Nah. Piece of cake. I give them five hundred rubles and the next thing I know I'll be in Poland or—"

"Finland?"

"Yeah. Or Finland. Then I go to the Russian embassy and get them to repatriate me so I can make my report. Or if there's a problem, they've given me a foreign passport so I can always *buy* a ticket to get back as a tourist!"

Mels showed him the British passport. The soldier's face was doubtful.

"But you'd need five hundred rubles to do this?"

"Oh, yes, but they gave me that, too. Anyone could do it. In fact, confidentially, one thing I'm supposed to do is recruit someone to come with me. 'Back-up,' you know."

He sipped his brandy and replenished the conscript's empty glass.

"'Back-up'?"

"Well, I can't be everywhere, can I? I mean suppose I get to Yugoslavia, how will I know how they send people to, I don't know. . . ."

"Finland?"

"Exactly. How would I know how they send someone to Finland? I mean, I can hardly go back a second time, can I? The only problem is finding an Estonian. You're Latvian, right?"

"Estonian."

"*You're* Estonian? I'm terrible with accents."

Mels tried his best to look as though a brainwave had just hit him. He had only drunk half a glass of brandy to the three that the younger man had drunk, but he knew his limits as far as alcohol was concerned. *Am I overplaying the part?* The Estonian noticed Mels' look.

"So, what do you think?"

"You mean do I think you'd do for the part?"

"Yeah! I can speak Finnish like a Finn. I mean, we used to watch Finnish television all the time in Tallinn. Half the time the signal came in stronger than the local station. It's OK to tell you that, isn't it?"

"Sure. You're a secret agent now! Look, I can see from your shoulder badges that you're with the Fortieth Army."

"*Will be* with the fortieth army. I haven't reported for duty yet."

"Even better—they won't miss you. I know a few people with the Fortieth. I'll explain that you're helping me. What's your name, soldier?"

"Palmiste. Aimar Palmiste."

"Well, Aimar, the problem is that you can't go in uniform. Do you have any civilian clothes with you?"

"Well, yeah. In my kitbag. Should I change?"

"Sooner the better. Go change in the Men's Room. You'd better leave that uniform with me. A draft dodger wouldn't be carrying any military items around."

After his liberal dose of Churbanov's brandy, Aimar Palmiste seemed to have some difficulty navigating his way to the Men's Room. Mels peered over the cutout Misha figure to observe the scene in the station while he waited. Had the KGB already been informed that he had been dropped there? Weeks of being on the run had left him with an inability to relax his guard. His eyes went from group to group.

Vacationing families sat on their luggage eating sandwiches

under an oversized bronze statue of Lenin. The statue had Lenin in his usual pose, the thumb of one hand under his vest while the other hand held a cloth cap with which he gestured vaguely into the distance. The anonymous team that had cast the arm had evidently not consulted with the team responsible for the head, which sported a second cap, giving the man an unintended comical appearance.

On a bench nearby, an old man with a chest full of world war two campaign medals pulled out a copy of *Pravda*, which he read through a small magnifying glass, mouthing the words as he went along. An energetic team of aproned cleaning women moved up and down the enclosed area brandishing wet mops, forcing people to move—including a group of students who were gathered round a long-haired guitar player, singing sentimental campfire songs. A group of collective farm workers in traditional kepkas were drinking kefir just inside the restaurant while unshaven vagrants kept watch for unfinished bottles.

The only militiamen in sight were harassing Caucasian construction workers for bribes. They had the relaxed demeanor of fat cats who know that their indulgent owner will eventually give them the cream they demand.

A fight broke out near the ticket window among people queuing for tickets. The militiamen abandoned their attempt at extortion and waded into the fight. Within minutes, an ageing combatant, rather the worse for drink and with several teeth missing, had his arms pinned back by the police. All told, it was an unremarkable slice of daily life that was probably being played out at a hundred railway stations across the Union. But the Misha figure reminded him not only of the bear's namesake, the decidedly un-cuddly KGB agent he had left back at the dacha but also of Hamlet's warning about the bear-like persistence of the Soviet security apparatus. He knew that as soon as they were told he had been dropped at the station they would come here whether it was this evening or a month from now. Then Palmiste reappeared, wearing jeans and a canvas windcheater. He had his uniform with him in a brown paper bag. Mels took it.

"Don't worry, Aimar. You won't have to stay long in Finland."

Palmiste tried not to look like a man suppressing a laugh.

"I don't have a foreign passport. And I need money."

Reluctantly, Mels put his hand in his pocket. He still had nearly a thousand rubles on him but the downside of his plan was the mischief five hundred rubles could get a drunk eighteen-year old into in the hours before he reached the National restaurant. *Still, what choice do I have?*

"Aimar, you're a brave man. You'll go on ahead while I arrange for a passport to be made for you. Look, I've bought you a ticket to Moscow. You'll be in first class so you won't have to talk to anyone. Tomorrow night, take the Metro to the Kremlin. You need the National restaurant on Gorkovo Street. I'll be there about ten o'clock. Go to the bar upstairs and tell the barman you're a friend of Hamlet's. Here's five hundred rubles. Now give me your military I.D. card."

"Why? I'll need that!"

"Do you have any other photographic I.D. on you? How do you think I'm going to get a passport made?"

As Palmiste handed over his military identification papers, loudspeakers announced the arrival of the train from Leningrad, en route to Moscow. The students grabbed their rucksacks and ran for the train.

"OK, Aimar. See you tomorrow night!"

As soon as Aimar was out of the way, Mels entered the pharmacy to buy linen bandages and safety pins. He occupied a stall in the Men's Room and wound the bandages around his head until his face was completely covered except for his eyes. Palmiste's uniform was a little tight—Mels had been eating too well on the cruise ship—so he left the tunic buttons unfastened, reasoning no senior officer was likely to call a serious burn victim to task over such an infraction. He checked his reflection in the grimy mirror in the restroom as the loudspeaker announced the arrival of the Leningrad train. *Not bad.* He undid his imitation Rolex and placed it in an inside pocket—that was not the sort of thing a private soldier would be wearing. With luck, at this hour he would be undisturbed all the way to Leningrad. If not, well, he seemed to remember from his youth that he had been able to turn on an almost unintelligible Estonian accent when required.

He was not sure if it was his imagination but there seemed to be considerably more militia in the station when he exited the restroom. He was asked to show his documents before boarding the train.

"Palmiste, eh? Estonian? You poor bastard. I thought we were putting the Tajiks and the Kirghiz on the front line down there?"

"Don't get me started on those damned Tajiks, Comrade!"

"Well, at least you won't be going back."

Mels saluted and turned to get on the train, but the other militiaman stopped him.

"Just a minute, Palmiste."

Mels' heart started to pound with adrenaline but the militiaman merely summoned a railroad porter over.

"Hey you! Give this war hero a hand. Show him to his seat!"

The first class compartment had space for four people. The remaining three passengers were already aboard and had pulled out the beds which converted the carriage to a sleeping car. Mels was helped into the lower bunk and slept all the way to Leningrad.

As he descended the long, steep escalator from the main line station into the Metro, Mels reasoned that he had only two, temporary, advantages. The KGB would not suspect anything amiss until he failed to show up at the National restaurant that night and he was fairly sure that—unless Palmiste did something stupid enough to attract their notice—they would not be looking for him in Leningrad dressed as a private. He looked behind him and smiled. The statistics were on his side. There were probably a hundred people using the escalator, of which he counted over two dozen in uniform. The other advantage he had was less tangible; total surprise was on his side. No one had ever done what he was about to attempt. At least no one had ever done so *and* lived to tell the tale.

He needed to contact both his daughter and Tanya. It was important that they both came with him where he was going, otherwise he knew the KGB would use them as hostages. He took the Metro to Vasilyevskiy Island and walked to the Institute of Applied Mathematics where he asked to speak with Natasha.

"She's not in today, soldier. It's Sunday. This isn't about her brother, is it?"

"Her brother?"

"Vassily, the soldier. I used to play soccer with him before he got called up. They haven't heard from him for a month. Her mother's frantic."

"Look, I really shouldn't talk to you about it. Do you have her telephone number?"

"Well, I, . . . OK, but he's not hurt, right? I mean, not badly?"

"Vasya's fine. But I would like to talk with Natasha."

As a "war hero," Mels was even allowed the use of the Institute's phone to call Natasha, and—through her—to telephone Luba's friend, Yulia. They arranged to meet in the Smolensk cemetery in an hour. Then he called Tanya's number. A male voice answered.

"Tanya? She's not here? Who is this?"

"A friend."

"Sasha, maybe? Where are you Sasha? Is Heather with you?"

He put the phone down and left immediately by a back exit.

Mels sat in a pew reserved for war invalids inside the Orthodox church at the cemetery. The church was filled with the acrid smell of incense. Devout believers—old women mostly—kissed the walls of the chapel of Saint Kseniya while the dirge-like service progressed. Yulia entered the church but did not recognize him. At first he barely recognized her. Her freckled face seemed to have aged seventeen years in as many days.

Yulia's amateurish attempts to cross herself attracted the ire of a bearded priest who berated her ignorance and lack of respect until Mels intervened. She recognized his voice immediately and followed him into the churchyard grounds.

"Is that real? Did they do something to your face?"

"No. And it's damned itchy, too. So is this uniform. I don't know how they can bear to wear them in Afghanistan."

"Well, it gets cold at night down there. It's mountainous desert."

"Smart girl. Like my daughter. That's whom I want to talk to you about."

"Oh, Mels L'vovitch. I thought you knew. They took her away."

"Took her away?! Where to?!"

"I don't know. The Big House, I think. It was horrible, apparently. I wasn't there but your father told me. He got a telephone call from someone—a woman—who said you were OK. Then the KGB arrived with a young Uzbek woman. She was the one that made the call."

"Tanya!"

"Oh, Mels L'vovitch. I'm really sorry."

"What happened?"

"They wanted to know where you were. I think they knew it wasn't worthwhile trying to beat it out of your father; he's a tough old bird. But his Achilles heel was right in front of him—your daughter."

"If they laid a finger on her—"

"No! That's the whole point. According to Lev Davidovitch, some high-ranking person arrived and told them he needed her for something else. He instructed them to take her 'somewhere safe.' He told them to use the Uzbek girl, instead. But then she apparently said something strange to him. Something about 'remembering what he told her.'"

"'Remembering what he told her'?"

"Yes. I think your father said it was 'dead people tell no tales.' Then she, she *killed* herself, Mels. She threw herself out of the window. I'm so sorry, Mels L'vovitch, I know this must be painful. Especially because, well, you know. Luba told me about your mother."

Mels said nothing. A deep emptiness had opened up inside him.

"Mels? Mels L'vovitch? Say something! I can't tell what you're feeling behind those bandages."

"Hmm?"

"There's something else. The last thing she said before she reached the window. It was a girl's name. An English name. I don't remember what it was, you'll have to ask your father."

"'Heather'?"

"Yes, that's right, 'Heather Yale.'"

"It's 'Heather Ale.' It's not a girl's name. It's a poem."

The emptiness inside him was filling rapidly with the desire for revenge.

"My father; is he OK?"

"Well, not really. I think they beat him pretty badly, though he wouldn't tell me."

"That's typical. Well, Yulia, you've done all you can do. I'm going to have to deal with this on my own from now on so I may not see you again. I'm afraid I won't be able to help you with your Math."

Yulia's chin trembled. Her freckled face was on the verge of tears.

"Be careful, Mels L'vovitch."

He gave her a hug.

"When have I been anything else?"

Mels took a bus past his father's apartment building to gauge the level of security before he decided to risk it on foot. The KGB had left only one guard outside. He saw them changing shifts from the bus. The new guard glanced disinterestedly at Palmiste's military identification papers and waved him past without asking any questions.

The front door lock had been removed from his father's apartment. Knowing it would be useless to knock because of his father's deafness, Mels pushed it open and stepped cautiously in.

He assumed that the apartment itself would be bugged but he was unprepared for the other changes that had taken place there. The KGB had wrecked the place with the methodical viciousness of a hyperactive mink. Photos and pictures were torn, the glass lampshade that hung from the ceiling had been smashed and the carpet that had once served as a wall covering had been thrown on the floor and smelled of urine. There was so much debris on the floor that his feet felt like icebreakers pushing their way through ice floes as he walked towards his father's small bedroom.

His father lay on the bed, sleeping. He looked every one of his sixty years. Mels tried to recall when he had ever seen his father asleep. The man was always up before him and always in bed after. He leaned over and looked at his father's face. There were yellowing bruises around the temples and a scabbed-over cut above his lip. He opened his eyes and looked into Mels.' Despite the bandages, his expression immediately showed he recognized his son. He beckoned him to come closer and whispered.

"I knew you'd come back."

He put his finger over his lips and gestured to the small bedside table on which lay a few scraps of paper and a pencil. Mels handed them to him. He wrote in a shaky hand:

"Luba—Big House. Uzbek girl dead. Bandages?"

Mels took the pencil from him and added:

"Disguise. Know about Luba and Tanya. Going to Big House. You OK?"

"Fine. Me too."

"No! Dangerous."

The elder Katz swung his legs out of bed and stood with some difficulty. He gestured to Mels to help him move the iron bedframe then tapped on the wooden tiled floor methodically with an iron nail. He gestured to Mels by cupping his hand around one ear. Mels understood immediately and pointed to the tile that gave a hollow, ringing sound. Lev Katz pressed down on one end of the tile and a small hinge lifted up the other. He reached in and pulled out an oilcloth-wrapped package that he handed to Mels.

Mels knew from the weight what it was before he even unwrapped it though he was surprised by its make. It was a German officer's nine-millimeter Luger pistol and a full clip of ammunition. His father promptly inserted into the clip into the grip then tucked the gun into his belt. He then reached back under the floorboard and pulled out another surprise—a dagger in a leather sheath that he strapped to his shin. He pulled the knife from the sheath and showed Mels the swastika and two lightning bolts on the black handle. He spat on the swastika then replaced it in its sheath.

Mels took an envelope and wrote down instructions for his father to follow. His father laughed when he read them, then picked up the telephone and dialed the Big House. Mels listened in as he shouted into the receiver.

"Hello? This is Lev Davidovitch Katz. No, it's useless trying to answer. I can't hear. Look, I'm deaf at the best of times but every time I pick up this damn phone to call someone I can't hear above the noise of your agents talking to each other. You can't even tap someone's line without screwing it up, you bunch of hopeless amateurs. Send someone to fix it!"

Mels nodded to him, raised one thumb, then gestured for him to put the phone down. His father handed him the Luger.

They did not have long to wait. An unmarked van turned into the courtyard within ten minutes. Two technicians got out and chatted to the KGB guard at the entrance before walking up the stairs to the apartment. Lev Katz waited behind the front door until they had both entered, then grabbed the second repairman by the neck and started to choke him. Meanwhile, Mels stuck the pistol in the face of his workmate and signaled him to make no noise. Within ten minutes they had the two of them stripped to their underwear and bound, hand and foot, with telephone cable. Mels unwrapped the bandage from his face and used it to make gags for one of them. He knelt down next to the other one and whispered in his ear.

"Call your buddy from downstairs to come up here. If you try anything funny I'll shoot your dick off!"

He dragged the terrified technician to the open window.

"Pyotor! Come up here a moment, will you? We need a hand."

"It'll cost you a pack of smokes!"

While the agent ascended the stairs, Mels gagged the second repairman. The two of them had little trouble overcoming Pyotor but Mels was disappointed to find that he was unarmed except for a lead-weighted leather blackjack. Lev Katz's expression, however, revealed that he had had recent acquaintanceship with this particular item. Evidently having something of a score to settle, he tied the agent's hands behind his back and placed him face down on the floor, with his knees bent. Then he formed the telephone cord into a noose and placed it around Pyotor's neck with the free end being used to secure his feet so that he would strangle himself if he tried to move his feet. He paused for a moment to admire his handiwork, then looked as though he had suddenly remembered something. He disappeared into the other room and returned with the urine-smelling carpet, which he placed under the agent's face.

As they walked down the stairs in the technician's overalls and caps he turned to his son.

"You know son, you look terrible. That hat makes you look like Lenin. Don't try to say anything—it's useless. I haven't been able to hear anything at all since they roughed me up the night they took away Luba. It's my fault that the girl—Tanya was it?—was killed. She got a message to me but I couldn't hear what she said. I made her stay on the line while I got my hearing aid. It could only have been a few minutes but the KGB must have traced the call in that time. She didn't say where you were, just that you were safe. They brought her here the next day. She looked in a bad way though I guess she hadn't talked. She must have known she'd break though. That's why. . . ."

His voice cracked. Mels reached across and touched his arm.

"Mels, the woman I loved threw herself out of that window and now the woman you loved, too. Now it's time. Time to fight back."

The guard at number four, Kalyaev Prospekt looked at the van's license plate then buzzed them through the security gate into a large underground garage. They left the vehicle near a pedestrian entrance and held the magnetic cards they had removed from the telephone technicians against a metal detector. The pedestrian entrance opened and they found themselves inside the Big House, KGB's Leningrad Headquarters.

Chapter 17

As luck would have it, it appeared that Sunday morning in the Big House was much like any other day of the week. The level at which they entered looked like a typical overstaffed government office. The atmosphere was not at all what Mels had expected. Far from being menacing, there was an ambience of bureaucratic sloth. Indeed, apart from its immense size—the size of a city block—the Big House bore a striking resemblance to his own Institute. The corridors were full of people loitering in doorways and chatting to the occupants. In Mels' Institute it was *de rigeur* to hold several sheets of fan-folded, green-and-white striped computer printout as cover for one's idleness. No one was fooled but if challenged one could always pretend to be discussing the contents. Here, Mels noticed, most held manila folders. It was strange to equate the prosaic use to which the folders were being put with their contents; the private lives and opinions of Soviet citizens.

They walked to the main bank of elevators in the lobby where Mels had expected to find an office directory. There being none, he pressed the button to summon the elevator and try his luck unassisted. With the presence of so many KGB employees, Mels had hoped that their own presence would seem less anomalous and therefore less subject to challenge by bored security personnel but a uniformed guard at the main entrance immediately summoned him.

"What do you think you're doing? You think you're going in there wearing overalls? Service elevator!"

Heart beating fast, it was all Mels could do not to laugh out loud. *So the Committee for State Security has a dress code!*

They arrived at the service elevator at the same time as a *babushka* pushing a cart laden with a samovar, small silver tea trays, napkins, cups, saucers, and an assortment of pastries (*Follow the napkins*, thought Mels). There were ten floors, three below ground and seven above. Unsurprisingly, the woman pressed the button for the top floor. There were uniformed guards by the elevators on each floor but they did little but glance at people's identification badges as they exited. On the top floor the *babushka* went on ahead, delivering trays of tea to each office.

There were no names on the office doors. Anticipating this, Mels' plan had been to check out only those offices to which the hallway carpets lead. Unfortunately, it appeared that *everyone* on the seventh floor was of sufficient rank to merit a contiguous carpet. He decided that their best bet would be to split their forces. His father should check out one side of the corridor while he did the other. This was too difficult to mime but he found nothing in his overalls on which he could write to explain the plan to his father. The sound of a faucet running indicated that they were standing outside a restroom. Given the rank of the facility's users, he reasoned paper was probably available within. Washing his hands at the washbasin was a tall man in civilian clothes. There was a strange scent in the room—at once musky and cabbagey—that touched off some memory in Mels. He gazed at the man—who in turn was looking at Mels' reflection in the mirror—then pulled the Luger from his pocket and held it to the man's head.

"General 'Asparagus,' I presume?"

The man replied in the well-modulated undertone of someone who never had to raise his voice to get people to listen.

"Mels Katz. And who is that with you, your father? I was expecting to see you later today but under different circumstances. You've saved me a trip to Moscow."

"Always glad to assist our security services. Now let's go to your office, shall we? I will have this pistol in my pocket. Keep your hands where I can see them. If you try any funny business I will willingly kill you."

They walked slowly to General Annichkov's office. He punched the combination into the lock and swung open the thick door. Inside the walls were covered in acoustic padding. The window faced into the courtyard and appeared to be as thick as the door. Surprisingly, there was no Brezhnev portrait but KGB Chairman Andropov shared wall space with Marx and Lenin.

The room was completely silent, without even the ticking of a clock.

"Zero reverberation. And your office looks inward. No view of the Neva for you, then?"

"One forgets that you're a physicist, Mels. You're right. We found some of our friends at the American Consulate had a habit of getting flat tires on the opposite bank of the river and training some sort of laser device—"

"An interferometer."

"Quite. Well, whatever it's called, we don't like our conversations being recorded so we moved to this side of the building. The other side now has computers. We also have a radio tuned to Radio Moscow's English language channel. It's only fair. Everyone else seems to listen to the propaganda broadcast by the Voice of America, why shouldn't the CIA listen to Radio Moscow?"

The general punctuated his speech with a humorless smile that did not quite reach his eyes. Behind him, at the end of the room, there was a door that led into another office. Mels signaled to his father to watch Annichkov while he checked it out. Lev Katz removed the SS dagger and held it to the general's throat.

The door was only half-open before Luba flew out and threw her arms around Mels.

"Daddy! And Grandpa!"

He handed the gun to his father.

"Luba, darling! You look pale. Have they hurt you?"

"No, daddy. They took me to mother's apartment. It was really weird. They tried to drug me but I spat it out and then some fat old man tried to, to *molest* me. No, don't worry. Once I started to resist he got frightened and seemed to lose interest. We were in a room that looked like a dungeon so I tied him up with a chain until he started to get really red in the face. Then another one came in but I kicked him in the, you know, between his legs. He actually started crying!"

She pointed at Annichkov.

"It turned out this pig had been watching the whole thing on a television screen and came in and dragged me out before I could really hurt anybody. He slapped my face then told me that I was a smart girl and if I cooperated with them then one day I would end up running their operation! He said I wouldn't have to go back to school and I'd get money for make-up clothes and could go to as many Aquarium concerts as I wanted—can you imagine! Like I was some stupid kid! So when mother came back I told her she was being replaced because she was too old. *She was so mad*! She told me I had ideas above my station and that there was no way she was going to teach me the tricks of the trade so I was locked up in a closet the next time the clients came round.

I think they must have complained to Asparagus because he showed up late that night. She really flew off the handle. It was great! He had to call his bodyguard to pull her off him! After that they took us both away and put us in some prison cell. Only I refused to be in the same cell with her. That was over a week ago, I think. I'm not sure because there were no windows. What day is it?"

"It's Sunday, sweetheart. Sunday the twentieth."

"Wow! Have I missed the swimming heats at the Olympics? The worse thing is that they wouldn't give me a newspaper. All they had to read were little kids' books. And they wouldn't let me exercise. Plus at night the male guards would peer through the cell bars and whistle at me. I told them to go fuck themselves. Oh, sorry, daddy. I know you don't like to hear me swear but you should hear the remarks they make when the female warden isn't around. They're like a bunch of sex-starved animals!"

Mels turned to Annichkov.

"You're going to pay for this."

Annichkov kept his silence. Luba continued her tale.

"And this morning I was brought up here. They put me in that room next-door and said I was going to Moscow today and I'd see you tonight. Asparagus is taking your files with him. I saw him take a bunch of manila folders out of a filing cabinet in there and put them in that document case that's by his desk."

Mels picked up the document case and handed the gun to his father. Lev Katz commanded the general to strip down his underclothes then crouch on the floor with his hands on his head. Unable to follow the conversation between his son and daughter he trained both the Luger and his full attention on Annichkov.

Mels' name was on two of the folders. The first folder contained a motley collection of surveillance reports, personal letters long since "lost," a letter from Ignatiev that discussed his work for the Institute and commentaries (generally favorable) by some of his colleagues. All had margin notes ("PERFECT," "EXPENDABLE," "APPROVED") in the small, neat capitals that Mels recognized from Zhanna's apartment. The second folder contained photos—including some of him with former girlfriends (*my god, I hope Luba hasn't seen these* . . .)—cassette tapes, two Intourist plastic bags (in one of which he counted four thousand two hundred rubles in large bills), plus the passports and tickets that Ignatiev had shown him in his office.

"That will save us some time. I thought we'd have to stop at the Institute. Luba, find the number of Aeroflot and call and confirm our flight reservations for today."

"What about Grandpa?"

"Grandpa will come later, dear. Don't worry."

While Luba called the airline and reminded them that the tickets had been booked by the Committee of State Security and therefore took precedence over anyone else who had subsequently been given seats on the aircraft, Mels looked through the other files. The thickest was that of Galina Brezhneva's husband, Yuri Churbanov, which had a "Top Secret" stamp on the cover. Inside were details of various business dealings that were of no interest to Mels. He looked in Zhanna's file. There were a set of keys (apartment, car, etc.), transcripts of telephone conversations, an old KGB photo I.D., some medical records, and a thick folder of pornographic photographs of her with personalities ranging from cosmonauts to Politburo members.

"Now this I don't understand, Asparagus. You're so intent on 'tripping the ballerina.' But what about these people. And what exactly did she do that made all this necessary? And what *was* that charade with Galina Brezhneva about?"

A brief cloud darkened Annichkov's otherwise impassive expression, which was quickly replaced by his creepy smile.

"You don't seriously think I'm going to tell you that, do you? Speaking of Zhanna, thank you for returning the five thousand rubles of State property. Hamlet was kind enough to mention that you'd left it with her. I guess she must have 'forgotten' about it, though once we jogged her memory she did try to blame you for the missing eight hundred rubles. Classical Zhanna. I'll miss her. It's a shame the fact that the money had been returned didn't make it into Timor's trial. He, by the way, was the person who told us about Tanya. I think he actually believed it was going to get him a lighter sentence. Rather naïve, that boy. Still, I imagine he'll be able to continue to trade on his good looks where he's going—for the first few years, at least. Somewhat touchingly, your American friend tried to intervene on his behalf before he was repatriated. No, don't look like that. It was nothing to do with us. Logan appears to have contracted some kind of pulmonary complaint. The Baltic air was too much for him."

"So Timor ratted on Tanya?"

"Oh, I wouldn't put it like that, Katz. She's been under surveillance for years. Though I confess we have yet to work out how you managed to telephone her without our being able to trace your call. In fact, there are several other questions that puzzle me about your whereabouts during the last three weeks. If I didn't know whom you were, Katz, I'd assume you had a sophisticated network of contacts. No doubt you'll tell us all this during your interrogation."

"I think you're getting ahead of yourself, Asparagus. I don't see you being in a position to interrogate anyone at the moment. Quite the reverse. And my father told me he was fairly adept at getting even tough, blond storm-troopers to tell everything they knew."

Annichkov's soft-spoken voice took on a harder edge.

"You wouldn't dare!"

"Wouldn't I? Firstly you're going to tell me about Zhanna. . . ."

"You pathetic fool! Frankly, you have quite an ego, Katz. You really think the KGB cares about framing a geophysicist and his slut of an ex-wife? Yes, Zhanna *is* at the end of her usefulness to us. She likes being the center of attention. She doesn't realize that her utility was dependent on her discretion. It was stupid of me to leave a uniform at Gorokhovskaya Street. It was too much of a temptation for her. I frequently *do* use doubles, but not to be seen in public with whores like her."

"So where is she now?"

"She's been assigned other duties. Not far from here, actually. And, Luba, you're right. Some of our young cadres *are* sex-starved animals."

"OK, so you wanted to punish Zhanna. *That* was why Tanya had to die? And Hamlet was working for you all along?"

Annichkov looked thoughtful for a moment.

"One of my predecessors once said that 'Russia has need of Armenia but—'"

" 'But it has no need of Armenians.' I've heard that before. From Hamlet actually."

"Well, I think that overstates the case. They tend to be too smart to work as field agents; always trying to pull some unauthorized scam like black marketeering when they are supposed to sit there and do nothing except watch people. But Hamlet actually helped us a lot, as soon as he realized he had no choice. He seemed quite fond of you, Katz, but once he saw it from a business perspective he realized you were just another commodity he could sell.

Ironic, really; your dancer friend didn't need to die at all. Timor's tip made us listen to our tapes of Tanya's incoming calls (you'd be astonished at how many clues the idiots that monitor the tapes actually miss) but we were genuinely puzzled about 'Malibu' and 'Detroit.' We ran them through our computers for a day assuming it was some sophisticated code! And of course, we tried to persuade Tanya to tell us. Quite a strong personality that girl. I confess I underestimated her.

For a while there, we wondered where you'd disappeared to after you left Mehri's apartment in Baku. Then another young friend of yours, a shepherd boy called Kasoum, managed to escape from a room in *Icheri Shekher* and your fate was sealed, Comrade Katz. Once the blood bond was broken, the shepherds no longer had any reason not to kill Hamlet. Fortunately, they decided the one thing that they preferred to killing him was selling him to us and letting us deal with him.

We haven't found your dandy friend Ardzinba, yet. But we will. And this 'Heather Yale.' And, of course, your contact in Leningrad. They will all sell you out, Mels, believe me. You don't know the Russian people like I do. This isn't Poland. You intellectuals think people crave freedom but you can't free the Russian people from themselves. They've always supported tyrannical rulers. Napoleon promised to free the serfs in Poland and they rallied to his side. When he came to Russia he found the same serfs opposing him."

"So you followed me all the way from Sukhumi?"

"Yes. Well, with a little help from our colleague from the Stasi."

"So why me?"

"Why you? Why *not* you? You think you're someone special? The KGB protects the Soviet State from enemies, without and within. In this case, those enemies are within. Oh, I may as well tell you since I can assure you that you are not leaving this building. Someone chose you, Mels Katz, to perform a task. Someone at the very highest level. It was a simple task. You were asked to present a paper. We even offered to reward you, substantially. Six months in Vietnam with your Vietnamese friends and you'd be driving a car. But because of your stupid obstinacy, two people so far have died. One was one of our better agents. Major Radchenko had close to a hundred percent success ratio in getting confessions. And of course, there was that little girlfriend of yours. Did you know she was Jewish, by the way? You *did*! I can tell by your eyes. You will not bear up well in interrogation, Katz."

"But I didn't present the paper."

"No. But you handed the diamonds to Galina Brezhneva. Like giving liquor to an alcoholic. And you told them they were genuine and you promised her more. And that, Katz, is *exactly* what you were supposed to do."

"So *she's* the ballerina?"

"No, you fool! Her father—*Leonid* Brezhnev—is the ballerina. Didn't you know that? That's his old nickname in the Politburo. Because of his ability to switch positions depending on who was in power. Only now the old buffoon is senile and there are more capable contenders for the position."

Now it was Annichkov's eyes' turn to betray him. They inadvertently traveled to the portrait of Andropov.

"Andropov? *He's* trying to depose Brezhnev?"

"Someone has to protect the interest of the Soviet State! Brezhnev is an embarrassment. He has to have someone button his flies for him. Half the time he's too sick to make it to meetings. He wasn't even in the Kremlin when they decided to invade Afghanistan! And when Brezhnev goes, so goes his whole corrupt family—his fat Jewish wife, his drunkard brother whom they so aptly call 'Dog Shit', and his crooked son and daughter. It's a den of thieves! Yuri Churbanov has been stealing from the Soviet State for years and he's the deputy head of the militia!"

"So you replace one crook with another. So what? I don't see what this has to do with me."

"You don't see what it has to do with you?! You don't know a 'sheep's bleat,' do you, Katz? Why did you go to Zhanna's apartment?"

"What? I was running away from your goons. And I, er, I had something I needed for Luba."

"Cotton wool."

"Yes. Cotton wool. I suppose Zhanna told you that."

"Eventually. And why do you suppose there is no cotton? Because Churbanov has been reporting non-existent cotton harvests from Uzbekistan for years. Every year another 'record harvest' and they never even planted anything. He's taken a million rubles in bribes and he's had protection from Schelokov, his boss, who just happens to be the husband of Galina Brezhneva's best friend, Svetlana Schelokova."

"So why diamonds? And why pretend they're synthetic?"

"Trust me, since that bitch was a little girl the only things she cared about were diamonds and the circus. Right now she's on top of the high wire but one day soon she's going to take a fall. And when she goes the whole family will come tumbling down. There's no safety net in real life, Mels. You fall and you hit the sawdust. She thinks those diamonds came from some science experiment but—believe me—the real owner of those gems is looking for them right now. And trafficking in stolen jewels is a serious offence—as well as being one ordinary Russians are more likely to relate to than economic crimes against the State. But you don't need to know about that. . . ."

"You're right. *I* don't need to know about that. But other people do, and they will."

He produced the cigarette lighter-tape recorder from his pocket and played it back.

"Senile or not, Brezhnev is still leader of this country, not Andropov. And Schelokov and Churbanov will be very pleased to hear your opinion of them, General Annichkov. Whether they get the chance depends on you. My father will wait in your office until that plane takes off for Saigon. You would not dare shoot down a passenger jet full of innocent people."

Annichkov smiled enigmatically.

"When we get where we're going, you'll send my father to meet us. If anything happens to him, that tape gets published. For as long as we stay alive that tape stays secret. You know I have nothing to gain by giving that to the BBC or the New York Times if it means a KGB hit squad pursuing us."

"A clever plan, Katz, but one that requires the cooperation of the Vietnamese authorities. You are aware, I presume, that the Americans have left 'Saigon' and that it is now called Ho Chi Minh City?"

"Thanks for the information, General. Let me worry about that. All you need to do is call your goons between here and Pulkovo and tell them that we are to be allowed to get to the airport unmolested. I will leave instructions for my father so he isn't tempted to kill you while we're away. Luba, hand him the phone while I write a note for Grandpa. Then we'll tie him up with the cable I brought."

"Very well, Katz. It seems you have won this round. Inform your father I shall need to remove my reading glasses from my breast pocket."

Mels picked up a pad from Annichkov's desk and removed a pen from the pocket of his overalls. He was pulling the top off with his teeth when he heard his daughter scream for her grandfather, followed by a dull "pop." He turned back to Annichkov to see him holding the palm-sized gun he had last seen in Zhanna's apartment. He was now aiming it at Luba's head. Lev Katz lay slumped on the floor in a spreading pattern of blood.

"First my uniform, then my carpet. I thought 'dirty Jew' was just an expression!"

"I'm sorry, daddy! He pulled it from the pocket of his jacket when I blocked Grandpa's view. He didn't hear me warn him."

"Hands in the air, Katz! Now come over here. You're going to tie up your daughter with that cable you thoughtfully brought along while I summon my bodyguard. A handy hint, Katz; always keep your eye on your opponent."

With the pen still in his mouth, Mels walked slowly towards him. Annichkov's eyes followed Mels' hands as he cautiously unhooked the telephone cable from his work-belt. Mels then took a quick intake of breath and blew through the ballpoint pen in his mouth. A cloud of *basturma* powder enveloped Annichkov's face. He fired, wildly but Luba's young reflexes were too quick for him. After three shots the popping noise had stopped. By that time, Mels had recovered the Luger pistol from his father's lifeless hand and had it pointed at the blinded Annichkov.

"Luba, get that jug of water from the table and throw it over the general, will you? I don't want him to miss this,"

She poured the water over Annichkov's face. Coughing and spluttering, his *sang-froid* manner had gone and he seemed for the first time to experience fear.

"Daddy that was amazing! How did you do that?"

"A little trick an old friend of mine taught me. The pen is indeed mightier than the sword! Actually I'd forgotten about it until I tasted the *basturma* spices in my mouth."

"Katz, don't be hasty! You know you'll never get out of here— I'm you're only hope! We can strike a deal. Turn in your network. Tell us who Heather Yale is. Don't be a fool; they'd sell *you* out in a heartbeat! You'll go free. I give you my word! At least let me call my men and make sure you get to the airport safely—"

"No more tricks, Asparagus. I've never killed anyone before. Radchenko was an accident. I always thought I'd have a hard time in a war because of what I've been told is my 'moralizing' nature. But actually I have no compunction about this whatsoever. . . ."

He fired the Luger twice into Annichkov's head.

"I'm sorry you had to see that, Luba. Now, let's go! Take the keys and the money from your mother's file. Clip her I.D. to your blouse. I'll take Asparagus' clothes and change on the way. Do you think you can drive while I do that?"

"We'll see. If I can drive a truck I suppose I can drive a Zhiguli."

It took twenty anxious minutes to find Zhanna's car in the capacious parking lot. Mels drove the first few kilometers from the Big House then handed over to his daughter while he rid himself of his telephone repairman uniform. The International Airport was a couple of kilometers beyond the domestic one. They passed several knots of traffic policemen but were waved on without incident. Just as they reached Pulkovo, however, Luba turned to her father.

"Daddy, there's a flashing blue light in the mirror! What should I do?"

Chapter 18

Mels watched the fat traffic policeman in the side mirror. He had a strange feeling of *déjà vu* as the figure sauntered towards them. The militiaman was alone, which was encouraging. It was less profitable to extort money from people if they had to share it so a lone policeman might simply be trolling for bribes. For all that, Mels was taking no chances. The gun was at his side and his finger was on the trigger. If worse came to worse, the airport traffic was light on a Sunday and there would be few witnesses. The departure terminal was ten minutes away, and then there were less than two hours to take-off. *We stand as good a chance of getting away with two murders as with one.*

The policeman walked over to the driver's side. Luba wound down her window.

"Going a little fast there, young lady. And you just strayed into the 'Zil' lane. That's reserved for officials. You're not an official, are you?"

There was an amused sneer to his voice that quickly disappeared as he put his head in the window.

"Oh, I beg your pardon, Professor, er, Suslov is it? Look, I was just doing my job. There's no reason to take offense."

The policeman hurried back to his car and drove off. Mels released his grip on the trigger of the Luger.

"What was that about, daddy?"

"Attitude, Luba. Sometimes it's more powerful than these things."

He placed the Luger inside Annichkov's jacket. When they arrived at the airport, he walked into the stalls in the first men's room they passed, stood on the commode and dropped it in the cistern.

After Luba's telephone conversation earlier, there was no problem with their tickets. In fact, Aeroflot had upgraded them to First Class. But to get to the First Class lounge, they first had to negotiate the last two hurdles of the Soviet Security apparatus—Customs and Immigration.

The Russian belief that anything worthwhile in life requires waiting in line was much in evidence at the next stop. Despite their enhanced status and the fact that they had no luggage, they were forced to join a long queue of their fellow passengers whose bags were being scrutinized. Each passenger was required to open every bag to reveal what they were smuggling out of the Soviet Union. For some reason, pencils seemed to be a favorite commodity as well as Soviet champagne and Bulgarian cigarettes. The pencils were all confiscated though the latter items were allowed through (*we don't want the Vietnamese to think we can write, too*, thought Mels).

After Customs came Immigration Control. There was a window through which one pushed one's passport and ticket. Non-believer though he was, Mels muttered the only Hebrew phrase he knew (*Baruch ata adonai eloheinu . . .*) while the unsmiling eyes of an Immigration officer stared back. Although it was obviously a brand new passport, the Immigration officer went through page by page from the back cover to the front. When he reached the page with Mels' name, he checked it against a mimeographed sheet he had in front of him. As Mels had dreaded, he found a match and reached out to the telephone on his desk. To Mels' surprise, Luba reached out and stilled the man's hand.

"Is there a problem, here?"

She leaned over so that Zhanna's laminated KGB photographic identification card swung inches from the man's face. His mouth froze open for a few moments while he wrestled with a nagging thought.

"This man is on 'your' list, Comrade."

"Yes, I know."

"I'm supposed to inform someone if he tries to leave the country."

"Well, I think you might assume we know that, Comrade."

"But, Comrade, I'm not supposed to stamp his passport—"

"Quite. Allow me."

She calmly reached across and stamped Mels' passport, then for good measure stamped her own, taking care not to show the name in her own passport to the surprised Immigration Officer.

"Thank you, Comrade."

"You're welcome, Comrade."

Luba removed the I.D. as they entered the First Class Departure Lounge.

"You know Luba, your mother was wrong about many things but she was right to warn me about the injections they gave you at school."

Luba looked puzzled but let it pass; there were other things in the First Class Lounge to fascinate her. Suddenly child-like again, she piled her plate with caviar sandwiches and Pushkin's Tales chocolates—tastes of the Soviet Union that she had never experienced until now, her moment of departure.

A separate bus took the First Class passengers to the plane and they buckled themselves in for take-off. Most of the other occupants of the cabin seemed to be Indians, senior military officers by their appearance, who were returning from training in the Soviet Union.

"Daddy, is it OK to talk here?"

Luba had waited until they were airborne to ask.

"I think so, sweetie."

"What are we going to do in Ho Chi Minh City? They're Communists there. Won't they send us back when they find Asparagus' body?"

"We're not going to Ho Chi Minh City. And, hopefully, they won't find Asparagus for a while. I changed the combination on his office door when we left. What worries me more is Grandpa's place. We left three of them tied up there and there's no lock on the door. It's six hours to New Delhi (the plane holds over there for an hour and a half before it continues to Ho Chi Minh City). That's where we're going to apply for political asylum. Your Grandpa said the guards at the apartment change every twelve hours."

"That's right. And they always checked in on us at least once during that time. That means they could notice his absence anytime from 9pm tonight to 9am tomorrow."

"But if they find Pyotor—"

"Pyotor? *That* piece of shit! Oh sorry, daddy."

"*If* they find Pyotor missing at the start of the shift they'll most likely check tonight. Plus they're going to start getting suspicious when I don't show up in Moscow. But that would be after the plane takes off for Ho Chi Minh City. We'll be in the American Embassy in New Delhi by then!"

Luba squeezed his hand.

"That gives me just five more hours to eat those little caviar sandwiches."

"Don't eat too many, Lubashka! There will be plenty to eat on this flight. I'm going to the bathroom to wash up."

Mels stood outside the First Class bathroom in the company of two turbaned Indians with curling white moustaches and beards who were furiously puffing on *bidi* cigarettes. Rather than wait there and inhale the strong-smelling smoke, he walked through the adjoining cabin to the next bank of toilets. To his delight he found Cuong, one of the Vietnamese who had been training at the Geophysical Institute, waiting there.

"Mels Katz! You not dead?"

Cuong's Russian was rudimentary at best but he had always been a favorite of Mels.

"No, Cuong. *Not* dead!"

"That good, Mels. You always our friend. You not like the other *nguoi Lien Xo*, that is Soviet people. You the only one who eat with us."

"Thank you Cuong. To be honest, I had forgotten you guys were leaving today. Is everyone on the plane?"

"Yes, everyone here. Even Nguyen."

"Which Nguyen? Aren't there two?"

"Three! This Nguyen helicopter pilot. He my friend. He fly us out to seismic boat, next week. He learn to fly big gunships in Russia. He say waste of time. What for he learn big gunships? He no go to Afghanistan. And Russian helicopters not good like Hueys."

Cuong looked suddenly embarrassed. Mels thought it would be wise to change the subject.

"So the boat has already left port?"

"It leave Vung Tau four days ago. Trials with new geophone cable in deep water."

"Oh, the calibration. For the 'signature deconvolution'?"

"That right. Just like you taught us. Then survey start next week."

"But you were supposed to *see* the testing. That was part of the training."

Cuong laughed.

"Oh, Mels. There no Vietnamese on board now!"

"Why?"

Cuong lowered his voice.

"Because boat go near Gulf of Thailand. They no let us go there without soldiers on board. Too tempting. . . ."

He grinned.

Just then there was an announcement that food was about to be served. The intercom was garbled and the flight attendant making the announcement spoke very fast. It was clear that Cuong had not understood.

"She says that—"

But Cuong was listening to the message being repeated in English. Mels switched to English.

"You understand English?"

Like Hamlet's, Cuong's English was near perfect, and American-accented.

"I sure do. Listen, Mels, keep it to yourself, huh? It's not like those assholes I travel with don't know but there are some things it's best to be discreet about. I got sent for 'Political Re-education' with Nguyen when the Americans left and was lucky to get out. My dad didn't make it."

"What did your father do?"

"He was a doctor. He worked in an American clinic. To 're-educate' him, they put him to work carrying sacks of rice. He couldn't do it. Maybe it's just as well. His assistant was released this year and now he's a *cyclo* operator—that's a bicycle rickshaw—in Saigon."

"Marxist-Leninism in action."

"That's right! I didn't realize you felt the same way, Mels."

"What about the rest of your family?"

"The rest of my family are in Orange County, California."

"But they let you travel?!"

"Are you kidding? To Russia? Am I going to defect there?"

"Well what about India?"

Cuong looked at Mels with pity in his eyes.

"Oh, Mels, you didn't really think you were going to skip at New Delhi, did you? The Indians are somewhere between the Finns and the Cubans. So long as the Russians give them Mig fighters, they'll give them back their defectors. I doubt if they'll even allow us off the plane. If they do, you'll find that transit passengers are put in a sealed lounge until the flight for Saigon—I mean Ho Chi Minh City—takes off."

As so often before, when the situation demanded it, a plan of sorts came to Mels.

"How well do you know Nguyen?"

He returned to his seat to find his daughter had ordered one of each menu item and was gorging on liver pate and eggs benedict.

"You're going to be sick, Luba."

"But daddy, I've eaten nothing but prison food for days. And they told me they're making *blini*!"

"Aeroflot *blini*? *That* sounds delicious! Please don't eat too much, sweetheart. I'm going to need you to be alert in the next twelve hours—there's been a change of plan."

The flight to New Delhi was uneventful. Mels left his seat three times to continue his conversation with Cuong and their new accomplice, Nguyen. After much soul-searching they agreed that Mels' original plan would not work. Nguyen was sure there would be a Huey at the airport that he could talk his way into, but the range of the helicopter—even fully fueled—was insufficient to reach safe haven in Thailand. Landing in Cambodia and trying to make it on foot to the border was out of the question. There was still a war going on between the Vietnamese-backed government and the Khmer Rouge. If they fell into the hands of either party they would undoubtedly be killed.

Their only hope was to fly out to the Russian-crewed seismic boat and try to persuade the crew to refuel them. They still would not have the range to get to the mainland but Nguyen and Cuong seemed convinced that there was some sort of barge maintained by an American oil company exploring for natural gas in the Gulf of Thailand which was used as a transit point for refugees. Mels had his doubts about this—he knew too much about the workings of large corporations to believe in corporate altruism—but the Vietnamese insisted.

"They have no choice, Mels. The idea is to keep the refugees from swarming aboard the production platforms. Listen, we worked for the Americans—half the things they do seem to make no sense! That's because it's all aimed at 'Public Opinion.'"

"It's true, Mels. You ask the *Viet Nam Cong San* who won the Tet offensive and they'll tell you the Americans did. But the Americans we worked for thought *they'd* lost—just because of the bad publicity it generated!"

"So saving Vietnamese refugees from Thai pirates is 'good publicity' for this company?"

"That's right. Good for them; good for us."

"Here's the problem. Sometime between when we take off

from Delhi and when we land in Ho Chi Minh City, the KGB could realize my daughter and I escaped. We get there at five-thirty in the morning; that's 1:30am in Leningrad. Optimistically, they won't know we're missing until after noon, Vietnam time. But let's assume the worse. If they're waiting for me at the airport, you guys just walk away. You didn't know I was on the plane and this conversation never happened. But if the coast is clear, is there enough space for you to land a helicopter near the plane?"

"You've got to be joking! That airport was built by the Americans. It's huge! And there are only a few civilian flights a week. Saigon isn't exactly a tourist spot! But it will take me a minimum of twenty minutes to get a helicopter. And I mean *minimum*. Don't worry Mels, I won't need to hijack it or anything like that. They know me over at the hangar, plus the Aeroflot plane will have just landed. I'll tell them I'm taking Russian technicians to the VietSovPetro base at Vung Tau. They're used to it. Ever since the Chinese invaded last year they bend over backwards to please the Russians. Those assholes are always commandeering helicopters because they can't be bothered to drive through the city's bicycle traffic."

"Then I'll stay on the plane as long as I can. I'll get off when I hear the helicopter. That is, if I can hear it from inside the plane"

"You won't mistake the sound of a Huey! In fact, even if there *are* military guys around you'll see half of them freak out when they hear it—too many bad memories!"

"All right. Let's leave it at that. It's still extremely risky. We won't have enough fuel to make it back to Vietnam if we don't find the seismic boat and even if we do find it, we don't know what the reaction of the crew will be. Cuong, my number one plan is still to try to get political asylum in India. Only if that fails will we try this."

But Cuong was right about the impossibility of defecting at New Delhi. They simply never came into contact with anyone to whom they could ask for asylum. The plane parked out on the tarmac. Most of the passengers disembarked at New Delhi into waiting buses. But when Mels and Luba tried to follow, their documents were examined and they were told to get back on the aircraft since they did not have Indian visas. When Mels insisted, he was told he had a choice of destination; either Ho Chi Minh City or Leningrad. As the buses drove off towards the airport terminals, he toyed with the idea of making a run for it but Indian soldiers had formed a cordon around the plane to forestall any embarrassing diplomatic incidents.

With so much on his mind, Mels had not been keeping an eye on Luba. Before they landed in New Delhi, she had been complaining about feeling queasy. But her appetite soon returned after the aircraft took off for Ho Chi Minh City and, with fewer people in the First Class cabin, there was no shortage of new flavors for her to sample. Three hours from Ho Chi Minh City the plane hit a patch of turbulence. Luba promptly withdrew to the bathroom, returning with a face tinged a very pale shade of green and dark circles under her eyes.

"Luba, you silly girl! I told you not to overeat."

Luba said nothing, but tilted her seat as far back as it would go and pulled her Aeroflot blanket over her head. Mels tried the same thing but before he dozed off he had the distinct impression that he was being observed by a member of the cockpit crew.

As they came into land, Mels shook Luba awake. She did not look well.

"Luba, as soon as we land, we both go into the bathroom and lock ourselves in."

"I—I made a mess in there, daddy...."

"Don't worry about that now. Just don't make any noise once we're in there. We're going to try to stay there as long as possible, then we'll make a break for it, OK?"

But it was less than a quarter of an hour after they had locked themselves in that they heard someone with an electric drill removing the door bolt of the First Class bathroom. Within minutes the door was open and they found themselves facing a pith-helmeted Vietnamese soldier toting an AK-47 and an unsmiling Russian in plain clothes, obviously from the embassy's KGB staff.

"Mels Katz, you are under arrest for treason against the Soviet State. Come with me. My Vietnamese Comrade has instructions to kill you if you resist."

Through the open tail exit they could see the lights of a Vietnamese military jeep waiting on the tarmac. The KGB agent brought up the rear as they were marched down the aisle of the now empty aircraft. Luba was passing the last bank of toilets when she suddenly turned to the soldier behind her.

"Please—I feel sick. . . ."

But the soldier misunderstood and assumed she was making a last, feeble attempt to barricade herself on the plane. Holding his Kalashnikov with both hands as a kind of human plow, he tried to push Luba towards the exit.

Escape, however, was not Luba's first priority at that moment and—even with the best will in the world—her reaction to a rifle being sharply pushed into a stomach that had been subjected to twelve hours of Aeroflot food could not have been any different. A stream of vomit projected itself from the girl into the face of the hapless soldier. The soldier was no inexperienced conscript. A ten-year veteran, and holder of the *Dung-Si Diet My* ("Order for heroes who destroy Americans"), he was nevertheless unprepared for this onslaught of Russian biological weaponry. The unthinkable happened. Taken by surprise, he dropped his AK-47 as he instinctively backed away. Mels picked it up and pointed it at the soldier while Luba completed her mission to the aircraft bathroom. Having no desire to match his service revolver against an assault rifle, the KGB agent already had his hands in the air.

"Goodness me. How quickly things change. I'll need your gun, Comrade . . . slowly, now. Hold it by the barrel. Thank you. You speak Vietnamese?"

"A little. We're trying to get them to speak Russian."

"Well tell your friend he's in luck. He can take off that smelly uniform."

"*Coi bo quan phuc cua anh ra!*"

As soon as Luba reappeared from the bathroom she was sent to wash off the vomit from the man's tunic.

"You're not going to make me strip too, are you, Comrade?"

"No. But I need information. Who's out there? How many?"

"The plane is surrounded and there are a dozen agents waiting around the airport, Katz. You won't escape."

"Maybe. What's wrong with your friend?"

The Vietnamese soldier had started to look nervous as if he had heard something. Mels looked out of the plane's windows but saw nothing but darkness. Then he heard it too, the "thwop, thwop, thwop" of a helicopter approaching.

They took the agent and soldier with them to the helicopter, intending to use them as human shields, but it turned out that the KGB operative had been spreading a little disinformation. Far from being "surrounded," the only other security personnel near the aircraft was an unarmed young conscript who had been driving the jeep. He too was taken at gunpoint onto the Huey helicopter.

They flew west with the rising sun behind them over the Mekong delta. As the darkness retreated, a panorama of green rice paddies and rivers the color of *café au lait* opened up beneath them. They flew low to avoid radar. Mels could smell the tropical foliage as they swept by—to him it seemed intoxicating, like the smell of freedom. The feeling was obviously infectious. On hearing that they were heading for Thailand the young conscript, whose name was Minh, immediately begged to come along. They dropped the KGB agent and the old soldier on an uninhabited island off the coast. Cuong recognized the place.

"Boy this place has changed. There used to be little barbecue stands and guys selling coca-cola. We'd take the Americans here for picnics. See how beautiful the beaches are? But these guys won't starve. There are fishing boats around. Not to mention the military base on Dao Phu Quoc that is tracking us right now on their radar."

"Actually I wasn't particularly worried about their welfare. If the military are tracking us, why aren't they following us?"

"Oh, they will. They already radioed to ask who we are. Nguyen has told them we're taking supplies to your seismic boat. They even gave him the location! Don't worry, they'll put two and two together soon enough. But they'll have to get a decision from their bosses in Hanoi before they send any Migs after us and those old men sleep late! Plus they'll probably want to talk with Moscow first."

"And those *even older* men will sleep even later with the time difference!"

"OK. Cuong, you, Minh, and I will get out of the helicopter. Luba, you'll wear the other soldier's uniform and sit in the co-pilot's seat. Put your blonde hair under the helmet and pull the sun visor down. The chances are that some of the crewmembers will recognize me—I've probably trained half of them! I'll tell them on board that I've come on a quick inspection tour with Cuong."

The helicopter was already down to its emergency fuel tank when they spotted the survey vessel. The boat was proceeding forward very slowly as the winch on the back deck was slowly pulling the two-kilometer-long hydrophone cable back on board. As they got close they could see two sailors standing on either side holding baseball bats.

"That's Elmar Shahtahtinsky! So they *did* send him here! But what the fuck—excuse me Luba—is he doing? They'll destroy the hydrophones!"

"Sea snakes, Mels! The deadliest in the world. The big males see that seismic cable being dragged by and they think that's the biggest damn female they've ever seen. Those guys on the back of the boat are there to make sure they don't get on board."

They landed and Mels disembarked with Cuong and Minh.

Mels was immediately surrounded by the crew, many of whom were old friends from many years back who were delighted to learn that he had not died. Shahtahtinsky rushed up and embraced him, kissing him, Azerbaijani-style, on the cheek.

"Mels! You have a habit of showing up in unexpected places, I gather you are en route somewhere?"

"I'm here on *an inspection tour,* Elmar. But perhaps you'd like to *accompany me* on our *next stop* . . . ?"

Shahtahtinsky's eyes looked sad.

"If I had my family here, Mels. . . ."

Mels nodded.

"I understand, Elmar. Look I need to speak to the geophysicist in command. I assume that's not you or they wouldn't have you clubbing snakes on the back deck?"

"No, Mels. There's one snake I wasn't able to prevent getting on board."

To Mels' horror, Shahtahtinsky was right. Mels and Cuong were taken to the recording cabin and introduced to none other than Academician Aleksander Ignatiev, the director of the Leningrad Geophysical Institute. There was no point continuing with his bluff.

"Katz! This is impossible! How did you get here? I thought—"

"You thought I would be dead by now, or at least in KGB custody. And it's no thanks to you that I'm not. I see they have you working for a change, Ignatiev. Punishment for giving your internal passport to a wanted criminal, was it?"

"Thanks to you Katz I have had to endure the shame and indignity of flying here to the 'wild forest' instead of going to Moscow to see my nephew present our joint work. Naturally I am on the boat. Do you think I want to stay in Vung Tau amongst worm- and dog-eating savages?"

"I'm sorry that I don't have time to listen to your problems, Ignatiev. Right now I need you to order the crew to refuel that helicopter then we will be out of what remains of your silvery hair."

"Ha! You think we carry aviation fuel on board? This is a calibration voyage."

"And you're supposed to keep aviation fuel on board in case the crew needs to be medivac'd in an emergency. You really have no idea how to run an operation, do you?"

"Well we didn't have medical evacuations in my day. People knew then that you can't make an omelet without breaking eggs."

"What the hell does that mean?"

"I mean people in my day accepted that sacrifices has to be made to build socialism. In any case that is beside the point, I'm afraid we cannot help you."

Mels produced the revolver from his pocket.

"Then I am assuming command of this survey. Sit there and shut up, Ignatiev. I have an announcement to make to the crew."

Mels switched on the ship's intercom and apologized to the crew for his earlier deception. He informed them that they were heading for Thai waters and that they were free to make a choice of defecting with them or staying aboard.

Even as he made the announcement, he realized that for the majority—like Shahtahtinsky—this was no real choice. All had been hand-chosen for this trip. By Russian standards they were being paid well and most of them had family commitments back in the Soviet Union. Nevertheless, he wanted to avoid "heroic" actions by crewmembers who felt that they were being coerced.

After an hour, the first Migs appeared, circling low over the ship and dropping flares. It was only when they started firing their cannons in front of the ship that Mels thought it was time to even the playing field. He sent out a distress call, which was picked up by an English-speaking radio operator of a vessel up ahead.

As it turned out, this was an American seismic vessel acquiring data on the Thai side of the border. The American boat and its support vessel formed an escort on either side of the Russian ship while the angry Migs buzzed overhead. Infuriated, one of the Mig pilots fired a rocket low over the bows of the ships. On the bridge of the Russian ship, Mels heard the American radio operator excusing himself, saying he could not endanger his own crew. The escort peeled off, leaving the Russian boat alone.

They were in Thai waters now and the refugee barge could be seen up ahead. The contrails of the two Migs could be seen curling through the sky as they lined themselves up for a final assault. But at the last minute they turned tail and flew back in the direction of Vietnam. On the opposite bow, they could see four Phantom F-4 jets with Royal Thai airforce markings streaking towards them. The Phantoms stayed with them while the boat anchored near the barge.

A rope basket suspended from a crane was swung over to the deck of the seismic boat and Luba and Cuong climbed aboard. Next to go were Nguyen and Mels. Minh stood waiting with the handful of Russians who had decided to defect. He was holding the AK-47 loosely—too loosely—while watching them being swung aboard. Suddenly Ignatiev, who had disappeared during the confrontation with the jets, rushed forward and grabbed the rifle. He turned it on the soldier then fired off a burst at the rope basket.

Cuong managed to maintain his grip but—more badly hit—Mels fell into the sea. Eager to administer the *coup de grace*, Ignatiev leaned over the ship's rail with the weapon, waiting for Mels to resurface. But before he could squeeze the trigger, Elmar Shahtahtinsky swung the baseball bat with which he had been clubbing sea snakes and smashed it against Ignatiev's skull. He toppled into the sea, to the applause of the crew on the Russian boat.

Before Mels had even hit the water, Luba had rushed to the rail and dived in after him. With strong strokes she reached her father in moments and supported him until a line could be thrown from the barge. Though Mels had been hit three times in his side and leg and was bleeding badly, the Red Cross personnel on the barge—accustomed to the atrocities perpetuated by the South

China Sea's pirates—were more than capable of handling the situation until the medivac helicopter arrived.

En route to hospital in Hat Yai and full of morphine, he turned to his daughter.

"Luba?"

"Yes, daddy?"

"I'm not dead, am I?"

"No, daddy. Not yet. But you're going to need to slow down once we get to the West—you're living pretty fast for a geophysicist."

Epilogue

It was another eighteen months before Yuri Andropov felt his position was strong enough to move openly against the Brezhnevs. Galina Brezhneva made it easy for him. A life-long fan of the circus—her first husband was a circus acrobat—she was involved in a scandal with one of her lovers known as Boris the Gypsy who was smuggling diamonds abroad in the stuffed bodies of circus animals.

Her hunger for diamonds was legendary and affected everyone with whom she came into contact. She tried to steal a diamond-studded crown from a museum in Tbilisi and once even demanded that her aunt give her the diamond ring that she was wearing at the funeral of her uncle Zhora. In 1981—informed about an impending increase in price of gold and jewelry—she rushed to the biggest jewelry store in Moscow with her friend, Svetlana Schelokova, and bought up the entire stock on credit. The next day she returned and demanded that they buy it all back at the increased price.

Andropov had to act cautiously against her at first because of the Brezhnev camp's high level infiltration of his own organization. His first deputy was General Semion Tsvigun, another of Galina's uncles. Tsvigun tried to obstruct Andropov's investigation of the diamonds stolen by his niece. Shortly thereafter, in January 1982, he was found dead in his office, just down the corridor from Andropov. Officially, the death was described as "suicide." Ten days later, Galina's friends were arrested and she was brought in for questioning while her father was at the State Funeral of Politburo member, Mikhail Suslov.

The campaign against Brezhnev rapidly escalated. Lonely and confused, his last days were made hell by a series of dirty tricks perpetrated by the KGB and increasingly captured on camera. On a visit to a tractor factory in Tashkent, a catwalk crashed down on him and he was rushed by ambulance to hospital. Brezhnev recovered but was then foolish enough to visit Baku at the invitation of Andropov's henchman, Geidar Aliyev. The entire Soviet Union was treated to television coverage of Brezhnev's speech to a huge rally of Azerbaijan's Communist Party. However, just before going on to the podium, Brezhnev was handed the wrong speech. He read several pages before he noticed the error and stumbled out an apology to the assembled delegates.

On November 10, 1982 Brezhnev's wife was informed by the KGB bodyguards assigned to her husband that he had died. She was refused access to his body until after it had been embalmed and put on public display. Andropov had now officially assumed absolute power.

Galina's second husband, Yuri Churbanov (third, if you count a three day marriage to an illusionist called Igor Kio) had been rapidly promoted from humble militiaman to the position of deputy head of the Interior Ministry after their marriage. His boss—of course—was Nikolay Schelokov. After Brezhnev's death, Nikolay Schelokov was immediately arrested, but Andropov had not figured on the strength of character of Svetlana Shelokova.

With her husband in prison, her son sent to Siberia for "parasitism" and her influential friends now powerless, she felt she had very little to lose. She lay in wait outside Andropov's apartment and was able to critically wound him before being herself shot dead by his bodyguards. Her husband thereafter committed "suicide" in detention. Andropov never fully recovered, though he was able to promote the advancement of his protégés, Mikhail Gorbachev and Edouard Shevardnadze before his death in 1984.

After the brief rule of the already terminally ill Konstantin Chernenko, Gorbachev became general secretary in 1985 with Shevardnadze as his foreign minister. With the break-up of the Soviet Union, the long-standing animosities between the peoples of the Caucasus escalated from verbal exchanges to open warfare. The town of Sukhumi was destroyed by Georgian troops battling the Abhazian insurgency. Ethnic cleansing became the norm in the dispute between Armenia and Azerbaijan over the territory of Nagorno-Karabakh. Edouard Shevardnadze and Geidar Aliyev assumed power of their respective homelands and their fellow KGB alumnus, Vladimir Putin, became President of Russia.

Yuri Churbanov was sentenced to twelve years in jail for taking bribes but was later pardoned by Boris Yeltsin. His wife, Galina Brezhneva died in 1998.

Mels Katz is now an unemployed geophysicist living in Houston, Texas.

His daughter went to Stanford Business School and is a millionaire. She has a home in Malibu.